BEST DETECTIVE STORIES
OF THE YEAR–1976
30th Annual Collection

BEST
DETECTIVE
STORIES
OF THE YEAR
1976

30th Annual Collection

Edited by
Edward D. Hoch

E.P. Dutton & Co., Inc. | New York, N.Y.

Copyright 1976 © by Edward D. Hoch
All rights reserved. Printed in the U.S.A.

First Edition

10 9 8 7 6 5 4 3 2 1

Published simultaneously in Canada
by Clarke, Irwin & Company
Limited, Toronto and Vancouver
ISBN: 0–525–06435–4
Library of Congress Catalog Card Number: 46-5872

For Frederic Dannay,
who has kept the detective
short story alive and well

Contents

Introduction

Twelve years ago, in his introduction to the 19th Annual Collection in this series, the late Anthony Boucher stated that at least a thousand detective short stories (in the broad sense of the term) were published in the United States each year. In 1975, as I took over the editing of this annual from the able hands of Allen J. Hubin, there were fewer than five hundred detective-crime-suspense short stories published in America—this despite the brief appearance of two new mystery magazines.

In that 19th collection Boucher selected stories from three publications no longer in existence (*This Week, The Saint Mystery Magazine, Manhunt*) and one other that no longer publishes fiction (*Argosy*). On the surface this twelve-year trend would seem to indicate that the future of the detective-crime short story is bleak indeed.

But there are hopeful signs on the horizon. Though the magazine market for short mystery fiction (and all short fiction) continued to dwindle during 1975, the publication of mystery anthologies and single-author collections actually increased to its best level in some years. And plans are under way for at least three publishing ventures which will offer limited editions of mystery novels, anthologies and collections to be sold primarily by mail order.

Another hopeful sign at the end of 1975 was the announcement that *Alfred Hitchcock's Mystery Magazine,* scheduled to be discontinued, had been saved through its sale to Davis Publications, Inc., publisher of *Ellery Queen's Mystery Magazine.* What effect this will have on the field as a whole remains to be seen, but it demonstrates there are still publishers around with confidence in the future of the mystery short story.

A few words about this year's collection: Because I've created several series detectives myself, it's not too surprising that you'll find a number of series characters represented here. The traditional story with a series sleuth may no longer win the top awards in the field, but since the days of Dupin and Sherlock Holmes it has remained the solid backbone of the entire genre.

I have expanded the Yearbook features in the back of the book, begun by Anthony Boucher and continued by Allen J. Hubin, to include an annual biographical feature. My Honor Roll listings are a bit longer than originally planned, mainly because two new mystery magazines, *The Executioner* and *87th Precinct,* produced some stories worth noting. Both magazines suspended publication after four issues, but at year's end there was hopeful news that two other new mystery magazines might soon be forthcoming from different publishers.

Unfortunately, my Necrology listings are also long this year. We lost an unreasonably large number of fine writers and editors during 1975, including two past presidents of Mystery Writers of America, Rex Stout and Lawrence G. Blochman, and two outstanding mystery editors, Hans Stefan Santesson and Leo Margulies. They'll be missed, by readers and writers alike.

My thanks to Jo Alford of E. P. Dutton & Co., Inc., who suggested the biographical feature, and to Jack Ritchie, Larry Sternig and Ernest M. Hutter who supplied material for it. Thanks also to Francis M. Nevins, Jr., who helped me choose a Hoch story for inclusion here, and to Allen J. Hubin, who made the editorial transition such a smooth one. (Happily he continues to edit the indispensable *Armchair Detective.*) And very special thanks to my wife, Patricia, who has helped me with every phase of this project.

EDWARD D. HOCH

BEST DETECTIVE STORIES
OF THE YEAR–1976

30th Annual Collection

This is Jack Ritchie's fifteenth appearance in BEST DETECTIVE STO-
RIES OF THE YEAR, *outdistancing any other writer. The story—one of
five nominated for this year's* MWA *Edgar award—combines his special
brand of off-beat humor with a private eye mystery that begins with a bathtub
full of Jello. You'll find a brief biography of Jack Ritchie in the Yearbook
section at the back of the book . . . just a few words here about the unusual
publication in which this story first appeared.* MD *is a monthly "medical
newsmagazine" for doctors—not the most likely place to find new detective
stories. But for more than a decade now each December issue of* MD *has carried
a pair of short stories in a special "MD's Companion" section. Among the
contributors have been Ellery Queen, Robert L. Fish, and other mystery writers,
along with mainstream short story writers. We hope someday an anthology of
these stories will make them available to a wider reading public.*

JACK RITCHIE
The Many-Flavored Crime

"There it is," Gerald Vanderveer said. Ah, yes. There it was. A
bathtub full of Jello. Basically red, but with occasional streaks of
green, yellow, and orange.

"When did you first notice this?" I asked.

"When I went to the bathroom this morning."

"What time did you go to bed last night?"

"About ten."

I nodded sagely. "Evidently someone sneaked past you last night
while you were sleeping. You didn't hear water running, did you?"

"No. I'm a rather heavy sleeper."

Gerald's brother, Colonel Frank Vanderveer, appeared at the
bathroom door, his face a bit pale. "Milstead has been stabbed. He's
dead. In my dressing room."

I frowned. "Who's Milstead?"

"The butler," Gerald said.

We followed Colonel Vanderveer to his rooms.

A middle-aged man in a maroon smoking jacket lay at the foot of
the tall windows. He appeared to have been stabbed in the back. A
knife lay beside the body.

The colonel and Gerald looked at me for leadership. After all, I
was a private detective.

I rose to the occasion. "I think we'd better call the police."

When the police arrived, a Lieutenant Tatum seemed to be in charge.

He studied me. "You say you're a private detective?"

I nodded. "However, I promise not to interfere. You work your side of the street, so to speak, and I'll work mine. I'm here to investigate the Jello."

Gerald hastened to explain. "Someone has been putting Jello into my things. Monday it was the washbasin. Tuesday the toilet. And today the bathtub. I finally decided to hire a private detective to get to the bottom of this."

Tatum strode to the bathroom door and looked. "I'll be damned," he said. Then he shrugged and came back. "Who knows about this?"

"Everybody in the house," I said. "The colonel here, his brother Gerald, and Gerald's daughter, Kitti. After all, you can't have a whole bathtub of Jello . . ."

"I mean the murder," the lieutenant snapped.

"Oh, that. Well, I didn't allow anybody to enter this room, but I suppose the news has gotten around, what with the sirens and all."

Two white-coated attendants put Milstead's body on a stretcher. They covered it thoroughly with a sheet and carried it out.

Gerald had been watching them. "Frank," he said to his brother, "Isn't Milstead wearing your smoking jacket?"

Colonel Vanderveer nodded. "Yes. I caught him wearing it several months ago and it turned out that when I was gone he often liked to put on the jacket and indulge in the private fantasy that he owned this house and the grounds. Told him to keep right on doing it if he wanted to. Seemed harmless enough to me."

The fingerprint man raised his head from his work. "No prints on the knife."

A police officer brought in Mrs. Milstead, a somewhat sturdy woman with dry, narrow eyes.

"Mrs. Milstead," Lieutenant Tatum said, "I'm afraid I have some bad news for you."

Her eyes went to the dark spot on the rug. "I know. One of the maids told me that he was dead."

Tatum seemed to wait for tears, but when there were none, he continued. "When was the last time you saw your husband?"

"Around three this afternoon when we had a cup of coffee in the kitchen with the cook. After that I went shopping and did some visiting. I got back a few minutes ago."

"How well did you and your husband get along?"

"We had our arguments. Everybody knows that."

"Was your husband's life insured?"

"Of course. Twenty-five thousand dollars."

"Isn't that a pretty big amount?"

She disagreed. "Not for these days. I tried to get him to take out more, but he was stubborn."

"Do you have any idea who might want to murder your husband?"

"No. Maybe it was just another one of those *accidents?*"

"Accidents?"

Her eyes went to Colonel Vanderveer. "The colonel was almost killed by an arrow last week. It missed him by just a few inches. And then on Wednesday a flowerpot fell—or was *pushed*—from a third story window just as he was passing below. If he'd been hit, it certainly would have killed him."

Gerald now nodded somewhat reluctantly. "Also yesterday somebody tampered with the brakes of my brother's car. Disconnected them, or whatever people do in a situation like that."

Tatum turned to the colonel. "You had an automobile accident?"

Colonel Vanderveer shook his head. "Actually no. Kitti—that's my niece and Gerald's daughter—happened to borrow my car. She ran into a tree."

"Was she hurt?"

"No. Just shaken up a bit."

Tatum returned to Mrs. Milstead. "You think that your husband's murder was an accident?"

She shrugged. "It happened right here in the colonel's dressing room, didn't it?"

"Yes."

"My husband is about the same size as the colonel, isn't he?"

"I suppose so."

"I heard my husband was stabbed in the back. Right?"

"Right."

"So the killer didn't get a look at his face, did he?"

"Possibly not."

She smiled grimly. "My husband had his back to the killer. Maybe the light was bad. The killer thought my husband was the colonel and stabbed him."

I cleared my throat. "Could anyone here tell me where I might find a yardstick or a foot ruler?"

Tatum stared at me.

"I'm going to measure the bathtub," I said. "Length, width,

depth. That sort of thing. One can't be too thorough, you know."

"There ought to be a ruler in that desk over there," Colonel Vanderveer said.

I found the ruler, went into the bathroom, and measured the tub. When I returned to the main room, Mrs. Milstead had been dismissed.

Tatum now questioned the colonel. "You are retired from the army?"

Vanderveer touched his brush mustache. "Quartermaster Corps. As a humanitarian, I tried mightily, but vainly, to eliminate creamed chipped beef on toast from the breakfast menu."

"Tell me about those accidents. What about the arrow?"

"Nothing much to tell. I was taking a stroll about the grounds when it shot out of the woods and struck a tree near me. Undoubtedly a stray arrow. The boys from Esterville often go hunting in the woods and have very little idea of property lines."

"And the flowerpot that almost killed you?"

"It missed me by at least six feet. A sudden gust of wind must have blown it off that window ledge."

"The auto accident?"

"Brakes *do* fail."

"Then you don't believe that someone has been trying to kill you?"

"I refuse even to consider such a thing," Colonel Vanderveer said firmly.

"In the event of your death, who gets your estate?"

"My brother Gerald."

"How much is it worth?"

The colonel shrugged. "Approximately four million."

Gerald nodded. "On the other hand, I haven't a cent to my name."

"Just one of those things," Colonel Vanderveer said. "Gerald and I both started out with the same modest inheritance. I joined the army and left all of my financial affairs in the hands of a trusted family lawyer. He made me rich. Gerald chose to personally supervise the investment of every bit of his capital. Lost everything."

Gerald smiled happily. "However my brother provides generously for me and mine. I might just as well be rich, for all that it actually matters. And I pay no taxes."

I had been doing some arithmetic on a page of my notebook. "Could you tell me where I might find the kitchen?"

Gerald gave me the directions and I found Mrs. Milstead alone in the kitchen having a cup of coffee.

"May I have a look at your Jello?" I asked. "If there is any left, of course."

She regarded me without enthusiasm and then led me to a small storeroom. She unlocked the door with a key and eyed the shelves. "We've got four boxes of Jello. Two lemon, one wild cherry, and one black raspberry."

"Might I examine one of them?"

"Which one?"

"Black raspberry. It's my favorite."

She handed me the box.

I read the directions and other data on the package carefully. "Why do you suppose your husband was wearing the colonel's smoking jacket when he was killed?"

"I don't know," she said. "Suppose you tell me?"

I decided to protect Milstead's private fantasy, even though he was now dead. "I haven't the faintest idea." I studied the package of Jello again. "Black raspberry. My neighborhood supermarket always seems to be out."

"Keep it," she said. "It's on the house."

I returned to the colonel's rooms.

Tatum was now questioning Kitti Vanderveer.

She was rather tall and slim, with coal black hair and equally dark eyes.

"Exactly what happened with the car?" Tatum asked.

"I was going to drive to town," Kitti said, "but I'd been having trouble with my own car, so I asked Uncle Frank if I might borrow one of his. He said yes, of course. As I neared the end of our drive, I stepped on the brakes to slow down for the turn onto the highway, only there weren't any brakes. I couldn't see just shooting out onto the highway into the path of some oncoming car, so I turned off the driveway and ran into a tree instead. Luckily I was only shaken up. As it was, though, the garage man estimated the damage to the car at one hundred and twenty-five dollars."

"You suspect that somebody tampered with the brakes?"

"Well . . . wouldn't you? In view of all of the other things—the flowerpot and the arrow, you know."

After Tatum finished questioning her, I followed her downstairs. "When you got into your uncle's car, was it parked in the driveway or was it in the garage?"

"In the garage."

"After you finished backing the car out, didn't you have to apply the brakes to stop the backward momentum? Why didn't the brakes fail at that particular point?"

She thought that over for a few moments and then brightened. "Actually the car had been put away by *backing* it into the garage. All I had to do was get inside and move *forwards.*"

"There is the matter of the damage to your uncle's car," I said. "I believe you mentioned the sum of one hundred and twenty-five dollars?"

"Well?"

I rubbed my jaw speculatively. "Considering the fragility of the modern automobile body, it seems miraculous that you could hit a tree and incur damage of only one hundred and twenty-five dollars. Even if you hit a stationary object at only five miles per hour—and I'm certain you must have been going faster than that—the average damage to the average car is in the neighborhood of *three* hundred and twenty-five dollars."

She laughed quickly. "Did I say *one* hundred? I meant to say *four* hundred and twenty-five dollars. Merely a slip of the tongue."

I shook my head. "I suppose it would be a relatively simple matter to phone your garage and find out *exactly* how much the damage to your uncle's car really is? And while I'm at it, I could ask if the garage had to do any work on the brakes? After all, they were supposed to have been disconnected or something."

We were jointly silent while she did some furious thinking.

Finally I said, "No one tampered with the brakes at all, now did they? You simply got into your uncle's car and deliberately ran into a tree?"

Reluctantly she fell back on the truth. "Actually I ran into the tree twice. The first time I chickened out at the last moment and barely touched the tree at all. So I had to back up a few yards and give it another try."

"But why?"

She sighed. "Well, there had been those two previous attempts on the colonel's life, and I didn't want him to think that *I* might be responsible for them. So I thought that if I could arrange things to *look* as though another attempt had been made on his life, but that I had accidentally stepped into his place all unknowingly, then he would think that I couldn't possibly be the one who was trying to kill him since I certainly wouldn't step into my own trap, now would I?"

I almost asked her to repeat that last sentence, but then decided against it. "Do you have any bows and arrows in the house?"

"I think there's a set somewhere in one of the attic storerooms."

"Are you any good at archery?"

"No. As a matter of fact, none of us is at all good at the sport, except for Colonel Frank."

I went back upstairs to the colonel's room.

I smiled. "How many boxes of Jello do you suppose are necessary to properly gelatinize the water in a bathtub?"

Everyone in the room—especially Lieutenant Tatum—stared at me, and obviously none of them knew the answer.

I supplied it. "It would require approximately 1,080 boxes of Jello to make the project a firm success. Give or take a dozen."

Tatum seemed to look up at the ceiling. "Is that the family-size box or the regular?"

"The regular. And in the mass, that would be about five and one-half cubic feet of boxes. Actually the Jello *itself* would be considerably less in volume. You know how deceptive packaging is these days." I turned to Colonel Vanderveer. "Do you have a local phone directory?"

He pointed to the phone on a small table next to the wall.

I opened the thin volume and turned to its half a dozen yellow pages. I discovered that Esterville had only two supermarkets. I dialed the number of the first and asked to speak to the manager.

Lieutenant Tatum watched me, his head cocked slightly to one side. It was difficult to gauge his expression. Possibly professional awe?

When the supermarket manager came to the phone, I said, "Have you recently—within the last few days—had anyone purchase an inordinately large amount of Jello?"

I almost heard him nod. "Now that you bring it up, it happened just yesterday. Bought us out completely. Had to send to the warehouse for emergency replacements."

"Ah," I said, "Did you by any chance get his or her license number?"

"License number? Why should I get his or her license number?"

That was a bit of a disappointment. "Could you perhaps give me a description of the purchaser?"

"I suppose I could. But wouldn't it be easier just to give you his name?"

"Well . . . yes."

"It was Mr. Vanderveer. Not the colonel. The other one. Gerald. Polite, friendly-type person."

I hung up and stared severely at Gerald Vanderveer. *"You* purchased the Jello!"

He flushed slightly. "Well, my brother simply would not face up to the fact that *someone* was trying to kill him. He refused to bring in the regular police or even a private detective to investigate the matter. So I concocted the Jello scheme for the sole purpose of introducing someone competent into the house—ostensibly to solve the Jello business, but actually to find out who was making these attempts on Frank's life. I was going to tell you about that later, but frankly I wanted to see how and *if* you operated and . . ."

Lieutenant Tatum interrupted. "Well, well, so you wrapped up the Jolly Jello Caper. Congratulations. Now I don't suppose you could do the same for the murder of Milstead?"

I pondered a moment. "Perhaps a few suggestions?"

"Be my guest."

"You might see if there are any fingerprints on that broken flowerpot."

He blinked and recovered. "It's probably scattered all over the town dump by now."

"Possibly. But on the other hand, broken flowerpots are tremendously useful as drainage material. No gardener could possibly think of just throwing them away. I would imagine that the colonel's gardener might have rescued the pieces for that very purpose." I smiled cheerfully. "As a matter of fact, there is such a shortage of broken flowerpots that some people actually take perfectly sound pots and break them just so they will have shards for drainage."

For some reason Tatum glared at me and then sent off one of his men.

"Also you might check the archery equipment in one of the storage rooms in the attic," I said. "You might find fingerprints on the bow up there."

He sent another man off.

We waited until both of them returned and handed their items over to the fingerprint man.

Tatum still glowered. "Anything else?"

I nodded. "Let us suppose for a few moments that the attempts on the colonel's life were not really genuine. That is, they were meant to fail."

Tatum now frowned. "Dropping a flowerpot on the colonel wasn't an attempt on his life?"

"As he says, it missed him by a good six feet."

"What about the brake tampering? And that damn arrow?"

I evaded the brake episode. "You have been assuming that the archer *inadvertently* missed his target. But suppose he did it deliberately?"

"The arrow came within inches of the colonel. It would have taken an expert archer to do something like that."

"Either an expert or simply a bad archer who got closer than he intended."

"What about Milstead's murder?" Tatum demanded. "There was no miss there."

"You are assuming that Milstead was killed by *mistake* and that the colonel was really the intended victim. But suppose Milstead was actually killed for himself alone and that *all* of the other incidents were concocted solely for the purpose of making us think that Milstead's death had been just another attempt on the colonel's life, once again bungled."

The fingerprint man looked up. "I'm getting matching prints on the flowerpot pieces and the bow."

I carefully removed the package of black raspberry Jello from my pocket and handed it to the fingerprint man. "You'll find my prints on this and Mrs. Milstead's. Hers ought to match those on the bow and the pot shards."

I looked about the silent room and smiled. "Mrs. Milstead claimed that the last time she saw her husband alive was at three o'clock in the kitchen. Obviously Milstead wasn't wearing the colonel's smoking jacket at the time, since that was a secret thing with him. And yet Mrs. Milstead *knew* that her husband was wearing that smoking jacket when he was killed. Only the murderer could have known that."

Tatum frowned. "She might have seen the body being carried out on the stretcher."

"No. It was completely covered with a sheet when it left this room."

His frown deepened. "I don't remember Mrs. Milstead saying that she knew her husband was wearing the smoking jacket at the time of his death."

I cleared my throat. "When I spoke to her in the kitchen and told her about her husband wearing the colonel's jacket at the time of his death, she merely *nodded*—which indicates clearly to me that she knew he was wearing the jacket at the time of his death and, as I said, only the murderer could have known that. If she *hadn't* known anything about the jacket, she would have been surprised enough to at least say 'Huh?' "

Tatum seemed to have trouble speaking. "You mean to tell me that you're building your whole case on the fact that she didn't say 'Huh?' when you thought she was supposed to?"

"Well . . . yes. I imagine she killed him for the twenty-five thousand dollar life insurance."

There was an utter silence. Actually rather long.

Finally the fingerprint man spoke up. "The prints on the pot, the bow, and the box of Jello match. I guess it really is this Mrs. Milstead."

Lieutenant Tatum looked at me.

I had the strangest feeling that he wanted to cry.

But instead he went to the door and spoke to one of his men. "Send Mrs. Milstead up here. I want to ask her a few more questions."

Jesse Hill Ford is a mainstream writer whose novels and short stories often mirror the violence of today's rural South. He first appeared in this BEST series three years ago and we're pleased to welcome him back with a deceptively simple story of stunning implications. "The Jail" received the Mystery Writers of America annual Edgar award as the best crime short story of 1975.

JESSE HILL FORD
The Jail

How I found the car was I went with the truck looking for some plows and a harrow and a mowing machine, horse-drawn stuff we had a chance to sell to a fellow who was farming produce on shares —tomatoes, in particular. You can't cultivate tomatoes with a tractor. The sticks are too high. He had located a pair of mules. He was a Do-Right, but that is another story. A Do-Right is a member of a small religion we have in west Tennessee wherein a man pledges that he will *do right* and if a Do-Right is not lazy, he's a fair credit risk. So he needed the implements and I said I'd go look and see if I could locate them over on my grandmother's place.

I got into the truck and drove over there. It was July and I looked over her cotton and beans and saw that everything looked good. She'd built her cage-laying shed spang at the other end of the 2000 acres instead of putting it on the main road like I advised her, and I crossed the stock gaps and the dust powdered on the hood of my green truck. I put up the windows and put the air conditioning on and turned up the music on the country station and presently I saw the laying house and drove on back to the barn, white-painted and neat. I found the key on my ring and unlocked the doors and swung them open and saw the implements almost at once and the stalls just as they had been left, cleaned out and swept after the last mule died. It was a fine old barn and maybe I still would not have found the car except that I went walking down the hall, looking in the big old box stalls and thinking how it was when I was a boy. It was the fourth stall down and when I saw the car, red and low and foreign, with a good bit of dust on it that had filtered down from the old loft above, I took a look at the outer wallboards and could see where they had been removed in order to put the car in there. My first thought was

of Sheriff, my little brother, for I well knew his love of cars. And I
thought, Well, Sheriff has bought a car and for some reason stored
it in here without saying a word to anybody about it. Then I stepped
inside the stall and stooped down and rubbed the barn dust off the
license plate. New York State, 1965—I crouched there in the silence
of the barn and pondered that. I could feel my heart beating. I stood
up and opened the car door on the driver's side. It sure needed
greasing, for it kind of groaned—a coffin-lid groan—and I looked
inside and saw that it was probably British and next saw that it was
a Jaguar. You don't see a whole lot of Jaguars in west Tennessee.
Fact of the business, you so rarely see one now that the interstate
has been put through that there just isn't any telling *when* the *last*
Jaguar came through Pinoak, Tennessee. The interstate, which cut
us off the mainstream of travel between Florida and the Midwestern
states, was opened in 1966.

I saw something on the steering column held by little coil springs
and celluloid. I took it off the column and read the name on the New
York driver's license. S. Jerome Luben, male, black hair, brown
eyes, age 26, address on Riverside Drive, New York City. Nobody
with a name like Luben could be mistaken for a member of the
Pinoak Missionary Baptist Church. I tossed the license, celluloid,
coil springs and all, onto the driver's seat and closed the door. It
shut with a sound that was somehow so final I stood there another
full minute at least before I could move. The dust of nine years in
a mule barn was on my hands.

The year 1965 was the year Sheriff left home for the Marines. I
recalled the day he left. I recalled a lot of things, including the way
he kept whispering something and nodding to Henry. Henry is the
nigger who has worked for my grandmother since he was a little boy:
he kind of waited on Sheriff and buddied around with him since
Sheriff was little.

Did I say my little brother is spoiled? Spoiled rotten. The baby
in the family. My mother thought she was in the change of life and
went around eight months thinking he was a tumor and probably
malignant until she finally went to the doctor after she had got our
family lawyer, Oman Hedgepath, to make her will, which would
have left most of her estate for the support of foreign missions.
Mother worried about the souls of the heathens. When Ocie Pentecost told her she was pregnant, I think she felt cheated. A month
later, here came Sheriff. That is not his name, of course. His real
name is Caleb Batsell Beeman Baxter. Mother had an uncle in
Somerton whose name was Caleb and he got into real estate and
insurance and put his signs up so they read: C. BATSELL BEEMAN FOR
EVERYTHING IN REAL ESTATE AND INSURANCE NEEDS. He put that sign

on every road leading in and out of town and had a fine income all his life right up to the moment he fell into the wheat bin and suffocated. Wheat is like water, you fall into it and you go under. Uncle Batsell could not swim.

Mother figured Sheriff would be a lawyer like Oman Hedgepath and have a sign on his door and a shingle hanging in the breeze on Main Street, reading: C. BATSELL B. BAXTER, which she thought would make everybody with any law business want to see her youngest son.

As for me, I was never in her mind otherwise than somebody to run everything. To gin cotton during ginning season and combine beans during bean season, to buy hay and manage for the silage and between times build rent houses and work in the store and manage the tractor-and-implement company and make private loans and buy farms and run the sawmill—or, in other words, just like my daddy always did, to run everything and see to everything and mind everything and when there was nothing else to do, to step in behind the meat counter and weigh hams.

Not Sheriff, though. Once it got through her head that he was not a tumor, she saw him in the practice of the law. Then he started to grow up and almost from the first word he spoke, it was obvious that all in the world he would ever want to do would be to be a sheriff and enforce the law. It was all that he spoke about, and because he was the baby, we gave him toy guns and little uniforms and hats and badges. He went around dressed like that and went to school that way. What else would we call him but Sheriff? Everybody in Sligo County thought he was cute as a bug, and during the strawberry festival every year we'd build him a float in the shape of a sheriff's patrol car with little wheels on it and the aerial and all and Sheriff would ride in it, with Henry and a couple of others pulling him in the children's parade. Time and again he won first or got an honorable mention from the judges who come each year from Memphis to judge the parade and the beauty contest.

Then he got to high school and we gave him an automobile and Grandmother gave him police lights for the top of it and my father bought him a siren from Sears. I got him a real badge from a pawnshop in Memphis. It saved us from having to wonder what to do for him when it came Christmas.

If something happened in Pinoak, we had Sheriff as our private police force to investigate things and make arrests and take people over to Somerton to the jail. Nothing official, understand, but a convenience in a small place like Pinoak, where you don't have a police force.

Sheriff, for the most part, confined himself to stopping out-of-state cars if they were speeding or if they looked suspicious. He'd pull them over, get out, walk up to the driver's side and tip his hat. He was young and blond and blue-eyed and had such an innocent face. Yet behind it there was always something that made folks do exactly what he told them to do. Show their driver's license, open their trunk lid, even open their suitcases. He confiscated ever so much liquor and beer, but never went so far as to actually arrest anybody . . . that I ever knew anything about.

He seemed happy and he seemed contented. When he asked if he could have a jail, my father consulted highway patrol. They advised against it. The law in Tennessee did not, they said, let folks operate private jails. That could cause problems, they said. Otherwise, as long as Sheriff never arrested anybody or gave a ticket or fined anybody, he could pretty well do as he pleased, for he was a deterrent to speeders. Pinoak got known far and wide as a speed trap. Back before they opened the interstate, the out-of-state traffic would drive through Pinoak so slow you could walk alongside it the whole two blocks. They'd come at a crawl sometimes, with Sheriff so close behind in his cruiser he was all but bumper to bumper, and Sheriff just daring them to make a wrong move or do anything sudden or reckless.

More than anything else, he liked to stop a car with a New York tag, for when that happened, like as not he'd get a loudmouth who would start to complain and bitch and raise his voice and Sheriff would end up practically taking the fellow's car apart in front of his eyes. New York drivers were a challenge to Sheriff. Looking at that red car gave me a chill in spite of the heat.

I went outside and stood just beyond the white-painted doors of the mule barn. I could see the cage-laying house and hear the hens and could smell that special odor of hen shit and cracked eggs and ground feed. I saw that Henry's truck was there, so I went down to the packing room and found him. He had collected the eggs and had them in the tank with the vibrator that washes them and he was grading them and putting them in big square cartons of 50. The cracked ones he broke all the way and put the yolks and whites into big pickle jars to be hauled to the poor farm and to the Somerton jail, because the old and the poor and the prisoners are just as well fed on cracked eggs as on whole ones and cracked eggs come a whole lot cheaper; besides, otherwise we'd have to feed the cracked ones to the hogs. Henry never looked up and the vibrator hummed and the water danced the hen shit off the eggs and the smell of spoiled eggs was in the room. The floor was a little wet. A black-and-white cat was asleep on the sofa Henry had made for himself by welding legs onto a truck seat taken from a wreck.

"S. Jerome Luben," I said. "That mean anything to you?"

He froze, egg in hand, just that quick.

"S. Jerome Luben," I said again.

He dropped the egg and it broke on the wet concrete between his black, down-at-heel shoes.

"Is he dead?" I asked.

Henry reached into the tank for another egg, got one, and then cut off the vibrator. He wiped the egg carefully on the corner of his apron. Flies were worrying about the floor, lighting at the edges of the egg he had dropped.

"Naw, sah, he ain't dead. Leastways he wasn't dead this morning."

"This morning? You saw S. Jerome Luben this morning?"

"Yes, sah. He looked OK to me." Instead of looking at me, he looked at the egg in his hand and pushed with his thumbnail at what might have been a speck on its white, curving surface. "How come you to know about him, sah?"

"I just saw his car."

"Little red automobile."

"Did you knock the wall loose?"

"I prised some of the boards loose. It wouldn't go in if I didn't prise some boards off. But now I nailed 'em back."

"Nine years ago."

"Something lack that," he said, still examining the egg. "It had to be after Christmas, wadn't it?"

"How would I know?" I said.

"It was after Christmas of sixty-five, I b'lieve it was," he said. He never looked blacker. I began to feel something between my shoulder blades in the middle of my back, a cold sensation. He was so utterly still. "Yes, sah. Sixty-five," he said.

"What happened?"

He was quiet a moment. "I tole 'em it was bound to cause trouble."

"Who—told who?"

"Your grandmother, Miss Mettie Bell. And him—Sheriff. He got on her about wanting her to give him a jail——"

"A what?"

"Jail. Tole her wouldn't nothing else make him happy that Christmas if he didn't git him a jail. Jest a teeny little jail. Two cells, he tole her. That's all he wanted Santy to bring him and what if he went away to—where was it he went?"

"Vietnam."

"Nam, that's it. What if he went there and got kilt and hadn't never had him the pleasure of a jail of his own? He started on her in the summertime in weather about like this and she sent to Birmingham for the contractor and they come and built it and she handed him the keys on Christmas Eve. I was standing in the kitchen next to the sink when she handed them keys to him and made him promise he wouldn't abuse his privilege and wouldn't make no trouble and wouldn't tell nobody local from around here anything about it. She tole me I'd have to feed anybody he locked up and keep the jail swept and mopped and cleaned good. She wadn't going to endure with no dirty jail, she said. So I promised and Sheriff, he promised, too."

I sat down on the sofa. The cat raised her head and gave me a green stare. Then, closing her eyes again, she laid her head back down. I heard the vibrator come on.

"S. Jerome Luben," I said. "Is he in the jail?"

"He was this morning when I carried him his breakfast."

"Where the hell is this jail?"

I no sooner asked than something dawned on me. It was like looking at the flat surface of a pool. You can look ever so long at the surface and you will see only the reflection of the sky and the trees, but then, sometimes very suddenly, you'll see below it—you'll see a fish or a turtle.

It had to be the poison house. We bought farm poisons in such quantities, all the new poisons and defoliants, the sprays and powders for controlling everything from the boll weevil to the cabbage butterfly, plus all the weed killers. I recalled drawing the check to the Birmingham contractor and wondering why Grandmother got somebody from Alabama instead of a Somerton builder, but it was Grandmother's money and if she wanted the poison house set off in a field on the backside of nowhere, then it was fine with me, because the poisons always gave me a headache when I had to be around them. I never went to the poison house, not I or my father or any white man. It gives you a headache, a poison room does. They say the stuff can collect in your system and shorten your life. So, for nine years, I'd been looking at a goddamned jail and had never known what it was. I had never before wondered why Grandmother would put up a two-story poison house and have a Birmingham contractor build it. Hell, *I* could have built the thing. Only when you are busy as I am all the time, with one season falling on you before the last one is over—starting with cabbage and strawberries and rolling right on through corn and soybeans and cotton and wheat and winter pasture and back to cabbage and strawberries again—you are so goddamned relieved when anybody will take even a little something off your back you never wonder about it and you get so you never ask questions. Nine years can flit past you like a moth in the dark. You never give it a second thought.

"Henry?"

"Sah?"

"Cut that goddamned thing off and come with me." I stood up, feeling light-headed.

"Cut it *off*?"

"You heard me."

"But I got to grade these eggs——"

"Who feeds him his dinner?"

"Sah?"

"S. Jerome Luben."

He cut off the vibrator, wiped his hands and reached beneath his apron and hauled out his watch. He looked at it and then shucked off the apron and threw it onto the truck-seat sofa before sticking the watch back into the pocket of his gray work trousers.

"No need you to go," he said. He started out and would have gotten in his truck as though to close the matter between us once and for all. I give him credit. He was letting me have my chance to stay out of it.

"Get in my truck, Henry."

He froze again. "You don't have to go," he said.

"My truck."

He gave a sigh and turned then and went slowly to my truck and climbed into the passenger seat and slammed the door. I climbed in beside him and started the engine and felt the air conditioner take hold and start to cool me. It was the first I knew that I was sweating so heavily; it was cold sweat and dried beneath my shirt and left me clammy.

I pulled the gearshift down into drive and accelerated out through the gate, over the stock gap and into the dusty single lane that spun between the pastures, deep and green on both sides of us. Next came cotton acreage, then a bean field with corn standing far down beyond it toward the bottoms, and beyond the corn the groves of virgin cypress timber far down in the flat distance like the faraway rim of the world, as though beyond that contained edge of green there would be nothing else, just blue space and stars. West Tennessee gives that feeling and if you grow up with it, it never leaves you. It's big and lonely and a million miles from nowhere—that's the feeling. I turned through the gate and the tires slapped on the iron pipes spanning the stock gap and the poison house was straight ahead. I pulled around behind it. Sheriff's car was there, parked ramrod straight on the neat gravel apron. On the side of its white front door was a seal and above the seal the word SHERIFF in dark gold, and below the seal in neat black lettering: OFFICIAL BUSINESS ONLY.

The sawed-off shotgun was racked forward against the dashboard and the two-way radio that he always left on was talking to itself when I opened my door, cut the engine and climbed down.

Henry didn't move.

"Get out," I said and slammed my door. He opened his door and climbed down.

"No need you to git mixed into this mess, Mr. Jim," he said, giving me another chance.

The radio in Sheriff's cruiser muttered something, asked something, answered itself.

"Follow me," I said and headed for the door. It was a glassed aluminum storm door and before I opened it, I saw the desk and Sheriff propped up behind it, reading a *True Detective* or some such magazine. His hat was on the costumer in the corner. When I went in, grateful because the building was air conditioned, he didn't stir. Maybe he thinks it's Henry, or maybe he just doesn't care, I told myself.

Henry was behind me. The door clicked shut. Sheriff licked his thumb and turned a page. His blue gaze passed over me as though I didn't exist. He looked almost the same as he had looked the day he left for the Marines, the same tan, the same blond crewcut, the same innocent baby face. Then he saw me. The swivel desk chair creaked and he came forward until his elbows were on the desk. Then I smelled it. Henry had gone by me now into what I saw was a kitchen adjoining the office. I smelled rancid food and unwashed despair and tired mattresses and stale cigarettes—I smelled the smell of every jail in the South, from Miami to Corinth, from Memphis to Biloxi to Charleston to Birmingham—I smelled them all and every little town between. Finally, it is the smell of human fear, the scent of the caged human animal—nine years of that, one year stacked on top of the last, palpable as dust.

"Nice place," I said.

Sheriff looked at me, not sure yet what I knew. Give him credit, he's cool, I thought: my blood, my kin, my flesh. And I had as much hand in spoiling him rotten as anybody. Maybe that's what they teach you at the University of Mississippi, where I played and raised hell for four years before the Army got me. They teach you how to come home and continue to spoil the little brother in the family by letting him do what he damn well pleases. Every family needs one at least with no responsibility at all to burden him. Here sat ours.

"You never seen it before?" Sheriff said. He hollered at Henry: "What you doing in there?"

"Fixin' his dinner, scramblin' his eggs." Henry turned and stood in the kitchen door, holding a pickle jar. I could see the yolks and the whites. So they fed him cracked eggs, the same as any other prisoner in Sligo County. Henry stood patiently. He was looking down at the jar. In the opposite hand he held the lid.

"Fixin' whose dinner?" Sheriff said.

"His—upstairs," said Henry. He didn't look up and his voice was low, a sunken, below-surface sound.

"What the hell you talking about?" said Sheriff.

"He knows," Henry said in the same sunken voice.

"I found the car," I said.

"Oh," said Sheriff.

"The red car and a driver's license and a name."

"Well, now you know about him," Sheriff said. "Figured you or Dad, one was bound to come to the poison house someday. I'd say it was my office and you'd go away and not worry. How come you to find the car, Jim?"

"Just unlucky. A Do-Right wants some old tools and machinery——"

"I told Henry I'd bust his ass if he ever let it out. Didn't I tell you I'd bust your ass, Henry?"

"Yes, sah. Want me to feed him? It's time."

"Goddamn it," Sheriff said. "Goddamn it."

"Just answer me one question," I said. I heard eggs hit the hot skillet.

"Shoot."

"Why would you lock a man up and keep him locked up nine years?"

"You mean Jerome? Why would I keep him so long? It's a fair question. I never intended to leave him in here longer than just overnight to teach him a lesson. He passed through Pinoak that night doing above ninety. I risked my life and never caught him until the son of a bitch was nearly to McKay—lights and siren and giving my car a fit. Goddamn him. He could have been the death of us both. See?" He looked at me with that blue stare of innocence and passed his fingers over the crown of his close-cropped hair. "And he swore at me."

"So you locked him up for nine years. You buried him alive because he cussed you and he was from New York. Do you know how long they'll keep you in prison for this? Did it ever dawn on you?"

"I know all about it," he said.

"God help us," I said. "God *help* us—Henry's in it. I'm in it!"

"Look—go upstairs and talk to him. Please? Go up and let Jerome explain how it happened. He understands it and—" He stopped talking and stood up and took some keys off his belt and went to the steel security door and unlocked and opened it. I climbed the concrete stairs with Sheriff behind me.

There was a hallway at the top with a cell on either side of it and two windows and a toilet and lavatory in each cell. The cell on the right was open and had bookshelves on every wall to the ceiling. The cell on the left was closed. I saw the prisoner, a slender, black-haired man wearing blue jeans and loafers and a T-shirt. He was clean-shaven and his hair was cropped close to his head like Sheriff's and he was working at a typewriter. A book lay open beside him on the desk.

"What's for lunch?" he said. Then he saw me and pushed his chair back. On the cell floor lay the rug that used to be in my grandmother's parlor, a pattern of roses. "Who's this, Sheriff?"

"It's Jim."

"What a surprise. I'm Jerome Luben." He came to the cell door, swung it open and put out his hand to me. We shook hands. "So what brings you here?"

"He found your car," said Sheriff. "And Henry told him."

"You just now found out? Told anybody?" He was handsome in a Jewish way and looked none the worse for wear. There was premature gray at his temples, just a touch.

"Not yet I haven't told anybody," I said.

Luben looked at Sheriff. "Why don't you leave us alone for a few minutes? Tell Henry to hold my lunch. Need to explain things to Jim, don't I?"

Sheriff nodded and turned and went back down the stairs. I heard the security door clank shut.

"We can sit in here, if you like," said Luben, leading the way into the cell on the right. "My library," he said.

I recognized two of Grandmother's parlor chairs and one of her floor lamps.

"You upset, Jim?"

"A little," I said.

"Don't be upset. Because what happened couldn't happen again in a thousand—a million—years. I'm not angry, you see that, don't you?"

"Yes," I said. "But what the hell happened? This is the ruination of my family—the end."

"It's not the end. Listen to me. It's back in 1965, I'm fresh out of Columbia Law School. I'm driving like a bat out of hell, with no respect for anything—asking for it. I've got long hair and a beard and I'm smoking grass and everybody who thinks the war in Vietnam is right is a pissant in my book, shit beneath my feet. Get the picture? I'm bigger and richer and smarter than the world, the entire fucking—pardon me—world. I know Southerners do not use those words."

"Not often, no," I said.

"So your brother stops me. Polite? A complete gentleman. I tell him to eat shit. I hit him. I spit on him. I'm begging him to lock me up so I can be some kind of goddamned martyr and get my ass in jail and my name in the papers and on television and go home to New York and be a fucking hero. Now, understand, my *father* has washed his hands of me three years earlier and put my money in a trust that keeps my checking account overflowing. I mean, he's rich and my mother was rich and she's dead and I've told him what a capitalist pig he is and he hopes to God he will *never* see me again. I'm scorching the highway in the backward, backwoods, medieval South, and who stops me? Your brother."

"Lord have mercy," I whispered.

"He brings me here. He and Henry have to carry me bodily. I'm not cooperating. Then I blew it all to hell."

"How?"

"I demanded my phone call."

"Phone call?"

"Phone call. My lousy phone call. And Sheriff had to tell me there isn't a phone. I said what kind of fucking jail was it with no phone? I said did he realize what was going to happen to him if I didn't get my phone call? Did he know that he had arrested a lawyer—a member of the New York bar, an officer of the court, a graduate of Columbia and much else? Did he know how fucking rich I was? Because I was going to make a career out of him. I had nothing else to do. I was going to make him and Henry and anybody else responsible for building a jail and leaving a phone out of it suffer until they'd wish they had never been born! *Oy!*"

I began to see. I began to see it all. He went on. He was smiling now, that was the wonder of it:

"And he finally had to tell me that his grandmother had built the jail and he wasn't really a sheriff, not even a deputy. I had rolled a joint and was blowing smoke at him and getting high and I told him as soon as he let me out, I'd see his grandmother in prison, and himself, and poor old black-ass Henry. And that did it. He was due to go to the Marines. He had already enlisted. He went away and left Henry to feed me."

I didn't want to let myself think what I was thinking. In the chambers of my mind's memory, I saw the red Jaguar in the mule barn. I heard the door chunk shut; I felt all the finality of our family's situation. Coming down to it, I saw that it was me or S. Jerome Luben.

Luben was saying, "I'm sure Sheriff will keep his word, in which event I'll be free next October. Not that I will leave." He frowned. "I find this hard to believe. I therefore know how difficult it may be for you to believe."

"Believe what, Mr. Luben?"

"That I'm finally rehabilitated. That I love the United States of America, that I'd go to war for my country if asked to serve. That I'd even volunteer. Inward things—I'm clean, I'm thinking straight. He'll unlock the door in October, you'll see."

I knew I'd have to kill him. I felt my heart stagger. He must have seen a change in my face. He looked at me quietly.

"After you're free, what will you do?" I asked. We'd bury him and the automobile. The easiest way would be to poison him, to let him die quietly in his sleep, and just as he had been carried into Sheriff's prison—unresisting but not cooperating—so would he be carried out of it and put deep in the ground. It was the only way.

Luben smiled. "Are you ready for this? I like your brother."

My look must have asked him who he was trying to bullshit, because he drew a breath, smiled again and went on talking. All the pressures of New York and the world outside and his troubles with his father and the other members of his family, the drug scene, the antiwar movement, the hippie underground, he was saying, all that passed away once he was locked up here, apparently for life. "All that shit, all those pressures were suddenly gone. I say *suddenly* like it happened overnight, when, of course, it didn't. I was maybe four years getting anywhere with myself, trying to bribe Henry to let me escape, screaming at night. Then I decided to cut my hair and get rid of the beard. Sheriff had already told me I could have anything I wanted within reason, as long as I bought it with my own money. These books, this library, the typewriter—I've got nearly every worthwhile book there is on penology. What started as a lot of shouting back and forth between Sheriff and me became long, leisurely conversations. He taught me how to play dominoes. I used to enter chess tournaments in my other life. Sheriff taught me dominoes—a simple game but really full of genuine American integrity. When I got tired of dominoes, he went home and got his Monopoly set. It was his kindness and his honesty and, at some point, it came to me that I liked him. I saw at last that there had been no forfeiture of equity on his part. You follow me?"

"I'm not sure," I said.

"All I'm saying is that I did wrong. He arrested me and when I threatened him like I did, in effect I locked the door on myself. Now, after ten years, almost, you see the result. You see what I've become."

"Which is what?" I asked. I got the feeling you have when a salesman goes too fast and gets close to selling you a bill of goods. In a desperate way, I wanted to believe there wouldn't be any need to kill him. The thing about him was that he was so goddamned nice and likable and, what's more, his voice and his accent reminded me of Sheriff's voice, just a touch, or maybe an echo, but it got to me where I lived. Yet I knew it couldn't be possible that he was really one of us. He was a New York Jew and a lawyer and he had to hate us. He was dangerous as a rattlesnake. "What are you now?" I asked.

"A model prisoner, a rehabilitated man. This is a copy of an essay for *The American Journal of Penology*," he said, opening the top drawer of a little olive-green filing cabinet. "Wrote it in my spare time," he said, laughing a quiet little laugh at his own joke.

I looked at the title page. "Some Problems of Local Authorities in Administering Small-Community Jails and Lockups" and, under it, "By Solomon Jerome Luben, B.A., LL.B." "Well, nice, real nice," I said. My hand was trembling.

"That's nothing. Take a look at these." And he grabbed a long tube of rolled-up papers from the top of the nearest bookshelf and started unrolling it on the library table.

Seeing the back of his neck, I thought maybe it would be better just to shoot him when he wasn't looking. If I knew Henry and Sheriff, they'd leave that part up to me.

"Don't you want to see this?" he asked.

"All right." And I moved in beside him and looked.

"Front elevation," he said. "Innovative design, eh? Wait till you see the modern features!"

All I saw was a long building.

"I'm financing the whole thing. We break ground in October, when I walk out of here. The end of the medieval monstrosity that has been the bane of every small community in the South." He peeled the top sheet aside. "Of course, there'll be a wall. Now, this is your floor plan, your maximum-security block. Dining hall is here. Exercise yard. Library, of course. Kitchen. Sheriff and I have been two years planning this little jewel. Like it?"

I stood dumbfounded. Again he said his fortune was sufficient to see the place built and maintained. He, S. Jerome Luben, would be the administrator. Sheriff would provide the prisoners, of course. Henry might need help in the kitchen, with so many additional mouths to feed. "We'll have to cross that bridge when we get to it." A dreamy look came into his eyes. Small-town mayors and city officials would be brought here, in greatest secrecy, of course, he said. It was his plan to see what he called "Sheriff's great idea" applied all over the South, for openers. "Ultimately, of course, it will sweep the globe. Once they see how it cuts all the red tape. No criminal lawyers getting some bastard, some baby raper, some fiend out just because his confession got the case thrown out of court. No trial, no court. Just the jail to end all jails, with an indeterminate sentence for everybody. No mail, no phone calls. Just. . . ." And he snapped his fingers.

"Where would you plan to build it?" I asked.

"Why, here, right here! Can you imagine a better location for the first one?" He peeled the next sheet away. "These are below ground —solitary-confinement cells, soundproof, totally dark. I tell you, Jim, when Sheriff and I get through with this thing, it's really going to be something! *Oy!*"

I couldn't think what to say. I couldn't think, period.

"What a plan, what a beautiful fucking plan," Jerome Luben was whispering.

The steel door opened and clanged below. Footsteps on the stairs; it was Henry—bringing the eggs.

Surely one of the most successful and long-running series of pastiches has been Barry Perowne's continuation of the Raffles saga created by E.W. Hornung. In fact, Perowne's pastiches are probably better known to American readers today than the Hornung originals! Raffles had an especially good year in 1975, starring in several excellent Perowne stories and also in a London stage production—Graham Greene's The Return of A.J. Raffles. *Oddly enough, the Greene play (his first in eleven years) involves Raffles with some of the same historical personages present in this story.*

BARRY PEROWNE
Raffles and the Bridge of Sighs

On the night he fell foul of the Mad Marquess, as that brawling nobleman who propounded Rules for the Prize Ring was generally known, A. J. Raffles was sitting with me at a table in Willis's Supper Rooms.

A celebrated London after-theatre resort, all red plush, gilding, and ornate gasoliers, the place was noisy with the confident voices of people of rank and fashion.

"You know, Bunny," Raffles said to me, his evening dress immaculate, his dark hair crisp, his keen face tanned from a recent cricket tour abroad, "no man can choose the name with which he's born, and in normal circumstances he goes right through life with it."

On our way here we had passed a theatre where a brave but vain attempt was being made to revive a witty comedy by a poet and playwright whose name, owing to a scandal just over two years before, it was not now prudent to include on the theatre posters.

I thought it was this which had prompted Raffles' remark, but he added "For a woman, of course, the matter of names is rather different."

Warming his brandy snifter between his fine brown hands, he glanced across with meditative gray eyes at the orchestra-dais, to which his only living relative, his sister Dinah, had gone to ask that a piece be played that she particularly wanted to hear.

A graceful, fair-haired girl of twenty-one, with a clean-cut quality and an air of friendly composure akin to her brother's, she stood chatting to the orchestra leader and his melodists in their Hungarian gypsy costume.

Understanding now what had prompted Raffles' remark about names, I said, "You mean different for a woman in the sense that she changes her name when she marries?"

He nodded, his eyes on Dinah. And a tension began to grow in me, for, oddly enough, I knew more about his sister than he did.

In accordance with the terms of their father's will, Dinah as a child of seven had been placed under the guardianship of an uncle in Australia, while the residue of the estate had been used to see Raffles, then 14, through his father's old school in England.

Dinah had been fond of her uncle, who had brought her up well, and on his recent demise she had decided to leave Australia and come to London. She had arrived, seeking her brother, while he was away on the cricket tour. So, naturally, I had appointed myself her brother-by-proxy.

Women being ineligible for residence in The Albany, the bachelor establishment where Raffles had his chambers, I had obtained accommodations for Dinah adjacent to my own small flat in Mount Street, so that I could keep an eye on her. In this I had had no difficulty. On the contrary, my difficulty had been to keep my eyes off her.

In fact, I soon had become conscious of aspirations concerning her that were quite incompatible with my role as brother-by-proxy, so it had come as a relief to me to be freed of that hampering status by Raffles' return from the cricket tour.

"Consider, Bunny," he said now, as he offered me a Sullivan from his cigarette case, "my way of life. At any moment, its criminal side may be exposed. My transgressions are different from those of that poor devil of a playwright——"

"Of whom," I murmured, "some wise Clubman remarked, 'I don't care what people do, as long as they don't do it in the streets and frighten the horses.' "

"It's not horses that are frightened of scandal," Raffles said. "It's London Society people. That playwright's transgressions put him in the same place my very different transgressions would put me—in the dock at the Old Bailey. I'm currently captain of the England cricket team, and every door in the land is open to me. If I were charged at the Old Bailey as a criminal, you can imagine the unholy scandal. What effect would it have on Dinah's prospects in life if the disaster happened while her surname still is Raffles?"

I took a gulp of brandy. My main aspiration concerning Dinah was that I might be able to persuade her, some happy day, to change her surname to my own, Manders.

"You want to see her married?" I said.

He nodded. "Safely, happily married, Bunny—though not, of

course, to an Englishman. If I come a cropper, I don't want Dinah
to be living in this country when it happens. I want her well away
from the scandal. Otherwise, I'd like nothing better than to see her
married to an Englishman—some sound, loyal chap. You, for instance. But that can never be, Bunny, because if some day I stand
in the dock at the Old Bailey, I'm afraid it's inevitable—God forgive
me for it—that you'll be standing there beside me.''

I felt as if I had been hit by a sledgehammer. Not only had he
made his point, he had impaled my heart on it. Fortunately, he did
not notice my emotion, for just then an altercation at the doorway
of the Supper Rooms attracted his attention.

"It's a small world, Bunny," he said wryly. "That playwright's out
of gaol now, living in obscurity abroad somewhere. But there's the
very man who, because of his titled and fatally attractive son's
friendship with the playwright, started the scandal that put the poor
devil in prison for two years."

At the doorway stood the most vindictive man in London, the
Mad Marquess. Short, thickset, choleric, he was slightly bowlegged
in his evening dress, for in his youth he had been notorious for
riding his horses in the Grand National till they burst their hearts.
Blackballed from decent Clubs because of his persistent brawling,
he was at it again now, fulminating like a balding, beetlebrowed ape
at the unfortunate Head Waiter.

The Marquess' usual cronies were shifty jockeys and mus-
clebound pugilists, and he had four of the latter with him now,
bullet-headed heavyweights, lumpy in their evening dress, and
there was also in the party a handsome, orange-haired woman,
flamboyantly gowned—a notorious courtesan known to dissolute
men-about-town, for reasons sufficiently reprehensible, as "Skittles."

"It's Skittles," said Raffles, "that the Head Waiter doesn't want
to admit."

"And no wonder," I said—for as the browbeaten Head Waiter
surrendered and reluctantly led the Marquess' party to a table, half
the women in the place, followed by their escorts, swept out with
their chins in the air.

The party, with the Marquess guffawing and Skittles wielding her
fan with an air of supercilious triumph, passed close by the orchestra
dais and the Marquess stopped suddenly.

"What, no music?" he said. "Play *The Beautiful Blue Danube.*"

The orchestra leader, violin and bow in hand, glanced uncertainly
at Dinah, with whom he had been talking.

"You heard what I said," bawled the Marquess. "Play *The Blue
Bloody Danube.*"

Raffles said, "Excuse me a moment, Bunny," and rose and walked over to the orchestra dais.

"Dinah," he said, "is *The Blue Danube* the piece you want to hear?"

"Why, no," she said. "I asked for one of Brahms' Hungarian Dances."

"And did the orchestra leader say he would play it for you?"

"Yes," Dinah said quietly.

"Then on the principle," Raffles said, "of first come, first served, that is what the orchestra will now play. Please go and sit down and enjoy it."

In the deathly hush, Dinah came and joined me at our table. Raffles remained looking without expression at the Marquess, who stared back with a dark flush slowly engorging his simian face. New shoes sqeaked on the red plush carpet as the four bruisers, massive and scowling, took station on both sides of their squat patron.

Tense, my heart pounding, I rose to go to Raffles' side. But the Marquess, just then, flung out a hairy forefinger at him and said thickly, *"I shall remember you!"* Turning, he exploded at the trembling Head Waiter, "What are you standing there for?"

The orchestra leader, with a glance at Raffles, tucked his violin under his chin, and the thrall that had held the people in the Supper Rooms immobile was broken by a buzz of voices as the melodists launched into the lilt of a Brahms Hungarian Dance.

Raffles rejoined us, saying, as he sat down, "Dinah, I'm sorry that should have happened."

"I'm not," she said, a little breathless, her gray eyes shining. "For I've found my brother."

True to his intention of putting Dinah in the way of making an advantageous foreign marriage, Raffles in the following week took her to Paris and, at the warm insistence of them both, I accompanied them.

Raffles had with him letters of introduction from people of social consequence in London to people of like consequence in Paris. As a result, the three of us were soon caught up in a whirl of *salons* and dinner parties, and Raffles received many compliments on the appearance and comportment of his sister.

"Which is all very pleasing, Bunny," he said to me, privately, "but keep your eyes open for some grist to the mill. With a foreign marriage my objective for Dinah, I have to bear in mind a custom of well-regulated European families."

"What custom, Raffles?"

"The custom of the dowry, Bunny."

To give Dinah a change from formal occasions, one free evening we took her over to the Left Bank, and among the places at which we dropped in, looking for amusement, chanced to be a Waxworks Museum.

The effigies were arranged in groups, each figure having propped at its feet a card bearing a number by which the effigy, with a brief history of its original's claim to celebrity, could be identified in the catalogue—which I was carrying and from which, when asked by Dinah, I read out to her the information relevant to such effigies as attracted her attention.

We came to a group of figures which, in the harsh glare of gas-light, leered out through the iron bars of a cage bearing a placard with the titles *Les Ames Damnées*—("The Damned Souls.")

Some of the figures in the cage wore the striped pajamas and frayed straw sombreros of felons condemned to Devil's Island, but I noticed, with a shock, one whose ample girth was clad in coarse trousers and tunic stamped all over with the broad arrows of the English prison system.

"Dinah," Raffles said, at once, "there's a group over there we mustn't miss."

He steered her firmly away from the iron cage—for several times, as I knew, he had dined at the tables of London Society people in the company of the poet and playwright whose effigy, with shoulder-length waved hair parted in the center and a slim volume open in one hand, stood now, branded, among the felons.

I lingered a moment, fascinated. Stenciled on the breast of the effigy's tunic was the prison number, C.3.3., and on the slim volume which the effigy held open at its title page—*The Ballad of Reading Gaol, by C.3.3.*—lay a shriveled green carnation.

Chilled, I turned away and, thrusting the catalogue hastily into the side pocket of my suit, joined Dinah and Raffles.

We had a late supper at the Closerie des Lilas, a lively restaurant in the *quartier,* and, later still, dropped in for a nightcap at a *café* in the Boulevard Saint-Michel. There were a half-dozen or so men standing in a row at the bar, but few of the tables were occupied—and we had only just sat down and given our order to the waiter when Dinah put a hand on Raffles' sleeve.

"There's a man over there," she said, "who seems to know you."

We followed her glance. And my heart sank like a stone.

In the all too abundant flesh, grown now bloated and debauched, the man looking at Raffles across the *café* was he whose effigy stood in the cage of *Les Ames Damnées.*

Meeting Raffles' eyes, the man turned away his head.

My heart thumped as I wondered what, with his sister with him, Raffles would do.

After an instant of hesitation, he excused himself to Dinah and walked across to the table where ex-Convict C.3.3., gross in his rumpled evening dress, sat in the company of a young man in his early twenties who could hardly have made a greater contrast, for his light tweed traveling-suit hung on his painfully lank figure as on a skeleton.

Rich and resonant, with a hint of brogue and a slur of drunkenness in it, the ex-convict's voice reached Dinah and me clearly across the *café.*

"Well, well," he said, as, still seated, he offered Raffles three fat fingers of a languid hand to shake. "An Englishman who doesn't cut me dead! But I suppose A. J. Raffles would consider that not quite *cricket?*"

"Bunny,"·Dinah murmured, "why did the man say that?"

"He's a man, Dinah," I said guardedly, "who made a mistake and has rather fallen in life."

"What was his mistake, Bunny?" Dinah asked.

His mistake, apart from having been too greatly charmed by the Mad Marquess' attractive but capricious son, had been in not getting out of England when he had the chance. Instead, with Irish insouciance and the green-dyed carnation of an aesthete defiant in his buttonhole, he had remained to stand alone, deserted by the Marquess' son, in the dock at the Old Bailey.

But I said, "His mistake, Dinah, was to be born out of his time. He'd have been understood in the Athens of Pericles, but he wasn't understood in the land of the Widow at Windsor, so people don't want to know him any more."

"*I* want to know him," said Dinah.

Before I could stop her, she rose and walked over to the table where Raffles stood talking with the two seated men, and I had perforce to follow.

"You're a fine brother," she said to Raffles. "You desert me."

"Sebastian Melmoth," the ex-convict said quickly, heaving up his bulk from his chair. "And may I present my gifted young friend, Aubrey Beardsley."

As the wand-thin youth, with his refined face of an almost transparent pallor, bowed to Dinah, the waiter approached with a tray and asked Raffles if the drinks we had ordered were to be served now at this table.

Making the best of the situation I knew he would gladly have avoided, Raffles said, "If these gentlemen will drink with us—?"

"Absinthe, *garçon*," said Melmoth, as ex-Convict C.3.3. evidently now called himself, and he explained to Dinah, as we all sat down, "The green hue of absinthe is restful to the cultivated eye." Cultivated as they no doubt were, his own eyes were also bloodshot, with bags under them, as he went on, "Young Beardsley here is only in Paris for one night. He's on his way to convalesce in the mild climate of Mentone, and we ran into each other on the quay named for that horrid little monkey of a genius, Voltaire."

"Is it Mr. Melmoth you're sketching, Mr. Beardsley?" Dinah asked, for the frail youth was adding touches, with a stylus pen, to a drawing on a small sketch-block.

He shook his head. "I'm sketching the backs of those men standing in a row, like a kind of frieze, at the bar over there. D'you like it?"

Tearing it from the block, he gave Dinah the sketch.

"Only their backs," she said, comparing the sketch with the row of men at the bar, "yet—somehow—you've caught them perfectly."

"For that kind remark," said Beardsley, "you shall have it. How are you called, Miss Raffles—by your friends?"

"I'm called Dinah, Mr. Beardsley."

"Then I shall inscribe this," said the artist, doing so, " 'For Dinah—*Arte per l'Arte*—Aubrey Beardsley.' "

As he presented Dinah with the sketch, the waiter came with a glass of warm milk for him and the absinthe for Melmoth.

"Your brother, Miss Dinah," Melmoth said, licking his sensuous lips at sight of the absinthe, "is instructing you in the ways of the world, I trust?"

"I'm learning something new from him every day, Mr. Melmoth."

"Raffles, the cricketer," said Melmoth, "in the role of Pygmalion. But how bizarre!"

"Bizarre?" said Dinah. "I don't know what you mean."

"Alas," sighed Melmoth, "I so seldom mean what I say!"

He drank his absinthe. But it was clear, as we sat talking, that his wit was gone, quenched by the vindictive persecution, with its dire results, of the Mad Marquess. Melmoth called for more absinthe, grew drunker and maudlin, until presently young Beardsley, taking a sip of his milk, coughed painfully and a sudden froth of blood appeared on his lips. He clapped his handkerchief to them, and I saw on Melmoth's big, vealy face a look of poignant concern.

"Aubrey," he said gently, "it's late, dear boy, for we decadents to be abroad, and you've a train to catch in a few hours. Look there at the window! Day breaks on the Boul' Mich'—*And down the silent, sleeping street/The dawn, with silver-sandalled feet/ Creeps like a frightened girl*. Come, Aubrey my dear, I'll take you to your hotel."

Bloated and rumpled, he heaved himself up, took from the table his silk hat and turquoise-knobbed ebony stick.

"Perhaps we shall meet again," he said to us, as he handed young Beardsley his traveling-cap. "Aubrey goes to the healing climate of Mentone, and I—who knows whither?" He clapped his silk hat on his straggle of shoulder-length, graying hair, and shrugged, with a wry smile. "Melmoth the Wanderer! Come, Aubrey."

The bulky, destroyed poet put an arm protectively about the thin shoulders of the young artist, and, as they left us, we sat down again; but somehow, for a while, we had nothing to say.

It was Raffles who, quite suddenly, broke the silence between us: "Dinah, let me see that sketch."

Dinah gave it to him, he glanced at it, then over at the bar, then handed the sketch to me. It portrayed, as a frieze in India ink, the backs of a half-dozen or so men of assorted shapes and sizes standing in a row. I looked over at the men standing at the bar. In the row there, a gap had appeared. I looked again at the sketch, which showed no gap—and my scalp suddenly tingled.

"Come on," said Raffles, tossing some coins onto the marble tabletop.

He hurried Dinah and me out, and he and I looked quickly each way along the Boulevard Saint-Michel. The breaking day was redolent of fresh-ground coffee and new-baked bread, but there was nobody to be seen except a man with a hose spraying the sidewalk trees and the gutters.

"What are you looking for?" Dinah asked us.

"A cab," said Raffles. "It's time you were in bed."

But what Raffles and I were looking for were two men whose backs appeared side by side in young Beardsley's sketch—a short man with the slight build of a jockey and a tall man with the burly build of a pugilist.

We had no idea where the ex-convict who now called himself Sebastian Melmoth was living in Paris.

"In any case, Bunny," Raffles said to me later, in private, "the fact that the Mad Marquess' chosen cronies are small jockeys and big bruisers is a pretty thin reason for warning Melmoth that it's possible he's being watched."

"Personally," I said, "I didn't notice the oddly assorted couple leave the bar. They *may* have been following Melmoth, but I think they were just a coincidence. After all, Raffles, the Marquess did, more than two years ago, what he set out to do. He wrecked Melmoth's life. What possible motive could the Marquess have now for having the poor devil spied on?"

"I don't know, Bunny," Raffles said. "Anyway, confound it, it's none of our business. Forget it! A dowry for Dinah, that's our business now—or mine, anyway."

He had no suspicion of my own feelings about Dinah and twisting the hooks in my own heart, I managed to say, "Your business, Raffles, is my business—as always."

He smiled. "Good old Bunny!"

So it was with a dowry for Dinah in the forefront of his mind that we left Paris, some days later, and took Dinah off to Venice, where Raffles had a letter of introduction to present.

On the day when the three of us, Dinah with a pretty parasol raised against the burning sunshine, disembarked from a gondola at a splendid old *palazzo* on the Grand Canal, the majordomo informed us that the Principessa was not in residence, having repaired to her country place in the Tuscan hills.

Raffles said that, in the circumstances, he would mail the letter to the Principessa's country place, and leaving our calling cards with the majordomo, we went back down the steps and Raffles told Salvatore, our gondolier, to take us to the Piazza San Marco, the hour being now hard upon teatime.

At the barber-pole mooring-posts of the Piazza gondola quay, Raffles tipped Salvatore handsomely and, with Dinah arm-in-arm between us and flocks of pigeons waddling away and flapping up before us, we sauntered across the great square, to our left the soaring Campanile, to our right the Doge's Palace and the lofty, tessellated porch of St. Mark's Cathedral topped by the equine statuary group once stolen by the greatest burglar in the annals of crime, the Emperor Napoleon.

We passed into the welcome shade of the colonnaded arcade to our left, where, on the sidewalk, the tables of the Caffè Florian were set out.

"Why, look!" Dinah exclaimed. "There's Mr. Melmoth!"

My spirits sank. The overweight aesthete, in a white alpaca suit that would have been the better for pressing, and wearing a boater with a faded ribbon on his straggling locks, sat alone with his absinthe at a table.

"So!" he said resonantly. "Melmoth the Wanderer and Pygmalion the Cricketer, with his malleable maiden, meet again!" With a majestic but wavering gesture, for he certainly had been looking upon the absinthe at its greenest, he made us free of chairs at his table. "I'm here, in this city of rendezvous, where the mercantile West meets the gorgeous East—with the permission of that old bore Wordsworth—to keep a rendezvous myself."

"A happy one for you, I hope, Mr. Melmoth," said Dinah.

"As to that, Miss Dinah," said ex-Convict C.3.3., *"King Pandion is dead/ All his friends are lapped in lead.* And yet—and yet, Miss Dinah —*I have had playmates, I have had companions—"*

He looked out with pouched eyes at the Piazza San Marco as though he saw, through the glaze of heat quivering there, English willows in summers gone, and himself, bland with success, idly propelling a punt for the indulgence of a graceful, capricious youth in blazer and straw boater, reclining on the cushions.

Suddenly, to my embarrassment, tears rolled down Melmoth's puffy cheeks.

"It *could* be a happy rendezvous," he murmured, "after so long. It *could* be." Groping for his turquoise-knobbed stick, he rose heavily. "I'm expecting a telegram. I must go to my hotel again and ask if it's come at last. Oh, I *do* hope it's come. Forgive me, Miss Dinah."

Blindly, he walked out under the arch of the colonnade into the white lightning of the sun. And Dinah, perhaps a little upset by the man's emotion, took up from the table the list of the Caffé Florian's ice creams and gazed at it, biting her lip.

I looked out at Melmoth. Pigeons rose before him as he made his way diagonally across the great square. An opening to the left of St. Mark's Cathedral swallowed him in shade. And two men strolled out from the cathedral porch on the far side of the square—two men in cloth caps, a little man like a jockey and a big man like a bruiser. The gap of shade that had engulfed Melmoth swallowed them.

I met Raffles' eyes. He stood up, saying, "I'm going to buy some cigarettes. I won't be long."

But not until I was dressing for dinner that evening did I see him again, when he walked into my room at our hotel looking out on the lagoons.

"Bunny," he said, "they followed Melmoth to his hotel. The little fellow's a baby-faced, sly-eyed young Cockney called Titch. He stayed to keep an eye on Melmoth's hotel. The big bruiser's called Josser. I trailed him to a back canal, where he went into a *Pensione.* It's evidently where they're lodging. Tonight, when Dinah's retired, you and I'll take a prowl around that *Pensione* and see if we can find out what their game is."

"What d'you think about this 'rendezvous' of Melmoth's?"

"I'm afraid, Bunny, it's the one rendezvous in this life he should not keep."

Venice in the small hours. Moonlight and uncanny silence. No hoofs, no whipcracks, no hansoms, no horses. A city without wheels.

By narrow sidewalks edging devious waterways, Raffles and I

reached the *Pensione*. The word was visible, in the moonlight, over the iron-studded door of the tall old building which, with its shuttered windows, stood at the junction of two canals.

"How does one get to it?" I asked, looking at the building across the gap of stagnant canal water.

"Plank drawbridge," said Raffles. "It was down when I followed Josser here. It's been pulled up now and chained beside the door over there." He put a hand on my arm. "Listen!"

A vague mutter of men's voices was coming from the direction of the side of the building. As we listened, a voice unmistakably Cockney rose louder, exclaiming, "Garn!"

We moved to our right. The narrow, cobbled sidewalk angled sharply to edge the other canal, at the side of the *Pensione*. From the one open window in the tall side of the building, dim lamplight fell across the stagnant water. The window was not much above our own level. High up, moonlight silvered the eaves of the building.

We moved along the sidewalk, against which barges stinking of rotten fruit and vegetables were moored in line, and we came opposite the lamplit window. The voices of the men in the room were clearly audible to us now across the canal.

"Garn, you big baboon, use your loaf, Josser! 'E got 'is bleedin' telegram, didn't 'e? 'Oo else would it be from but young Lord Alf, the Marquess' dandy son? 'E laid low, did 'is young lordship, when the beak at the Old Byeley sent Melmoth down for a stretch. Never wrote to 'im in the clink, neither. So Lord Alf's conscience 'as bin troublin' 'im, givin' 'im socks, bet yer life. An' now 'e reckons it's safe to meet Melmoth again, on the quiet, an' see 'ow 'e's made out."

" 'E'll get a bleedin' shock when 'e sees that, Titch!"

Shadows moved on a wall in the room across the canal there. Liquor glugged audibly from a bottle.

"It's like the Marquess told us, Josser. 'E's suspicious because 'e's 'eard 'is fancy son's rented a villa—Villa Giudice at Posilippo, on the B'y o' Nyples—an' the Marquess reckons Lord Alf may take Melmoth there on the sly. An' you know what the Marquess told you when 'e 'anded you that thahsand pahnds you got in yer baggage there—"

" 'Get Melmoth for me, Josser,' the old bleeder said, Titch. 'I don't care 'ow you do it, or 'oo you 'ave to bribe, or 'ow much, but fix Melmoth for keeps, Josser!' The Marquess an' 'is bloody *Rules o' the Prize Ring,* eh, Titch?"

"Gentry's different, Josser. They makes their own rules as they goes along. No skin off our nose. Tomorrow we fixes Melmoth, and

it don't cost a blind farthing. All I does is watch my chance to walk
up to 'im tomorrow an' ask the time, an' say wot a nice bit o' weather
we're 'avin.'. Then I walks off to the police station where them
Venice coppers lolls around in admirals' 'ats an' white gloves. An'
I tells 'em, indignant-like, I'm a innocent young tourist passin'
through which a grown man 'as just made remarks to that interpre-
tations could be put on.''

"You crafty little baby-faced, Titch!"

"So then I tells 'em, Josser, that I recognizes the grown man as
an old lag wot was 'ad up at the Old Byeley. An' I tells 'em 'is real
name. That'll do it, Josser. *They'll* 'ave 'eard of 'im. 'Oo 'asn't? An'
it'll be a case o'—'Give a dog a bad name,' see?''

"They'll run 'im in on the spot, Titch!"

"What's more, Josser, the British Consul ain't goin' to stir 'imself
overmuch for an old lag. So Mr. Alias Bloomin' Melmoth'll be in the
same fix as them Venice blokes in old-fashioned times 'ere. They got
frogsmarched across that there Bridge o' Sighs an' flung in the
dungeons of The Dodger's Palace—an' that was the last anyone
ever 'eard of 'em!''

"Blimey, Titch, the Marquess'll laugh 'is bleedin' 'ead off! All
right, we'll do it to-morrer. Now, go on, get out o' my room an' rest
yer brains. I needs my sleep.''

Raffles murmured in my ear, "While he's settling down to repose,
Bunny, let's see if we can get a drink somewhere to wash a bad taste
out of our mouths.''

We found, not far off, a small *caffé* that was on the point of closing.
The proprietor served us reluctantly with a couple of glasses of
rough Tuscan wine from a barrel, and Raffles asked for a few tooth-
picks. Puzzled, I watched him arrange four of them thus:

▬▬▬▬   ▬▬▬▬   ▬▬▬▬   ▬▬▬▬

"What does that signify?" I asked, with a frown.

"It signifies," Raffles said, "the position of the barges now lying in
line, each moored fore and aft, against the sidewalk side of the canal
back there. Now, if the fore end of the second barge were unmoored
and given a push, it would float out to this position.''

He revised the position of the second toothpick to:

"The barge," he said, "would then be aslant across the canal, and its fore end, I fancy, would just about be touching the wall of the *Pensione* almost exactly under Josser's window."

"A bridge!" I exclaimed.

"A pontoon bridge," Raffles agreed, "a Bridge of Sighs for the Mad Marquess, because it'll cost him the thousand pounds he entrusted to Josser in a bad cause, and enable us to divert the money to the worthier cause of laying a foundation on which to build Dinah's dowry."

When we returned to the canal that flanked the side of the *Pensione*, snores sounded audibly from the wide-open window and shutters of Josser's room. Raffles untied from its mooring-ring the rope at the fore end of the second barge. We stepped down into a slime of rotting vegetable matter on the floorboards of the barge. There we found the heavy, slippery bargepole. With this we thrust hard against the sidewalk parapet. The barge, still secured at its stern, swung out gently over the stagnant canal and knocked against the wall under Josser's window.

Raffles leaped up, gripped the sill, pulled himself higher, and, silent as a leopard, vanished into the darkness of the room.

I stood holding the bargepole jammed down into the mud of the canal bottom, to keep the barge in position. Sweat poured down inside my evening dress. Mingling with the snores from the open window just above my head, another sound became audible—the throbbing of an approaching *vaporetto*, a steam-launch. I peered along the dark canal to where, at its further end, about a hundred yards off, it debouched into a moonlit cross-canal.

The throbbing grew louder, then slower. I could hear the water churned by the screws. Would the launch turn into this canal blocked by the barge? My heart pounded. Suddenly Raffles dropped down beside me into the barge.

"Don't move," I whispered. "Look there!"

The *vaporetto* had steamed into view, there in the moonlight of the cross-canal. It was a police patrol launch. The epaulettes and cocked hats of two policemen were clearly visible as, their launch scarcely moving, they peered toward us along the dark canal.

Clearly, a voice reached us: "Niente! Andiamo!"

Smoke belched from the launch's short stack, the screws churned the water, the launch moved on, and its purposeful throbbing died away.

We tied up the barge in its original position and, leaving Josser's snores behind us, made our retreat quickly along the footwalks that edged the jigsaw of waterways. Not until we came out of the Piazza San Marco did I ask Raffles if he had found the money in Josser's baggage.

"It's in hundred-pound notes, Bunny. It's in my pocket." He stopped dead. "There's Melmoth!"

The pigeons had gone to roost. Nothing moved on the moonlit expanse of the great square slanted across by the shadow of the Campanile, but a few figures still sat at the sidewalk tables of the Caffé Florian in the arcade. Among those sleepless beings, the figure of Melmoth, alone at a table, brooded over his absinthe.

"The folly of the man!" I muttered. "How can he have brought himself to make a rendezvous again with the young lordship who wrecked him?"

"Mel*moth*," Raffles said dryly. "An apt alias, Bunny. The moth with scorched wings can't help scorching them again—even to death —in the same flame."

"He's forgotten the lines he himself wrote," I said, "in the ballad composed behind prison bars: *For who can tell/ To what red hell/ His immortal soul shall go?*"

"Bunny," Raffles said, "I don't know whether it's possible to help a man who's lost the will to help himself. But one can try. Go on to our hotel. I'll see you when I see you."

Leaving me in the moonlight, he walked on and passed under the gas-globes of the arcade to join Melmoth the Wanderer.

Broad daylight filled my room at the hotel when Raffles woke me. He had bathed, and changed from evening dress to a suit of light gray flannel, with a pearl in his cravat, but his keen face had a haggard look.

"It's 6 A.M., Bunny," he said, offering me a Sullivan from his cigarette case. "Melmoth's gone. I saw him off, an hour ago, on the first train out across the causeway. He's not going to keep his rendezvous today, or any other rendezvous ever, I think, with the young milord. I gather that Melmoth has just one steady, wise, compassionate friend—a man called Robbie—who's at Taormina in Sicily. I've given Melmoth two hundred pounds—all he would accept from me, though he doesn't know it's the Mad Marquess' money—and he's on his way now to Taormina."

"What about Titch and Josser?"

"No sign of 'em at the station, Bunny. Still snoring in the *Pensione* I imagine. When they wake up to find they've lost the Marquess' thousand pounds, then find they've lost track of Melmoth as well, I doubt if they'll go to the police—who'd be suspicious about how a precious pair like that got their hooks on a thousand pounds in the first place. No, I fancy they'll be catching the train today for Paris and London, which leaves at four this afternoon. To be sure they go, we'll take Dinah for a gondola ride, and I'll have a quiet word with Salvatore to see to it we're in the vicinity of the station about four this afternoon."

The clocks of Venice were nearing that hour when our gondola, lazily propelled by Salvatore's huge oar, drifted us into view of the broad, water-lapped steps to the arched entrance of the glass-roofed station.

From gondolas and from an awninged *vaporetto,* a public Grand Canal steam-launch, travelers were disembarking and going up the steps into the station. Among them trudged, bad-temperedly humping their carpetbags, Titch and Josser.

Evidently a train had just come in, for newly-arrived travelers were emerging from the station.

"Oh, look!" said Dinah idly, as she reclined on our gondola cushions in the shade of her pretty parasol. "What an attractive young man!"

Following the glance of her cool gray eyes, I saw that the young man in question, accompanied by a porter burdened with expensive luggage, had just emerged from the station. Of graceful build, immaculate in white flannels and a pink blazer, a boater jauntily tilted on longish hair almost as fair as Dinah's, he stood at the head of the steps, tapping a malacca cane languidly on his palm as he cast patrician glances over the throng of travelers, as though he expected somebody to be awaiting his arrival.

"He looks like a young Adonis," said Dinah, "just, as I imagine, Lord Alfred must look."

It was an instant before, in the gently rocking gondola fifty yards out from the station, the impact of her remark struck me. I stared at her.

Raffles said, very evenly, "Lord Alfred, Dinah?"

"Mr. Melmoth's ex-friend," Dinah said. "Poor Mr. Melmoth, I know his *real* name and why he changed it."

"Indeed?" said Raffles.

"But of course," said Dinah. "Because when we met Mr. Melmoth with Mr. Beardsley in that Paris *café,* I had a feeling that Mr. Melmoth looked rather like the poor convict, with the broad arrows on him, that I caught a glimpse of in that iron-barred cage at the Waxworks. So I read all about him, and his green carnation, in the catalogue later on."

"But, Dinah," I blurted, *"I* had the catalogue."

"Yes, Bunny," she said, "I noticed it in the side pocket of your suit as we were talking to Mr. Melmoth and Mr. Beardsley."

From the shade of her pretty parasol, as she reclined on the gondola cushions, she smiled at us with indulgent composure.

"So I *stole* it," said Dinah Raffles.

Appalled, I glanced at Raffles. And I knew then, very surely, he would see to it that his sister changed her surname as soon as he had amassed her dowry. For A. J. Raffles was looking up speculatively at where, high on the cathedral roof not far off, the only horses in Venice pranced nobly against the blue of the sky—the priceless golden horses of St. Mark's.

AUTHOR'S NOTE

Although various biographers of Lord Alfred Douglas and Mr. Oscar Wilde (self-styled, in exile, Sebastian Melmoth) mention an arrangement between those gentlemen for a joint sojourn at the Villa Giudice, Posilippo, no explanation for the abandonment of that arrangement has been forthcoming until Mr. Manders' account of the above adventure was made available by the authorities.

Lord Alfred is known to have been present, however, when, ultimately, Mr. Wilde's remains were interred in the Père Lachaise Cemetery, Paris, under the epitaph he had composed for himself:

> And alien tears will fill for him
> Pity's long-broken urn . . .

Young Mr. Aubrey Beardsley, whose unique talent illustrated so much of the best work from Mr. Wilde's pen, died at Mentone at the age of 24, shortly after the meeting described in Mr. Manders' narrative.

If there exists any account by Mr. Manders of an attempt by his friend A. J. Raffles to make off with the golden horses of St. Mark's, it remains among the many private writings of Mr. Manders which, following their seizure at his Mount Street flat by Scotland Yard, the authorities have not yet deemed it prudent to release.

The first new story about Ellery and Inspector Queen in more than four years.

ELLERY QUEEN
The Reindeer Clue

"Ellery!" Inspector Queen shouted over the heads of the waiting children. "Over here!"

Ellery managed to work his way through the crowd to the entrance of the Children's Zoo. The weather was unusually warm for two days before Christmas and the children didn't mind waiting.

If the presence of a half-dozen police cars stirred any curiosity, it was not enough for anyone to question Ellery as he edged his way forward.

"What is it, dad?" he asked, as the Inspector closed the wooden gate behind him.

"Murder, Ellery. And unless we can wind it up fast there are going to be a lot of disappointed kids out there."

"Are they waiting for Santa Claus?" Ellery asked with a grin.

"The next best thing—Santa's reindeer. It's a Christmas tradition here to deck the place with tinsel and toys and pass one of the reindeer off as Rudolph."

Ellery could see the police technicians working over the body of a man sprawled inside the fence of the reindeer pen. Off to one side a white-coated man kept a firm grip on the reindeer itself as the police flashbulbs popped. Another white-coated man and a woman were standing nearby.

"Who's the dead man?" Ellery asked. "Anyone I know?"

"Matter of fact, yes. It's Casey Sturgess, the ex-columnist."

"You've got to be kidding," Ellery exclaimed. "Sturgess murdered in a children's zoo?"

The old man shrugged. "Looks like he was up to his old tricks." Sturgess had been the gossip columnist on a now defunct New York tabloid.

When the paper folded he'd continued with his gossipy trade, selling information in a manner that often approached blackmail.

Ellery glanced toward the woman and two men. "Blackmailing one of these?"

"Why else would he come here at eight in the morning except to meet one of them? Come on—I'll introduce you."

The woman was Dr. Ella Manners, staff veterinarian. She wore straight blond hair and no makeup. "This is a terrible thing, simply terrible!" she cried out. "We've got a hundred children and their mothers out there waiting to see the reindeer. Can't you get this body out of here?"

"We're working as fast as we can," Inspector Queen assured her, motioning Ellery toward the two men.

One, who walked with a noticeable limp, was the zoo's director, Bernard White. The other man, younger than White and grossly overweight, was Mike Halley—"Captain Mike to the kids," he explained. "I'm the animal handler, except today it's more of a people handler.

"Our reindeer is tame, but it's still a big animal. We don't let the kids get too close to it."

The Inspector motioned toward the body. "Any of you know the dead man?"

"No sir," Bernard White answered for the others. "We didn't know him and we have no idea how he got in here with the reindeer. We found him when we arrived just after eight o'clock."

"You all arrived at once?" Ellery asked him.

"I was just getting out of my car when Captain Mike drove up. Ella followed right behind him."

"Anyone else work here?"

"We have a night crew to clean up, but in the morning there's only the three of us."

Ellery nodded. "So one of you could have met Casey Sturgess here earlier, killed him, and then driven around the park till you saw the others coming."

"Why would one of us kill him?" Ella Manners asked. "We didn't even know him."

"Sturgess had sunk to some third-rate blackmailing lately. You all work for the city, in a job that puts you in contact with children. The least hint of drugs or a morals charge would have been enough to lose you your jobs. Right, dad?"

Inspector Queen nodded. "Damn right! Sturgess was shot in the chest with a .22 automatic. We found the weapon over in the straw. One of you met him here to pay blackmail, but shot him instead. It has to be one of you—he wouldn't possibly have come into the reindeer pen before the place opened to meet anybody else."

Ellery motioned his father aside. "Any fingerprints on the gun, dad?"

"It was wiped clean, Ellery. But the victim did manage to leave us something—a dying message of sorts."

Ellery's face lit up. "What, dad?"

"Come over here by the body."

Ellery passed a bucket that held red-and-green giveaway buttons inscribed, "I saw Santa's Reindeer!" He ducked his head under a hanging fringe of holly and joined his father by the body. For the first time he noticed that the rear fence of the reindeer pen was decorated with seven weathered wooden placards, each carrying eight lines of Clement Clarke Moore's famous poem, "A Visit from St. Nicholas."

Casey Sturgess had died under the third placard, his arm outstretched toward it.

"He could only have lived a minute or so with that wound," the old man said. "But look at the blood on his right forefinger. He used it to mark the sign."

Ellery leaned closer, examining two lines of the Moore poem. *Now, Dasher! now, Dancer! now, Prancer and Vixen!/ On, Comet! on, Cupid! on, Donder and Blitzen!*

"Dad—he smeared each of the eight reindeer's names with a dab of blood!"

"Right, Ellery. Now you tell me what it means."

Ellery remained stooped, studying the defaced poem for some minutes. All the smears were similar.

None seemed to have been given more emphasis than any other. Finally he straightened up and walked over to the reindeer that was drinking water from its trough, oblivious of the commotion.

"What's its name?" he asked the overweight Captain Mike.

"Sparky—but for Christmas we call him Rudolph. The kids like it."

Ellery put out a gentle hand and touched the ungainly animal's oversized antlers, wishing that it could speak and tell him what it had seen in the pen.

But it was as silent as the llama and donkey and cow that he could see standing in the adjoining pens.

"How much longer is this going on?" White was demanding from the Inspector.

"As long as it takes. We've got a murder on our hands, Mr. White."

He turned his back on the zoo director and looked at his son. "What do you make of it, Ellery?"

"Not much. Found anyone who heard the shot?"

"Not yet. The sound of a little .22 wouldn't carry very far."

Ellery went back for one more look at the bloody marks on the Moore poem.

Then he asked Ella Manners, "Would you by any chance be a particularly good dancer, Doctor?"

"Hardly! Veterinary medicine and dancing don't mix."

"I thought not," Ellery said, suddenly pleased.

"You got something?" his father asked.

"Yes, dad. I know who murdered Casey Sturgess."

Sparky the reindeer looked up from its trough, as if listening to Ellery's words. "You see, dad, there's always a danger with dying messages—a danger that the killer will see his victim leave the message, or return and find it later. Premeditated murderers like to make certain they've finished the job without leaving a clue. You told me Sturgess could only have lived a minute or so with that wound."

"That's right, Ellery."

"Then the killer was probably still here to see him jab that sign with his bloody finger. And are we to believe that in a minute's time the dying Sturgess managed to smear all eight names with his blood, and each in the same way? No, dad—Sturgess only marked *one* name! The killer, unable to wipe the blood off without leaving a mark, smeared the other seven names himself in the same manner. He obliterated the dying man's message by adding to it!"

"But, Ellery—which reindeer's name did Sturgess mark?"

"Dad, it had to be one that would connect instantly with his killer. Now look at those eight names. Could it have been Donder or Blitzen? Hardly—they tell us nothing. Likewise Dasher and Prancer have no connection with any of the suspects. Dr. Manners might be a Vixen and White could be a Cupid, but Sturgess couldn't expect the police to spot such a nebulous thing. No, dad, the reindeer clue had to be something so obvious the killer was forced to alter it."

"That's why you asked Dr. Manners if she was a dancer!"

"Exactly. It's doubtful that the limping Bernard White or the overweight Captain Mike are notable as dancers, and once I ruled Dr. Manners out as well, that left only one name on the list."

"Comet!"

"Yes, dad. The most famous reindeer of all might be Rudolph, but the most famous comet of all is surely Halley's Comet."

"Captain Mike Halley! Somebody grab him!"

Moments later, as the struggling Halley was being led away, Bernard White said, "But he was our only handler! We're ready to open the gates and who's going to look after the children?"

Ellery glanced at his father and smiled, broadly. "Maybe I can help out. After all, it's Christmas," he said.

Charles Boeckman is a relatively new writer, and this is his first appearance in BEST. *But after reading this sensitive tale of an old beggar and his banjo, I think readers will be looking for more of his work.*

CHARLES BOECKMAN
Mr. Banjo

A murder trial brought me back to my home town, Whitaker. I would never have gone back there if a certain wealthy doctor's wife and her boyfriend had not decided to knock off the good doctor in a "hunting accident." Their clumsiness got them arrested for capital murder. They wanted, and could afford, the best criminal lawyer in the state. So they hired me, Roger Spencer. I come high, but I have a national reputation. Since they were guilty as hell, they were going to need the kind of courtroom miracles I could pull off.

Whitaker had changed little in the thirty-odd years since I left. I drove into town in my new car and turned slowly down Main Street, the setting of a thousand boyhood memories. Old Hester's pharmacy was now a chain drugstore. The front of the Bijou had been remodeled and was now the Ciné, but for the most part, the storefronts had the same depressing, slightly seedy look as when I'd grown up here. It was as if the Great Depression had settled here and never left. I had the spooky feeling that if I walked into the barbershop, the calendar on the wall would read "1936."

Then I passed the corner where the First National Bank was still located, and suddenly I could hear a banjo plunking. It was a trick of memory, of course, because that was the corner where old Mr. Banjo used to sit on his apple box and play for nickles and dimes. After all these years, I could still see him clearly, a frail old man, his sightless eyes looking nowhere, his faithful old dog Rascal curled beside his box, and his banjo strumming merrily away.

Then the memories became chilling. I shivered and speeded up to get away from there but the ghostly banjo music followed me down the street. I drove to the new motel where I had a reservation.

For the next twenty-four hours I was extremely busy, meeting with my clients and their local attorney, preparing for the first day of jury selection.

I was leaving the courthouse about four the next afternoon when a rather nondescript, gray, middle-aged man approached me. "Mr. Spencer—Roger . . . remember me?"

I put on my professional, public-relations smile. "Why yes, I think so. Let me see now . . ." (Actually, I hadn't the vaguest idea who he was.)

"Dick Frazer. I—I guess we've all changed," he said, apologizing for my not remembering him.

Again flashed a flood of memories—the banjo ringing faintly down the corridor of years—and a slight chill rippled down my spine. "Dick! Of course I remember," I said with genuine warmth, shaking hands with him. "Why, we were good friends. We hunted squirrels and rabbits after school."

"Had to," he laughed. "Food came scarce in those days. Remember the rattlesnakes we used to trap and sell?"

I shuddered. "Don't remind me! Like you said, though, money was hard to come by. So you're still living here."

"Yes. I'm running the town's newspaper—still a weekly like it always was. I took it over after my father passed away. Listen, do you have a minute for a cup of coffee? You're a celebrity now. I'd like to get a story about you for this Friday's edition."

I could do that much for my boyhood chum, Dick Frazer. He'd been the only person in this entire town I'd given a hang about. I hadn't even come back for my old man's funeral. His sister, my Aunt Cynthia, sent me a wire the night his booze-riddled liver finally gave out. The wire said "Your father died at 11 P.M. tonight." I had a strong urge to wire back "So what?" but I guess we're all slaves to our conscience. I wired several thousand dollars to the funeral home here, told them to plant the old man in their best casket. I made only one stipulation—that they put a quart of cheap bourbon beside the body.

Over coffee at the local cafe, Dick said, "Roger, I guess you know this story I'm going to write will have the old 'local boy makes good' angle. You were the only one in our school crowd who had the sense to get out of this town and make something of yourself. Remember Kate Lowery, the prettiest girl in our class? Everybody said she'd be a Broadway star one day. Well, she's still here, running a dingy little dance studio for kids, supporting her no-good husband. Cecil Buford, our football captain—well, he's running a service station. Some of them are dead now . . ."

I knew what he was thinking; me of all people—Roger Spencer, son of the town drunk—the least likely of us all to make it big. Life has some curious twists.

We had our coffee and chat and Dick made his notes for the story he was going to write about me—the story I told him, of course. Nobody knew the real story except me and a couple of other people who have been dead for a long time. That's the one part of my life about which even my wife Ellen doesn't know.

We left the cafe together and walked to the parking lot. On the way, we passed the First National Bank corner.

"Hey, Roger, remember that old tramp that played the banjo here on the corner?" Dick asked.

"Sure," I said, hurrying a little to get to my car.

"Mr. Banjo, we used to call him. He was a fixture on that corner for years. Remember how somebody got the crazy story started that he was one of those eccentric misers who went around in ragged clothes while he was hoarding a bunch of money hidden somewhere in his shack?"

"Yeah, I remember."

"Would you believe it, for years after he disappeared folks in this town rooted around that shack where he lived, hunting for his buried treasure. Of course, they never found anything. Poor old guy never had more than the clothes on his back. But people like to dream. I often wondered what became of that old man. One day he just disappeared."

"Not much telling. Well, I've got to get back to the motel, Dick. Have a lot of briefs to read. Sure nice talking to you again after all these years."

"Same here." He looked admiringly at my car as I slid behind the wheel. "So glad for your success, Roger. Again, congratulations."

He said it a bit wistfully. I understood. He was one of many men who suddenly look around and find that middle age has arrived and they must face the fact that life is never going to deliver the promises it made when they were young.

"It's all in the breaks, Dick," I said, and that was true. I'd just been one of the lucky ones. We shook hands and I drove out of the parking lot. Dick and I had been close, but that was more than thirty years ago. Now we had nothing in common, and I probably would never see him again. I preferred to leave the past where it belonged.

In my motel room the large vanity mirrored my reflection: a tanned, still handsome man, gray over the temples, but a body kept trim by the best-equipped gym in town plus regular golf at the country club. I took off my expensive suit, my imported Italian shoes and the fancy wristwatch guaranteed not to lose over two seconds in two months. I put it on the dresser beside the picture of Ellen, my lovely wife, and Pam, our daughter, that I always carried with me.

I mixed a drink, then stretched out on the bed in my shorts. I'd brought along my banjo. I began idly strumming some chords. Playing the banjo was a hobby going back many years. I played for kicks and for charity shows back home. I'd found it an excellent therapy for unwinding the knots of tension that go with my profession.

Now the instrument brought the memories back again, this time in sharp focus.

Those had been hard times, growing up in Whitaker back in the thirties, but we kids made our own fun. My greatest treasure was a single-shot .22 squirrel rifle. Somehow my old man managed to stay sober enough one Christmas season to give it to me. Most of the time he spent in an alcoholic fog in some bar while I roamed around town and into the country pretty much as I pleased. As Dick said, we spent a lot of time on the river bottom hunting squirrels and rabbits, and I had developed a little business trapping and selling rattlesnakes to an outfit in Florida that canned the meat. That paid for my .22 cartridges and clothes my old man never quite managed to get around to buying for me. School was a sketchy affair, but I'd inherited a high I.Q. from my mother who died when I was four. I read a lot on my own and made good grades despite all the times I played hooky to hunt.

I picked up music from that old blind beggar we called "Mr. Banjo." I'd once heard that his last name was Jones—Banjo Jones. I don't know for sure if that was really his name. He never told me. He probably didn't know himself.

He lived in a one-room tar-paper shack out of town a way, between the city dump and the river. A familiar sight in our town was Mr. Banjo trudging in every morning to take his place on his apple box beside the bank. He'd be carrying his banjo and holding the leash of his dog Rascal. Rascal wasn't one of those fancy Seeing Eye dogs. He was just a big old mongrel, but he sensed with some kind of canine intuition that Mr. Banjo was blind and did a pretty good job of leading him around.

Kids like Dick and myself were fascinated by Mr. Banjo. We'd stop by the bank on our way home from school to hear him whanging away on his banjo. All we had to do was drop a coin in his tin cup, and he'd start off like a jukebox. If we didn't have a nickle or penny for his cup, we'd drop a steel washer in. He didn't know the difference. He seemed to enjoy playing. He'd whang that old banjo like he was performing on a stage with a spotlight, showing his toothless gums in a grin and nodding his gray head to the time of the music.

I guess I made friends with old Banjo because we were both what you might call town outcasts. I was "that ragged Spencer kid," son of the town drunk. Most of the nice kids in town—like that snooty Kate Lowery that I had a hopeless crush on because she was so pretty—wouldn't have anything to do with me. The town just tolerated old Banjo because they felt sorry for him, I guess. In those days, every place had its town beggar. Mr. Banjo was ours.

My roaming around the countryside with my squirrel rifle sometimes took me down to the city dump and past old Banjo's shack. Sometimes on Sundays (the only day he wasn't in town) he'd be sitting in front, sunning himself, Rascal curled at his feet. I began stopping off to talk to him. He was a strange old guy. I don't guess he had a full set of brains, but I liked to listen to him. He wouldn't talk much to people in town, so everybody thought he was a half-wit. I think it was because he was suspicious of people; but he trusted me. I'd get him started and he could tell stories by the hour. According to him, he'd been all over the United States before he came to Whitaker. He talked about cities like San Francisco, New Orleans, Memphis. To a kid who'd never been out of his home county, that was exciting stuff, even if most of it was lies. I guess it was listening to Banjo tell those stories that gave me the itchy feet that wanted to shake the dust of Whitaker forever.

Old Banjo taught me what I know about music. He'd put my fingers on the strings of his beat-up old instrument, showing me the way chords were made. I guess I had a natural ear because it wasn't long before I caught on. He must have liked me pretty much by then, because he hardly ever allowed anyone else to touch his battered old, treasured banjo.

I don't know who the idiot was that started the rumor about Banjo having a fortune hidden in his shack. I guess it was the hard times. People were so desperate for money, they liked to believe stories like that. It probably got started when somebody read about a ragged bum who died on skid row and the police found a bunch of money sewed up in his mattress. Things like that do happen all the time—misers who live in rags, with hardly enough to eat, accumulating a fortune, penny by penny, until they have hoarded a bunch of money they hide in their dwellings because they don't trust banks.

Of course it was ridiculous to think poor old Banjo had anything besides his dog and his banjo and the shack he lived in, but I heard the rumors. Guys down at the barbershop who didn't have anything better to do would speculate on how much Banjo had stashed away. It got to be a kind of game around town, guessing the amount. "See that old bum," somebody would say when Banjo shuffled into town holding Rascal's leash. "He collects a lot of nickles and dimes and never spends a cent except for a few cans of beans every week. He's a miser. Must have hoarded thousands of dollars. No telling how much he's got hid." Somebody added fire to the rumors by claiming they'd seen Banjo ride the bus into the county seat with a heavy tin box under his arm—and come back without the box.

It might have been a harmless game if Sheriff Buck Mayden hadn't decided to get serious about it. You saw a lot of law officers like Buck in the small towns back in those days—men short on brains, but long on muscle. Buck was a big, sullen man with a mean streak. Everybody was afraid of him. His way of keeping law and order was to pack a big six-shooter on his hip and bully people into respecting him.

Buck got to be sheriff when old Sheriff Honer died. Well, Buck hadn't been sheriff long before he started making life miserable for old Banjo. I saw him talking to Banjo in front of the bank one day. The next day, Banjo didn't show up in his usual place. That was the first time in my entire life I could remember that I didn't see Banjo with his dog, his cup and his apple box on Main Street.

I went out to his shack, expecting to find him sick, but he was sitting out front on his apple box, looking sad. "Sheriff says the city's got a law against beggars," he told me. "Sheriff says I got to buy a license. I ain't no beggar. I play music for a living," he said with a stirring of pride.

"How much does the license cost?" I asked.

"Sheriff says it's twenty-five dollars to start and ten dollars a week after that. The old sheriff never told me nothin' about a license like that when he was living."

I whistled softly. That was a big sum of money in 1936. "You goin' to pay it?"

"Where'm I goin' to get money like that? Guess I'll have to move along. Don't much feel like it, though. I'm gettin' too old to go driftin' around the country. Always figured to spend the rest of my days here."

The next several days, whenever I went down to Banjo's shack, he was sitting in the same place out front, staring straight ahead, his blind eyes looking at nothing. I figured he didn't have anything to eat, so I cooked up some rabbit stew and took it out to him.

One afternoon, when I was approaching the shack, I saw the sheriff's car parked there. Buck drove one of those black 1934 Ford V-Eights that Clyde Barrow liked.

I sneaked closer to see what was going on. Buck was standing over Banjo, yelling at him. The old man looked scared. "You got that twenty-five dollars. I know you have. That and a lot more! Now where is it?"

Banjo made some kind of frightened, pleading sound, holding up his hands as if to protect himself. He kept shaking his head vigorously when Buck asked about money.

Buck uttered a scorching swearword and stomped into the shack. I heard him throwing things around in there. It sounded as if he was tearing the place apart, board by board. I hid behind a bush. My heart was thumping. Like everyone else in the county, I was afraid of Buck Mayden. Wasn't a thing I could do but sit there and watch.

After a while, Buck came out, looking mad and frustrated. "Where is it, you old fool? Where you got that money hid?"

"Ain't got no money hid," Banjo whined.

"Th' hell you ain't! You stingy old miser. You been hoarding them nickles and dimes for years. Where you got them hid?"

Banjo just kept shaking his head. Buck suddenly grabbed him and gave him a hard shaking. It was like shaking a sackful of rattling bones.

Rascal was growling fiercely. Then, to protect his master, he charged Buck. He sank his fangs in Buck's leg. Buck let out a howl of pain and fury. He shook the dog loose, then drew his big old six-shooter and shot Rascal dead.

Poor old Banjo let out a cry of grief. He knelt on the ground beside the dog that had been his companion for so many years. Buck grabbed Banjo again and started giving him a terrible pistol whipping. He'd stop from time to time, sweating and panting, and demand to know where Banjo had his money hidden, but Banjo would only shake his bloody head and beg the sheriff to stop hitting him.

Finally Buck yelled, "Well, if you ain't got no money, then you're a vagrant and you're goin' to jail! Get in there!" and he threw Banjo into the back seat of his car.

I sat behind the bush a long time after they'd left, feeling sick. Finally I went down and dug a hole behind the shack and buried Rascal. I made the grave as nice as I could, and put a piece of broken concrete that I dragged over from the dumping grounds for a headstone and wrote "Rascal" on it with a pencil.

There wasn't much left inside the shack. Buck had ripped the mattress apart, torn up the flooring, cut Banjo's few clothes to shreds. I found the old banjo and tin cup in the wreckage and carried them home with me.

Next day, I went down to the jail. The sheriff's office with its two-cell jail was situated in a little brick building near the outskirts of town. Respectable people never went near the place. I knew where it was because my old man spent a lot of Saturday nights there, sleeping off drunks.

Buck was leaning back in his swivel chair, his boots crossed and propped on his scarred desk. He was chewing a match and reading the *Police Gazette.* When I came in, he glanced up. "What do you want, kid? I ain't got your old man in here today."

"I wonder if I could see Banjo," I said.

He went back to reading. "Can't nobody see him. He's a dangerous prisoner. Got him in solitary confinement."

I screwed up my courage to ask, "How come he's in jail?"

"Attacking an officer, resisting arrest. Vagrancy. Mostly vagrancy."

"How long's he gonna be in jail?"

"Till he can pay his fine."

"Where's he gonna get the money?"

"Oh, he's got it. He's got a lot of money hidden somewhere, but he's too tight-fisted to tell anybody. He'd rather rot in jail. Now go on, beat it, kid."

I stood on one foot, then another, thinking fast. "Well," I said, "me'n ol' Banjo's pretty good friends. I'd sure like to see him get out of jail. Maybe if I could talk to him, he'd tell me where his money is. He trusts me."

Buck slowly lowered his *Police Gazette,* gave me a thoughtful look as he sucked on his match. Finally he spat out some frayed match pieces, got up and took the cell key out of his pocket. "You find out where he keeps his money so's he can pay his fine and we'll let him go."

"How much is his fine?"

"That depends. First you find out where his money is."

Buck unlocked the cell door. I went in. Poor old Banjo was lying on a smelly bunk. He looked real bad. The blood was dried and crusted on his face and in his gray hair. It was plain to see he'd had no medical attention. Probably nothing to eat, either.

"Hi, Banjo," I said, trying to sound cheerful. "It's me, Roger. I came to see you."

He turned his sightless face slowly, painfully in my direction. "Hello, boy," he whispered faintly.

I said, "I brought your banjo. Figured you'd like to have it. It wasn't hurt none."

For the first time he showed a little life. He reached out with shaking hands. I put the banjo in his hands and he hugged it close. Some tears rolled out of his eyes. That surprised me. I didn't know blind people could cry.

I looked around to see if Buck was listening, but he'd gone back up front to his desk. "Here's a candy bar," I whispered, sneaking it out of my pocket. He thanked me, but he put it beside him without eating it. I guess he was too sick to eat.

"Buck said he'd let you go if you'll pay a fine," I said.

He shook his head. "Ain't got no money to pay a fine." He turned his face to the wall. "I'm going to die here."

He wouldn't say anything else. I finally called Buck to let me out of the cell. I looked back once. The old man was lying there, hugging his banjo, his face turned to the wall.

"Well?" Buck demanded. "Did he tell you?"

I shook my head and Buck muttered some cuss words.

I went home, got my rifle and spent the rest of the day down on the river bottom, plinking around and checking the rocks for rattlesnakes. I was feeling pretty low. I couldn't sleep much that night, thinking about poor old Banjo. There wasn't any use talking to anybody in town about him. Nobody was going to cross Buck Mayden over a worthless old beggar. Banjo was going to die in that jail cell, just like he said.

Sometime during the night I hit on a way I could save Banjo. I sat straight up in bed, sweating and scared, my heart pounding. I tried to stop thinking about it, but I couldn't. Finally I knew I was going to do it.

The next day I skipped school and made a trip out to Banjo's shack. Then I hiked back to town. It was early afternoon when I got to the jail. Buck scowled when I walked into his office. "You back again?"

I wet my lips and swallowed hard. "Could I please see Banjo one more time? I sure want to get him out of jail. Maybe he'll tell me today about where his money's hid."

Buck was in a real mean, sullen mood. "Don't know why he'd tell you when he won't tell me. That's the stubbornest old miser I ever saw. He'd rather lay there and die than tell me where his money's hid."

"Let me try," I pleaded. "He came close to telling me yesterday."

Buck gave me a hard, suspicious look. "How do I know if he tells you, you won't run out there and dig the money up and keep it yourself?"

"Then how could I get Banjo out of jail?" I pointed out. "Please; he's gonna die if I can't get him out soon."

I guess I did a good job of convincing him. He scowled at me hard but said, "Well, it won't hurt to try. He's sure not going to tell me. But let me warn you, you're in big trouble, boy, if you try to make off with that money. I'll throw both you and your old man in jail."

He took me back to Banjo's cell and left us alone for a while. Banjo was worse than the day before. He was only partly conscious. I leaned over his bunk, whispering to him.

When Buck came to get me out of the cell, I said, "Well, he told me."

Buck's eyes lit up like the electric sign in front of the Bijou. "You tellin' the truth, kid?"

"Sure. I know where to find it."

"Well, I'm not trusting you. Come on. We'll go out there and you'll show me where it is."

Buck got his Stetson hat and buckled on his big six-shooter. We drove out of town fast in his V-Eight Ford. We went down the dirt road to Banjo's shack in a cloud of dust. When we got there, I led the way around the shack in the direction of the dump grounds. Finally I pointed to the rusting remains of a Model T. "Under there. He's got it buried there."

"Whoopee!" yelled Buck. "You stay back here, kid," he warned. Then he ran to the wrecked car and started digging wildly, throwing trash and loose dirt aside. There were dark sweat stains around the arms and neck of his shirt. Then I heard him give a panting exclamation when he came to the can. He clawed the lid off and plunged his hand down for the money.

Then he let out a bellowing scream and leaped to his feet. Dangling from his arm was the big, diamond-backed rattlesnake I'd put there earlier that day. The snake's fangs were sunk in Buck's wrist. He screamed again with pain and fright. He shook the snake off, yanked out his six-shooter and blew its head off.

I'd stood there, petrified. Now I broke into a dead run, back to Buck's car. I grabbed the keys out of the ignition and sprinted toward the woods.

Behind me I heard Buck's enraged bellow. "Come back here, you lousy kid!"

I ran all the faster, zigzagging around the trash in the dump grounds. I heard the roar of his six-shooter. The buzz of .45 slugs whirred around me like angry hornets. Then I reached the woods and plunged into the brush. I heard him coming after me, crashing limbs. He was sobbing and bellowing with a mixture of pain, fright and anger.

For a long time I ran through the brush along the riverbank with Buck floundering and crashing behind me. Luckily, I'd spent so much time down here I knew every trail and bush. I don't know how long Buck chased me but at last I heard a final crash in the brush behind me, then silence. I crept back to make sure it wasn't a trick. It wasn't. Buck was sprawled out on his back, staring up at the sky with glassy, scared eyes. Sweat was pouring off him. His arm was swollen up like a balloon. It was turning purple.

It took a long time for Buck to die. I sat on the ground and watched. He got delirious. He'd cuss for a while, then he'd sing. Sometimes he'd try to get up, but he'd fall back down and lie there. Finally, at sundown, he died. I waited a while, then went over and looked down at him. His bulging eyes were staring straight up at the sky like glass marbles about to pop out of the sockets. I forced myself to reach in the pockets of his sweat-soaked clothing for the jail keys. Then I ran back to his car.

It was dark when I drove up to the jail. I made sure no one was around; then I went inside, turned on a light and unlocked Banjo's cell. "It's me, Roger. Come on. I'm going to get you out of here."

Two things: I had to get us away from this town before people started looking for Buck, and I had to get Banjo to a doctor.

The old man was so weak I half-dragged him out to the car, but he wouldn't leave his banjo behind. He lay down on the back seat, still hugging his banjo while I drove out of town.

I figured it might be several days before somebody found Sheriff Buck Mayden, but I drove all night to be on the safe side, crossing the state line about dawn. The first large town I came to, I asked how to find a hospital that had a charity ward. It wasn't long before I had Banjo in the county hospital and a doctor was working on him.

I went to get some breakfast and I ditched Buck's car on the other side of town.

When I got back to the hospital, they'd cleaned Banjo up and he looked nice and peaceful in a hospital gown on a bed in the charity ward. He was sleeping. The awful look of pain was erased. A nurse told me they'd given him a shot to make him comfortable.

I hung around the hospital most of that day. I told them Banjo was my uncle and that he got all banged up when he fell off a horse. His foot was caught in the stirrup and the horse dragged him. I'd read about that happening to a guy in a pulp Western story.

That night I slept on a park bench. The next morning I went to see Banjo again at the hospital, but his bed was empty.

The doctor saw me and called me aside. He explained that Banjo had died peacefully in his sleep during the night. "We did what we could for him, but he was a very old man." He asked if we had any money and I said we didn't and he said that he'd arrange for the county to bury the old man.

They gave me a small bundle, the bloodstained rags he'd been wearing when I brought him in, and his banjo. I went down to the park bench where I sat alone and cried a little.

I hit the road after that. I did what a lot of young guys were doing those depression years. I worked the C.C.C. camps and rough-necked in the oil fields.

In 1938, I was roughnecking in an oil field near Seguin, Texas.

Wherever I went, I always took Banjo's beat-up old instrument with me. I was in my rented room one night, plunking some chords, trying to learn a tune that was popular that year. The head on the banjo split. I took it apart to see if I could fix it. It was easy—a blind man could do it. When I removed the head, I found pasted inside the banjo five one-thousand-dollar bills. That was a lot of money in those days—enough to take a smart kid out of the C.C.C. camps and oil fields and put him through law school.

I've liked banjo music ever since.

William Brittain, a teacher himself, has been writing short stories about Leonard Strang, gnome-like high school science teacher, since 1967. This is one of the best in the series.

WILLIAM BRITTAIN
Mr. Strang Picks Up the Pieces

It was Mr. Strang's free period. The little old science teacher was at the demonstration table in his classroom, preparing a chemistry experiment and wishing he could grow another pair of arms. If he held the Erlenmeyer flask in place on the ringstand with his left hand, he could insert the rubber stopper with his right. But that meant more than a yard of glass tubing would be projecting horizontally with no support whatever. Flexing his gnarled fingers, he glared at the laboratory equipment on the table before him. Then he tucked the tubing into his armpit, gripped the flask awkwardly, and giving a perfect imitation of a man wrestling with a transparent octopus, he brought it toward the dangling stopper.

At that point there was a knock on the classroom door.

"Oh, Mastigophora!" muttered the teacher, laying down the apparatus with a clatter. He walked stiffly to the door and opened it.

The muscular young giant who entered the room wore a conservative gray suit and gripped a briefcase in one hand. He extended his other hand and smiled. "Good morning, sir."

"How are you?" said the teacher, a bit less testily. "And who are you? I'm rather busy now——"

"They told me in the office that I could come right up. I thought you'd remember me."

"You know, now that you mention it, you do look familiar. But over the years I've had several thousand students in my classes here at Aldershot."

"Do you recall the time about ten years ago when somebody in your biology class dyed all the guinea pigs and hamsters bright green?"

"Of course I do. I could never prove it, but I always suspected a lad named—" As Mr. Strang's memory leaped back through his years at Aldershot High School, a grin spread across his face. "Kempel," he murmured. "Brewster Kempel. Welcome back, Bruiser."

Brewster Kempel, known throughout his high school years as "Bruiser," gripped Mr. Strang's arm with a huge paw that in earlier days had hurled footballs and paper wads with equally devastating accuracy. The diminutive teacher had often itched to tan young Kempel's britches. But Kempel's infectious grin and outgoing personality made it impossible not to like him.

"By the way, did you ever get the green dye off those animals?"

"I did. At the cost of a good deal of elbow grease. Can I assume this is a confession?"

"Yes, sir. But I'll have to remind you that the statute of limitations has run out on that one."

"Umm. I take it then that you followed through on your plan to become a lawyer."

"That's right. Passed my bar exams just a couple of months ago. Matter of fact, the law is why I'm here."

"Oh?" Leonard Strang's eyebrows shot up in the direction of his receding hairline. "Have I become involved in something illegal?"

"Not as far as I know," grinned Kempel. "But I could use a statement from you."

"What kind of statement?"

"Well, I'm with the county public-defender's office. Our job is to assist people who can't afford a lawyer. Right now I'm on a case that —well, it looks pretty open-and-shut. Of course, my client insists he's innocent. Anyway, I thought if I could get one or two people to testify to his good character, it might help him when his trial comes up."

"I'd be glad to help if I can," said the teacher. "Who's the client?"

"Clifford Whitley."

"I see." Mr. Strang pursed his lips and stared at the floor. "So that's why he's been out of school the last couple of days. I've got to be honest, Bruiser. I don't know how well I'd serve as a character witness for him."

"Tell me something, Mr. Strang," said Kempel in a flat voice. "Are you shying away from this because Cliff's black?"

The teacher reacted as if he'd been slapped. His eyes flashed as he looked at the younger man, and when he spoke his voice was little more than a whisper.

"I think perhaps you'd better leave, Brewster," he said. "If you don't know me better than that last remark would indicate, I doubt that we have anything more to say to each other."

Kempel nervously shifted his weight from one foot to the other, like a small boy caught cheating on an exam. "Look, Mr. Strang, I'm sorry. I don't know of anybody who didn't get a square deal in your classes. But this is my first real case and I want to do as well as I can by Cliff. I just—well, spoke out of turn, I guess. But why won't you go to bat for him? He's a good student, isn't he?"

The teacher nodded. "His tests and homework are quite satisfactory. But he's also extremely militant. That's understandable, up to a point. But he can become violent at anything he considers an insult. The slightest remark can set him off, and when that happens there's no reasoning with him. Now if he's hurt somebody during one of those tantrums of his, he's got to take what's coming to him. What's right is right, regardless of skin color."

Kempel stared curiously at Mr. Strang. "Who said anything about Clifford hurting somebody?"

"If he needs a lawyer, I naturally assumed——"

A smile crossed the young man's face. "Clifford Whitley's charged with burglary, pure and simple. Smash-and-grab out of a store window. Nobody hurt, nobody even threatened. And Cliff didn't put up any resistance when he was arrested."

Kempel jammed his hands into his pockets and rocked back on his heels. "It's improper to jump to conclusions. You taught me that, Mr. Strang."

"A hit, Bruiser, a direct hit. I stand properly rebuked." Mr. Strang sat down at his desk. "Of course, under the circumstances, I'll do everything I can to help. But I find it hard to believe that Clifford is guilty. He might break a few heads over a chance remark, but I don't think he'd ever steal. He has too much pride for that."

"Mr. Strang, you don't even know the facts of the case."

"And you, Bruiser, don't know Clifford Whitley the way *I* do. Now before we get to my statement, I want to hear just what did happen."

"But there isn't time—"

"Of course there's time. The next period doesn't start for fifteen minutes. Sit down there, please."

Mr. Strang pointed imperiously at a chair, and Kempel slumped into it with a sigh. From his briefcase he took a yellow legal pad and began thumbing through its pages.

"It happened Tuesday evening. About seven o'clock. Bainbridge's Jewelry Store, down in the village. Do you know where it is?"

"Of course," said the teacher. "It's in that section called Peacham Lane, the area they advertise as 'a little bit of olde London towne.' Pseudo-Nineteenth-Century architecture, narrow cobblestone streets, and so forth."

"That's the place. The way Louis Bainbridge tells it, he and his clerk Jerome Osborn spent about an hour after he'd closed the store working on inventory. Finally Bainbridge told Osborn to go home. Maybe five minutes after he'd left, Bainbridge was in the back room when he heard a loud crash in the front of the store, and at the same time his burglar alarm began bonging away. He came out to see what was going on."

"And what was going on?" asked the teacher.

"The display window in the front of the store was smashed. And Clifford Whitley was running off down Peacham Lane toward Main Street."

"A couple of questions, if you don't mind," said Mr. Strang. "First of all, I've always understood that most jewelry stores have some kind of special glass in their display windows. Devilishly hard to break. What about that?"

"The place was originally set up to be a boutique," said Kempel. "When the guy who was supposed to move in broke his lease, Bainbridge took it over. He was always going to put in one of those special windows, but he never got around to it. So he settled for installing that metal tape around all the windows and wiring it into an alarm system. He thought it would be safe enough for a while."

"Umm. I see." Mr. Strang took out his briar pipe and blew into the stem. "Another thing. At seven o'clock it must have been quite dark in Peacham Lane, even considering the lighted shop windows. How can Bainbridge be so sure Clifford Whitley was the boy running away?"

"Easy," grinned Kempel. "It seems one of the local cops, a man named Joe Bell, drives his patrol car up Peacham Lane every evening at just about seven for a look around. He heard the burglar alarm and spotted Cliff right away. Bell didn't have any trouble catching him. Cliff practically ran right into the front end of the police car. Before he had time to turn and go the other way, Bell was all over him. Cliff insisted he was just out for a walk and got scared when the window broke, but—" The lawyer shrugged.

Mr. Strang sucked absently at the empty pipe. "And I assume there was something missing from the window display at Bainbridge's. Otherwise the most you'd have on Cliff is malicious mischief."

"Right. A couple of detectives were sent over and had Bainbridge sort through the stuff in the window. There were all kinds of things in there from men's watches to gold keychains to who-knows-what. Plus a lot of broken glass. Bainbridge and the detectives went over the whole shebang. Finally it was discovered there were three engagement rings missing. Rather good stones in all of them. Worth close to four thousand bucks altogether."

"And the rings, of course, were found on Clifford."

"No," said Kempel. "He was clean when they searched him. And he insists that he doesn't know a thing about the rings. But Sergeant Roberts figures he must have tossed them away somewhere when he saw the police car."

"Wait a minute," interrupted the teacher. "That wouldn't be Paul Roberts, would it?"

"Yes, that's the one. He's the detective in charge of the case. Why, do you know him?"

"Yes, quite well, Bruiser. He should be able to help us cut a lot of red tape once we begin looking into this."

Kempel was puzzled. "Looking into what, Mr. Strang? All I want from you is to be a character witness for Cliff."

"Bruiser, from what you've told me so far, this case doesn't strike me as being open-and-shut. A window is broken and a scared boy runs away. Nothing criminal there."

"But, Mr. Strang, Cliff was the only one near the window when it was broken. It had to be him."

"Who says so?" asked Mr. Strang. "According to what you told me, Bainbridge was in the rear of his store when the window was broken."

"Two separate eyewitnesses, that's who says so," replied Kempel.

"Oh." The pipe between Mr. Strang's teeth drooped. "And who are these witnesses?"

Kempel flipped through the pages of the legal pad. "The first is Milton Gage, who owns a haberdashery right across the street from Bainbridge's. Gage was working on a window display of his own. When he heard the glass break he looked up from a jacket he was fitting on a dummy. There, on the other side of the street, was the smashed window and Clifford Whitley running away."

"And the other witness?"

"Jerome Osborn, Bainbridge's clerk. He must have seen almost the exact same thing Gage did. You see, he was standing right outside Gage's store, in front of Gage's window, reading his paper. Since he'd worked late, he'd phoned for a taxi and was waiting for it to pick him up."

"Let me get this straight," said the teacher. "Both men were on the street directly opposite the jewelry store. Is that right?"

"That's it. In a perfect position to see what happened."

"Yes, but if what you tell me is true, neither one of them actually saw Clifford break the window."

"Of course they did!" cried Kempel. "I just got finished telling you that——"

"You told me," said Mr. Strang in his most professorial manner, "that at the instant of the crash, Gage was involved in dressing a dummy in his own window and Osborn was reading his paper. Neither man saw the alleged crime itself. Just the aftermath—the broken window and Cliff running away."

"Mr. Strang, be reasonable," said Kempel. "Okay, technically you're correct. But the fact is, *there was nobody else* in Peacham Lane at that time. How could the window have been broken if Cliff didn't do it?"

"Have you considered the possibility of a projectile of some kind?" asked the teacher. "Fired or thrown from some vantage point?"

Before Kempel could reply, there was the sound of a bell in the hallway outside, followed by hundreds of shuffling feet. The period was over.

Mr. Strang got up and stuffed his pipe into his pocket.

"My chemistry class wouldn't be the best place to continue our discussion, Bruiser," he said. "Tell Sergeant Roberts we'll be calling on him tomorrow—about four."

By 4:10 the following afternoon, Detective Sergeant Paul Roberts had a few thousand well-chosen words he felt like using on Brewster Kempel and Mr. Strang; but with a reluctant bow to the squad's public relations, he limited himself to just one.

"No."

"But, Paul," said the teacher, "we just wanted a few moments to discuss——"

"No."

"If only you'd—" Kempel began.

"No." Roberts shook his head, annoyed. "Kempel, I thought we had a deal. You'd advise young Whitley to plead guilty and we'd go as easy on him as we could. Now you want me to help you get Whitley off. I'm not out to railroad anybody, but in this case the prosecution has all the marbles. You've got nothing at all on your side. So why make trouble?"

"I no longer think it's that clear-cut," said Kempel. "Mr. Strang and I talked on our way over here. And he was pretty convincing."

"Yeah, he usually is," grumbled Roberts. "Okay, Mr. Strang, we can put Clifford Whitley right next to that window the exact moment it was broken. Two eyewitnesses across the street saw him there. Now you mentioned to Kempel the possibility of some kind of an object being thrown at the glass from a distance. Out of the question, and you know it. A bullet would have made a single small hole in the glass. And any object big enough to smash the whole window would have been lying around somewhere.

"We went over the display case behind the window with a fine-tooth comb when Bainbridge was checking what was missing. But there was nothing. And don't give me any of this jazz about some kind of sonic beam, either. We considered that possibility—for about fifteen seconds. Setting up a rig like that would cost more than this whole caper was worth."

"Paul," said the teacher. "If the glass was broken from the inside——"

Roberts shook his head. "Except for a couple of small hunks on the sidewalk, all the glass fell *into* the display case. The window had to have been hit from outside. And Whitley was the only one who could have done it. The only one. Period."

"But there are still a few things that aren't explained, Paul," said Mr. Strang.

"Yeah? Like what?"

"Well, for example, why did Cliff pick up the engagement rings rather than a watch or a keychain or something more in keeping with a boy's interests?"

"I dunno. Maybe he just took the first things he laid his hands on. Anyway, the rings were a lot more valuable than any of the other stuff."

"Another thing," Kempel cut in. "Cliff's a fairly sharp boy. Why try a stunt like this at the one time during the day when a police car could be expected to come by?"

"He didn't know about it, that's why," growled Roberts in annoyance. "Who do you know who checks patrol-car routes?"

"Perhaps," said the teacher. "Although if I were contemplating a crime, I'd take the trouble to find out about them."

"This wasn't planned ahead of time, Mr. Strang. Whitley saw a chance and took it. That's all."

"I see. But about those two men across the street—Gage and Osborn. They both heard the crash and immediately looked up. How long would that take? A fraction of a second?"

"I guess so," said Roberts, his patience beginning to wear thin.

"Then how could Clifford Whitley possibly have had time to reach into the window after he'd broken it and grab anything?"

There was a long moment of silence. Then Roberts slouched lower in his chair and pointed a finger at Kempel. "That last question—that's your case, is it?"

The lawyer nodded.

"Well, lemme tell you something. Time is relative. Maybe Gage and Osborn looked up right away and maybe they didn't. Maybe they were confused about where the sound came from and spent a couple of seconds looking up and down the street. I can't tell you that. But if that's the best you can come up with, take my advice and plead young Whitley guilty. It'll be easier on him."

Fifteen minutes later Brewster Kempel and Mr. Strang were riding back toward the teacher's roominghouse. "Sergeant Roberts is right, you know," said the lawyer glumly. "With what we've got right now, Cliff hasn't got a chance."

"That's why we're going to my place," said Mr. Strang. "You and I are going to spend the evening figuring out what really happened on Peacham Lane."

Mrs. Mackey, the teacher's landlady, seemed to sense the seriousness of the situation. Usually as garrulous as a stuck phonograph record, she served supper to the two men in Mr. Strang's room without a word.

By eight o'clock the floor of the tiny room was littered with scraps of paper, each covered with a diagram of Peacham Lane. Arrows and dotted lines were slashed across them, indicating the possible movements of Clifford Whitley, Bainbridge, Osborn, and Gage at the time of the burglary.

By 8:30 both men had to admit they were getting nowhere. Devices as varied as boomerangs, gigantic yo-yos, and trained monkeys had all been considered and discarded. The broken window and the theft of the jewelry remained a mystery.

Unless, of course, Clifford Whitley was indeed guilty. Reluctantly Mr. Strang admitted to himself that it seemed the only logical answer.

At nine o'clock there was a soft knock at the door of the room. "It's me, Mr. Strang," said Mrs. Mackey through the closed door, her voice like a breeze from off the Lakes of Killarney. "I thought ye might like some coffee."

Mr. Strang took the tray and thanked his landlady. Closing the door with a hip, he offered one cup to Kempel. "There's sugar and cream if you want it," said the teacher. Kempel took a large spoonful of sugar from the bowl as Mr. Strang went back to his small desk.

"Any new theories?" asked Mr. Strang, sipping from his cup. "Because if not, I'd suggest we close down Kempel and Strang, Private Investigators, forthwith. I guess I had Clifford Whitley wrong. Much as I hate to admit it, he has to be guilty. It's the only answer possible."

"Pfoo!" cried a guttural voice behind him.

"I beg your pardon, Bruiser?"

"Ugh!" gasped the lawyer. "It's this coffee."

"Mine tastes all right," said Mr. Strang.

"That's because you take it black. Mine's full of—of salt."

"Why, it can't—" The teacher stopped, then nodded knowingly. "Yes, it can, too. Mrs. Mackey keeps her cans of salt and sugar next to each other on the bottom shelf in the kitchen. Sometimes she's not too careful which can she picks up. Just last week she made a similar mistake and served a candied beef stew that had my taste buds begging for mercy. Wait here and I'll go down and get you some—"

His voice broke off suddenly. For a moment his mouth was just a small round opening between nose and chin. And then a grin spread across the old teacher's face.

"That's it, you know," he said to Kempel.

"What's it?" asked the lawyer, heading for the bathroom to rinse the salt from his mouth.

"The way it was done. The broken window. Oh, what prime idiots we've both been! It wasn't that the thing was too complicated. On the contrary, it was too simple."

"What are you mumbling about, Mr. Strang?"

"About Clifford Whitley. I didn't think I could be that wrong about him. He didn't steal anything. He's taking the hobo's blame, or whatever you call it."

"A bum rap?" suggested Kempel.

"Yes, that's it."

"How do you figure?"

"No time now, Bruiser. Look, here's what I want you to do. Get in touch with Paul Roberts. Call him at home if he's not at the squad room." Mr. Strang began scribbling words on the back of one of the diagrams. "Give him this."

"And where'll you be, Mr. Strang?"

"Down on Peacham Lane. Where else?"

Peacham Lane was deserted when Mr. Strang got there. Three streetlamps, designed to look like old-fashioned gaslights, were all that illuminated its length. Fortunately one was directly across the street from the boarded-up window of the Bainbridge Jewelry Store.

Mr. Strang shivered, only partly because of the cold. The atmosphere of the place was effective, he had to admit that. He half expected Bill Sykes, Abel Magwich, or some other sinister Dickensian character to move out of the deep shadows.

He found what he was looking for at the curb directly in front of

Bainbridge's. His gloved hands fumbled for several minutes, but finally he was ready to leave. As he got stiffly to his feet, he heard the grinding rumble of a distinctly modern garbage truck headed in his direction.

When he arrived at Paul Roberts' house, the detective and Kempel were waiting for him. "Can you cut this short, Mr. Strang?" asked the detective. "The news is coming on the tube, and I don't want to miss it."

"As short as you like, Paul," was the answer. "I just want to show you a couple of things and ask if you'll arrange a meeting of everyone involved in this case. Tomorrow after school, if that's possible."

"Sounds crazy, but I think I can arrange it if you've got something really important. What did you want to show me?"

"These." The teacher extended his hands toward the detective . . .

The little interrogation room in the precinct house seemed jammed almost to overflowing by the time Mr. Strang got there. In one corner Brewster Kempel was murmuring something to Clifford Whitley and patting the shoulder of the scowling youngster reassuringly. Opposite them, Louis Bainbridge and Jerome Osborn were whispering excitedly, waving their arms in broad gestures. At the table in the center of the room Milton Gage was explaining to Paul Roberts the problems of having to close his store in the middle of the day.

As Mr. Strang entered, Roberts got to his feet. "Glad you got here," said the detective. "I didn't know how much longer I could hold 'em without somebody threatening to walk out. I hope you can make good on what you told me last night. I sent a couple of men out, but they haven't phoned in yet."

"Hey, Mr. Strang!" called out Clifford. "You the dude what's gonna spring me? Man, I sure hope so. This cat what they got for my lawyer sure ain't been much good so far."

"If you keep talking that way, I may just let them keep you here," replied the teacher. "Your street vernacular is like something from a bad movie."

"I'm sorry, man—uh—Mr. Strang."

"Well, I'm sorry you called this ridiculous meeting," snapped Bainbridge. "I've got a store to run. And it's going to be twice as hard attracting customers with my display window gone. Let's get on with this."

"Very well," said the teacher. Then, carefully, he removed his glasses and polished them on his necktie. That finished, he waved them about in his right hand, at the same time inserting his left into a jacket pocket.

"Problem," he began. "How does one break a window and remove some of the most expensive jewelry behind it in the twinkling of an eye without anyone observing the actual theft?"

"But we did see—" Gage began.

"No, sir, you did not. All parties involved heard a crash and then saw Clifford running off down the street. The actual theft of the jewels was never seen."

"So what?" said Osborn. "Did the diamond rings jump out of that broken window by themselves? This young man had to be the one who stole them. There's no other way anybody could have got at them."

"Oh, but that isn't quite true." Mr. Strang turned to Bainbridge. "Is it?" he asked.

"Well, I don't see how else——" Bainbridge began.

"Oh, come now. All those watches and things didn't leap into place through the solid back wall of the display case. How do you arrange the display in your window, Mr. Bainbridge?"

"The back of the case opens up inside the store," was the reply. "That's how we get things in there."

"Exactly. And that's the way they were taken out, too."

"Hey, wait a minute." Bainbridge was on his feet, his face a fiery red. "I was inside the store, remember? And I'd have seen anybody who——"

"Of course you would. Assuming the jewelry had been stolen at the time the window was broken. But of course that wasn't the case. The rings, in fact, had been taken earlier that day. With the number of objects in that window a few missing items wouldn't be noticed, except on close examination."

"You know," said Bainbridge, "I don't like the way this conversation is going."

"Neither do I," chimed in Osborn. "Are you saying that Mr. Bainbridge stole his own stuff? For the insurance or something?"

"Of course not," said the teacher.

"Then what——"

"Mr. Bainbridge couldn't have taken it. Because you did, Mr. Osborn."

Osborn rushed to the table where Roberts was sitting and began shouting at the detective. Roberts took it for almost a minute. Finally he rose, towering over the smaller man, and grasped him by one arm. The detective half led, half carried him back to his chair.

"Let Mr. Strang have his say," murmured the detective softly.

"Then, if he's wrong, we can all sit around and tell him he's got rocks in his head. Go on, Mr. Strang."

"Very well. Mr. Osborn here removed the rings during the day —very probably while you were out to lunch, Mr. Bainbridge. He just put them in his pocket, I'd imagine. However, he knew that eventually they'd be missed. So he'd developed a little plan to make the missing jewelry look like a simple burglary. All he had to do was break a window. Simple as that."

"Yeah, and that's where your half-baked theory falls apart," snapped Osborn, stabbing a finger in the teacher's direction. "When that window was broken I was standing on the other side of the street. I was right outside the window where Milt here was working. Couldn't have been more than a couple of feet from him."

"That's true, Mr. Strang," said Gage. "Of course I was busy dressing the dummy, but I'm sure I'd have seen Jerry run across the street and back. When the window shattered, I looked up almost immediately."

"Oh, Mr. Osborn didn't run across the street," Mr. Strang replied calmly. "He remained right there in front of your store, Mr. Gage."

"Then how could I have broken the window?" Osborn demanded.

"It was easy. You threw something at it."

Osborn stalked over to the detective again. "I'm telling you, Roberts, this—this schoolteacher is the one who should be locked up. You were on the scene. You and Mr. Bainbridge examined the window. How could I have——"

"Mr. Gage," interrupted Mr. Strang, "just before you heard the glass break, Osborn was standing right outside your window. And he was doing what?"

"Why reading his newspaper."

"A newspaper which had to have been bought earlier in the day," said the teacher, "because all the stores were closed on Peacham Lane by the time he got out of work."

"Yeah, yeah," said Osborn. "I got the paper at lunchtime. I always do that. So what?"

"But you also purchased something else on your lunch break, didn't you? Something you had wrapped up in that newspaper when you left the store. And then you waited in front of Mr. Gage's haberdashery, knowing he'd furnish you with a perfect alibi.

"At last you spotted Clifford coming toward you on the opposite side of the street. The perfect person to complete your plan. Who'd believe him, no matter how often he denied any knowledge of what had happened? Finally he passed the window. And that's when you took the object from inside your newspaper and hurled it across Peacham Lane so that it crashed through the window of the jewelry store opposite you.

"Mr. Gage didn't see that quick movement of your arm because he was involved in his work. And the Lane is so narrow you could hardly have missed. Clifford was startled and ran away. That's when Officer Bell picked him up."

"Wait a minute, wait a minute," said Bainbridge. "Jerry's been working for me almost a year now. I'm not going to believe he took those rings unless you can do better than that, Mr. Strang. I mean, what *kind* of thing could he have thrown across the alley *that nobody could find?*"

"I didn't figure it out until yesterday," replied the teacher. "It was when my landlady made a mistake and used salt for sugar. Those two look so much alike that—well, it's almost impossible by just looking at them to tell them apart."

"But what's that got to do with Jerry throwing something?"

Mr. Strang reached into a pocket and took out a small piece of paper. "I made a few phone calls during my lunch period today. One of them paid off. I have here a salesslip from the Aldershot Hardware Store. The clerk is ready to swear that Mr. Osborn made the purchase written on it."

"What purchase?" Bainbridge demanded.

"One pane of extra-thick glass twelve inches square."

"Glass? But——"

"Don't you see? Osborn kept the glass inside the newspaper. Then, at the proper moment, as Cliff passed the window, he scaled it across the narrow street in much the same manner that children fling those toys shaped like plastic discs. The glass struck the window and shattered it. At the same time the piece Osborn had purchased broke, either by hitting the window or by falling to the street. Just a few bits of extra glass that nobody would notice—something to pick up and put in the trash. Who'd go to the trouble of reconstructing a whole window, just to show there were some pieces of glass left over? Especially when there was a ready-made suspect."

"Y'know," said Bainbridge skeptically, "all this sounds very fine, Mr. Strang. But it's just a theory. No proof."

"There's proof, Mr. Bainbridge," said Roberts. "Last night Mr. Strang went back to Peacham Lane. He was lucky. You had a trash can full of broken glass set out on the curb, but the collection truck hadn't gone by yet. He found two pieces of glass. Two special pieces."

"Yeah? Why special?"

"Because one of 'em's only about two-thirds as thick as the other. It doesn't matter which is which. The fact is, there were *two kinds* of glass in that mess where your window was. But the window itself was just one solid piece. So the second kind of glass had to come from somewhere."

Before Bainbridge could put his next question, a uniformed officer came to the door of the interrogation room and motioned Roberts outside. As he left, Osborn turned to the teacher, a smirk on his face.

"Maybe you think you're going to hang this on me," he sneered. "But I bought that glass to fix one of my fish tanks. Yeah, I keep fish as a hobby. Anybody in my apartment building will tell you that. So where's your fancy theory now, Mr. Schoolteacher?"

Before Mr. Strang could reply, Roberts was at the door again. He looked at Kempel with a smile. "You and Cliff can go any time you want," he said. "But I think, Mr. Osborn, that you and I had better have a little talk."

"Me? Why?" asked Osborn.

"Because on the strength of the difference in those two pieces of glass that Mr. Strang found, I got a judge to issue a warrant to search your apartment. My men have been over there since shortly after you left the place. They found the stolen rings hidden in the gravel at the bottom of one of your fish tanks."

*Pauline C. Smith's memorable tale of murder in a southern California commu-
nity—with detective work by a District Attorney's wife whose success comes as
a surprise even to herself—contains overtones of the sort of family relationships
one might expect in the novels of Ross Macdonald. In fact, I think this is a
story Mr. Macdonald would enjoy reading.*

PAULINE C. SMITH
Death Across the Street

I

The bearded youth parked his car at the curbing and bounded up
the steep driveway past the garage door, which was closed and
meant that Mrs. Morrison was home so he could pick up his check
and take off for the beach. He took the steps in giant leaps, walked
between potted plants on the long front porch and pressed the
button by the door. He could hear the chimes distinctly.

He waited, tips of his fingers thrust into tight hip pockets, rocking
on bare feet as he gazed out over a strip of the city into the glare
of the ocean beyond and the rolling waves as they broke against the
shoreline. "Good surf," he observed to himself and unwedged his
hands from his pockets to rub them together in impatient anticipa-
tion. Where in hell was the old girl? Maybe in the backyard on a day
like this.

He pressed the button again, listening to the whisper of chimes
as he glanced in through the glass of the picture window at his left.
Probably where she was all right, out in back, fussing with her
begonias.

He whirled to gallop between the potted plants and came to an
abrupt halt at the top of the steps. *"Huh?"* he grunted, the exhala-
tion of disbelief squeezed from him at what he suddenly remembered he might have seen through the window.

He backed up slowly and reluctantly until, even with the window
and turning his eyes without moving his head, he caught a glimpse
of what he thought he had seen and raced back along the porch to
the steps. He made a flying leap, landing with a jarring thud on the
cement walk, jumped to the sloping lawn and tore down the driveway to his car.

The houses on the high side of this hill street, above garages, stair-stepped quietly and emptily. Those on the low side, even with the street, remained calmly tranquil. The youth swept the street with apprehensive eyes. He saw a truck parked two doors down. Then he climbed into his car and took off.

His girl, a lanky young colt with a dirty blond mane, said, "You mean you went up to this Mrs. Whatchamacallit's house to pick up your money and you saw her in there dead?"

The youth rubbed a hand over his hairy face. "I think that's what I saw."

"You *think!* Don't you *know?*"

"Well . . ." He explained the porch, the glare of the ocean sun in his eyes, the picture window, shadowed room and a body on the floor—"like someone bashed her."

"Did you see blood?" asked the girl.

"*No!*" he shouted, wondering if perhaps he had during that first subliminal impression, wondering if it was that which had backed him up for another sidelong glance. He dropped his head to his hands, trying to think. Maybe it wasn't a body at all, through the glass and on the shadows of the floor, but a light-colored cloth dropped there.

"Well, you'll have to call the police."

"The police?" He jerked his head from his hands. "The *police!* Are you nuts?"

"Why not? You didn't do anything."

"I know that, but *they* won't know it." The youth's voice became high and truculent. "If anything happens, the cops say right away, 'Where's Eddie Hoffer?' "

"Oh, they do not. Just because you're on parole——"

"Probation. How many times I got to tell you that? It's probation I'm on. That's a hell of a lot different than being on parole."

"Okay. But you've got to call the police just the same."

"No way. What do you want me to say? 'Officer, sir, this is Eddie Hoffer, sir. I just seen a murdered woman layin' there dead.' "

"How do you know she's murdered?"

"I know. That's all. It's my kind of luck."

"You saw her laying there. Right?"

"Right." The visual flash was becoming increasingly clear in Eddie's memory. "I sure did."

"Dead—right?" said the girl.

"Well, sure. She was layin' there on the floor."

"What if she wasn't dead?"

"Why would she be layin' there then?"

"Maybe she was hurt. Maybe she fell and broke her hip. Maybe she had a heart attack. Maybe she isn't dead at all, but if somebody doesn't get to her in a hurry, she *will* die. And if you don't call, Eddie Hoffer, it'll be all your fault."

Eddie yelped in guilty anguish. "But I *can't!*" he moaned.

"Well, look, don't tell the police who you are. Just call and tell 'em someone's sick in there, or dead maybe, and you're doing your civic duty. Then hang up." The girl tossed her untidy hair away from her eyes. "Tell 'em there's this woman in there and all you want to do is save her life."

Eddie moaned again.

"Start the car, Eddie. You've got to find a phone. You've just got to."

Mrs. Miriam Clark swung into her garage that afternoon, got out of her car, opened up the trunk and gazed with astonishment at the junk piled inside. She was always surprised at the assortment she had collected after one of her Friday forays. "You're a garage-sale-alcoholic," Nick often told her.

She pounced, remembering the gift she had purchased and came up with the cut-out metal sign that betokened PEACE IN THIS GARDEN, just right for Mrs. Morrison's peacefully lovely garden, which she had actually entered. "Bulled your way in, you mean," accused Nick, uttering a halfway truth since Mrs. Morrison was neither overly neighborly nor even slightly hospitable.

Miriam untangled the metal stake from Christmas decorations (in August) and held it high in triumph. She'd take it over there right now. Mrs. Morrison was probably in her garden this very minute, fussing over her beautiful begonias.

Hurrying, handbag swinging from her arm, garden sign held aloft, Miriam crossed the street, climbed the steep driveway and the curved cement steps. She stepped along the sidewalk, unhooked the gate and called, "Mrs. Morrison."

The garden, enclosed by ivy-covered walls, was a flower-bower of color, an Eden of quiet as Miriam's steps tapped a faintly mellow sound on the brick paths. Her voice called with less assertion as she peered self-consciously around giant elephant ears and through the green lace of fern in search of Mrs. Morrison, who might be hiding from her—"You're always trying to 'bring her out,' " Nick often charged. "Maybe she wants to stay in her shell, did you ever think of that?"

Mrs. Morrison was not hiding in the garden after all, so she must be hiding in the house, Miriam decided after her search. "She likes to be alone," Nick had often pointed out, "so leave her that way."

Since the sign felt awkward and heavily unappreciated in her hand, Miriam laid it on the edge of a planter and retreated from the garden. With her hand on the gate, she glanced at the open windows. What if Mrs. Morrison was sick in there? Too sick to hear, too sick to answer? Miriam bounded up the steps to tap at the back door, lightly at first and then with more authority. She cupped her hands around her eyes to peer in through the screened half of the door and see part of the kitchen with a slice of hallway.

Softly, she called, "Mrs. Morrison," and tentatively tried the doorknob, which was locked as she was sure it would be.

She backed off, descended the steps, unlatched the gate and walked the slope alongside the house. When she reached the stairs leading to the front porch, she abruptly stopped, hesitating for only a moment before she ran up and across the porch to lean on the buzzer, hearing distinctly the four-note chime. It was then she turned toward the picture window to note, with shock, the tightly closed drapes Mrs. Morrison never closed—those on the picture window beyond the porch, yes, to shut out the afternoon sun that beat a Pacific glare—but not here, shaded and protected by the porch roof.

Something was wrong.

Miriam hurried down the steps, yanked open the garage door and knew that Mrs. Morrison was home, for there was her car, placidly shining in vintage elegance. Miriam wrung her hands and peered up and down the curved street, which was quiet as usual, for nothing ever happened here to confuse the serenity, nothing to break the quiet.

She thought, for a moment, of running across the street to use her own phone and summon the police. . . . "You're always making mountains out of molehills," Nick often accused her, and a phone call might be one of her molehill mountains. She decided not to call.

Long ago, when she first took her under her friendly wing, Miriam had suggested that Mrs. Morrison leave a key in some safe hiding place—"in case something should happen with you here all alone. Or when you're away on those trips you take."

"You just want to know where she goes," Nick accused, "and she wasn't about to tell you. *Right?*" Right. She made the trips regularly, once a month, gone a day and a night each time, leaving the garage open and empty—an invitation, really.

Despite Miriam's gentle urging, Mrs. Morrison remained politely unperturbed until, at a garage sale, Miriam found and presented her with one of those small magnetic metal key cases and told her, "Here is just the thing."

"Good God, you're pushy!" Nick exclaimed.

Miriam felt along the inside edge of the gutter pipe that extended down the side of the garage, quite certain in her mind that Mrs. Morrison would long ago have removed the case, when her fingers touched it. She pulled it off in surprise, slid the lid open and there was the key.

II

The desk sergeant at the police station cradled the phone and looked up. "Some kid," he said, "says there's a body up on Seaview Drive. A body, he says, or maybe someone sick or hurt. He saw it through a window. Could be he's playing games, but you'd better go on up there and check it out. Here's the address." He reeled it off in quick syllables.

Miriam stood still in last-minute reluctance just before she hurried back up the stairs. Lightly she crossed the porch, fitted the key in the keyhole, turned it and silently opened the door, calling, "Mrs. Morrison," softly and with a quaver, into the silence.

She focused her eyes from sunshine to shadow, moved cautiously inside the room and repeated her call. Turning slowly, she saw the crumpled heap on the carpet and stifled a scream with the back of her hand.

The police car turned into the driveway and braked before the open garage. An officer emerged, climbed the stairs, stepped through the open front door and found Miriam Clark kneeling beside the body of Mrs. Morrison.

"Migod!" cried Nick over his martini. "So now you're a murder suspect!"

"Not after I explained about bringing over the present," said Miriam.

"What present?"

"Just a present I got her. Then I explained about the key."

"What key?"

"Her door key, still in that magnetic key case I gave her, there on the gutter pipe. But it wasn't until I told them I was the District Attorney's wife that they were pretty sure I wasn't a killer."

"Good God!"

"But the worst part of it all, I put that poor kid on the spot and now they're sure he did it."

"What kid?"

"The one who does Mrs. Morrison's gardening. Eddie Hoffer. They said someone called the police station and told them he'd seen something through the window and then he hung up, so they asked me if I saw anyone around the house this afternoon and I said no. Then I said it might be Eddie, this being Friday, his payday. It just popped out and I feel awful because, right away, I could see what *they* thought.

"I think it, too."

"Well now, he wouldn't *notify* the police that poor Mrs. Morrison was lying there dead if he'd killed her. Not only that, if he was the one who called and said he saw her through the window, that big window that looks out on the porch, he couldn't have because when *I* got up on the porch, those drapes were closed tight."

"So? He went in and drew the drapes and killed her and forgot to open them again—then, forgetting he forgot, he called the police."

"Oh, *boy!*" Miriam said scornfully and departed for the kitchen to finish the dinner preparations.

Nick followed her. "Look, Miriam," he said in his calm, logical, D.A. voice, "stay out of that over there."

"How can I?" she said, yanking a roast from the oven.

"Because I said so. I've got a position to maintain."

"So have I," she said.

"But only as my wife. Remember, you're not a social worker any more. You don't have to save the Eddie Hoffers of the world."

Miriam felt, and not for the first time during their twenty years of marriage, that they were on opposite sides of the fence—he the prosecutor, and she the defender.

It was ascertained that Mrs. Morrison died as a result of a blow from a blunt instrument. Instantly, stated the coroner, death occurring at some time between 2:00 and 2:30 P.M.

"But I don't *remember* what time it was," whimpered Eddie.

His mother, hands clasped so tightly in her cotton lap that the knuckles looked bleached, sat by his side. At his other side, his probation officer looked worried. "It was afternoon and I was just up there to get my pay. Maybe it was about two o'clock, a little after, a little before, I don't know. I never done nothin'. I just went up to get my pay."

"And you saw her through the window," suggested the detective with the mean eyes and soft voice.

"I *thought* I saw her," cried Eddie. "I mean, I thought I saw something layin' there on the floor in the house. I just thought I saw it."

"Through the window," prodded the detective softly.

"Well, sure, through the window—that window that looks out on the porch." Eddie's eyes, bright blue flowers of frightened inno-cence, peeked through his hedge of hair.

"But Eddie," murmured the detective, "the drapes were closed on that window. Shut tight. So how could you see anything if you were standing out there on the porch?"

Eddie shot to his feet, then dropped again to the chair and moaned. "I saw it. Or I saw *something*. Them drapes were wide—wide open the way they always were. Wide open, and I saw some-thing out of the corner of my eyes through the window." His mother unclamped her fingers and patted her son's shoulder. "I saw it through the window and them drapes were open."

The probation officer laid a gentling hand on Eddie's arm.

"You say this was at two o'clock when you stood on the porch and 'saw something out of the corner of your eyes?' "

"About two," corrected Eddie. "I *think.* "

"I understand," said the detective consulting his notes, "that your anonymous telephone call notifying the police that you'd seen a body——"

"Or something," interrupted Eddie.

"Okay. 'Or something,' that your call came in at two-thirty. Why such a long time, Eddie?"

"Why what, such a long time?"

"Why did you wait so long, once you had seen this body 'or something,' to notify the police? A half hour, Eddie!"

The cornflower eyes in the hedge became wary. "I told you I didn't know *what* time it was when I was up there. Maybe it was after two. I don't know. Anyway, I didn't want to call."

"Why not, Eddie?"

"Because I knew it would be like this. I knew you'd be out after me."

"Why would we 'be out after you,' Eddie, if you didn't do any-thing?"

"Because you always are. You hang everything on me." Eddie's voice rose to a whine and his probation officer pressed the hand more firmly on his arm. "Well, the thing is, I wasn't going to call at all, but my girl made me. She said if I called and didn't give my name, it would be all right, but it isn't all right." Eddie began to cry.

Eddie Hoffer, three months short of eighteen, was detained in Juvenile Hall only long enough to be questioned, warned to keep himself available and released in the custody of his only parent, his mother, and under the control of his probation officer.

He had not mentioned the truck he had seen on the street that day—he had forgotten it.

The detective next spoke to Eddie Hoffer's girlfriend.

"You mean this Mrs. Whatchamacallit was actually murdered?" Her eyes were excitedly horrified. "Sure I told him to call. He didn't want to. But I said if she wasn't dead, it would be his fault if he didn't call so she could be saved. We didn't go to the beach that day. What he thought he saw, and I guess he really did see it, put Eddie off. Surf was up too."

She stared at the detective with sullen eyes. "He was scared you'd be after him. He was scared from the beginning. I told him you wouldn't know who he was when he called. I said you wouldn't be after him, but I was wrong."

"Not really, Laura," said the detective. "We're just asking questions—trying to get some answers." He smiled, but she did not smile back. She lowered her head, allowing strands of dirty blond hair to fall over her eyes, and gazed back at him malevolently from under frowning brows and through the stringy curtain.

III

The neighbors on Seaview had seen nothing that Friday afternoon, not even a truck on the street. Who notices trucks with meter readers, soft-water and bottled-water service, bread, milk, roto-rooter men? Each neighbor, upon being questioned, displayed a defensive nervousness, as if murder so close to home were an ambient taint, a personal dishonor. Except for Mrs. Miriam Clark, of course, known to some in the law enforcement field as the wife of the District Attorney, and to others as "the volunteer lady." She was concerned and cooperative.

"You're not messing around in that business across the street, are you?" Nick asked her that evening.

"What do you mean by 'messing around,' and what do you mean by the 'business across the street?' "

"You know what I mean."

"Well, I'll tell you. They come over here and ask me questions and I go over there and answer them."

Her house proved to be no more welcoming than Mrs. Morrison had been. It was neat, stiff, decorous and dull, as unimaginative as a motel accommodation. Miriam thought of the garden, bursting with color and inspiration.

"There were no signs of forced entry," stated the detective. "Nothing apparently disturbed. It had to be a friend—or, at least, someone she knew. The only people she knew, apparently, were you, Mrs. Clark, and Eddie Hoffer."

Miriam sneered.

"Did she speak of a husband, former husband, deceased husband?"

"No," said Miriam, having gone through this before. She sighed openly.

"Children, nieces, nephews? Where did she live before she came here?"

"I don't know," said Miriam.

"She lived here for fifteen years. We checked the tax records. Did you know that, Mrs. Clark?"

"No."

"Fifteen years, with no friends in the neighborhood. How long have you lived across the street, Mrs. Clark?"

"Five years."

The detective shook his head in wonder. "Eddie Hoffer has done her gardening for how long now?"

"Three months. I recommended him. I do volunteer work at Juvenile Hall. The kid had been in trouble and needed a job. The gardening was beginning to be a little too much for Mrs. Morrison, so I brought them together."

"Very commendable, Mrs. Clark," said the detective, wishing to God that former social service workers would retire decently into domesticity instead of scattering about the blood of their bleeding hearts, "but don't you think it was rather unwise to bring those two together? A helpless old lady and an unpredictable delinquent?"

"Mrs. Morrison was not helpless and Eddie is not unpredictable."

"The courts ordered Mrs. Morrison's bank accounts to be revealed and her safe deposit box opened. She's in good financial shape. What if she bragged a little?"

"Not Mrs. Morrison."

"And Eddie got the idea all those riches were just sitting in the house waiting for him."

"*Ridiculous!*"

"To bash in her head and rip her off."

"Was anything taken?"

"Well, no. Her purse was found in a dresser drawer. But the kid panicked."

"He panicked, yanked the drapes closed, raced out and called you, saying he'd seen the body through the window."

"That's right."

"Oh, for goodness sake! Why don't you find out where Mrs. Morrison went every month? Every single month she drove off somewhere and didn't come back till the next day."

"I didn't know that."

"You didn't ask it, so I'm telling you now. I don't *know* where she went, but maybe you'd better get off Eddie and onto where she took her trips. Then maybe you'll find some friends or relatives—maybe the killer."

Miriam's eyes were blazing. The detective's eyes blazed back. "Well, we'll do that, Mrs. Clark, and thank you for the tip. We shall certainly investigate Mrs. Morrison's travel habits. We have so few clues, you know. Would you believe that the only fingerprints in the whole house are Mrs. Morrison's own? The back doorknob is smudged—so is the front, except for one clear print. Yours, Mrs. Clark."

The fingerprinters and photographers, the search team and detectives were through with the house, having found Mrs. Delia Morrison's checkbook, a file of paid utility bills, her purse containing cash, a driver's license, an automobile insurance identification card and nothing else, no notification as to next of kin, no credit cards, no wallet photos.

Having found nothing of a personal and usable nature in the house, they assigned a final "thread by thread" search as they called it, to Lieutenant Lila Albright.

"That's the way they do it," she told Miriam. "When there's nothing left to find, they tell me to get busy."

Having worked together on juvenile cases, Miriam as social service volunteer, and Lila as law enforcement officer, they knew, admired and understood each other.

"It's as if she died long ago. There is no clutter," observed Miriam as they emptied neatly sparse drawers unlittered by never-used cookie cutters, pencil stubs, old prescription bottles, loose blue-chip stamps, a baby's teething ring and outdated price-saving coupons.

"Migod!" Nick usually exclaimed if he were searching for a bottle opener or cuff links. "Don't you throw *anything* away?"

"It's as if she cast everything out and moved in yesterday," said Miriam. "Where are her dreams, her hopes, her memories?"

"Maybe she never had any," said Lila.

But she had, they discovered, all wrapped up in out-of-fashion wardrobe and bound together in books. The dresses, beaded sheaths of the '20s, chiffons of the '30s, swinging '40s skirts, Empress Eugénie hats, cloches, turbans, flimsy stiletto-heeled slippers were packed in a closet. The books, old movie magazines and trade papers, too, lined up in a bookcase beside Mrs. Morrison's bed, formed a library of Golden Age show business. Miriam leaned over and switched on the portable TV set at the foot of the bed, almost expecting it automatically to light up with Norma Talmadge and Ronald Colman. What she got was a game show in full color. She switched it off.

"She watched the late-late shows on TV," said Miriam. "Ann Harding, Chester Morris, all of those." Remembering the night, no, the morning a year ago, after she and Nick had returned from seeing their son off at the L.A. Terminal—a fledgling, entering an eastern university—and waited up for his call that he had arrived safely. Miriam saw the light then from Mrs. Morrison's bedroom.

"Knock it off," said Nick when she expressed her concern. "The old girl probably isn't sick at all, she's just watching television." Nick had been right that time, for there had been many nights since then that Miriam had checked to see the light from this window at one, two, even three o'clock in the morning when the tired old movies romped across the screen.

"So that's what she did, she watched the old movies and read about the old times, living them all over again," said Miriam as they fanned through the pages after finding yellowed newsclippings, inserted like bookmarks, "remembering those times when she went by the name of Adele Vanderveer and was one of them."

The clippings indicated a career of remarkable mediocrity, one that followed the direct and simple promotional approach of the times—cheesecake, posed modestly while offering the appearance of audacity. They leaned over the old clippings, two women reading fuzzy history about the "new starlet in Hollywood's firmament," and found it rather more sad than glamorous.

"If this Adele Vanderveer really was Mrs. Morrison," said Lila, "she was really quite pretty."

They studied the doll-like features with two carefully placed spit curls above pencil-thin eyebrows, the cupid-bow lips delicately smiling. "Does it look like her?"

"Well, no." Miriam thought not and could not remember the embittered face that lived so alone. "Maybe that's where she went each month, somewhere in Hollywood, back to her old haunts, a kind of rhythmic nostalgia—maybe to see an old lover—"

"—who is now living out his days in the Actors' Retirement Home."

"Or just to look at the stars' names on the pavement of Hollywood Boulevard and remember the people she used to know."

"And stay overnight in one of those bungalows, if they are still there, where she used to live."

"*Right!* She has an old friend there who now subsists on an occasional TV commercial," said Miriam.

They conjectured widely and wrongly, and Lt. Lila Albright took the clippings back to headquarters to begin research into the life and times of a long-ago minor actress in an attempt to discover relatives or acquaintances, one of whom might have become murderous and killed her.

IV

"What's happening to Eddie?" Miriam asked Eddie Hoffer's probation officer.

"Well, nothing really. At least, not yet. He was questioned and told to keep himself available and he's been drooping around ever since. He's broken up with his girlfriend because he thinks she gave him a bum steer. He's not even doing any surfing. 'So what's to hang five?' he says, whatever that means. I want him to finish high school next year, get himself settled down, but he doesn't even know if he'll go back. What's the use, he says, they probably won't let him anyway, meaning the law. He needs a job to keep busy."

Miriam thought of her own son, less than two years older than Eddie, ready to enter his second year of college as soon as he returned from a Student Humanities Tour of Europe. She was convinced that the difference between the two was only a matter of generic and genetic luck. "Tell him I've got some jobs for him."

The probation officer was shaking his head. "You live too close to that woman's house. I don't know. He doesn't want to be reminded."

"Well, you tell him he won't be reminded of anything that'll hurt him. I'm in his corner and I need help."

Miriam was all ready for Eddie. She led him down the side stairs to the backyard and set out pruning shears and hand clippers. The hedge that circled the yard was waist high with scraggly leaf fountains giving it a mountain-ridge appearance.

"As you can see," said Miriam brightly, "the hedge needs clipping." She followed him, watching with interest while he worked—*snip-snip.* "This backyard is certainly not as nice as Mrs. Morrison's, is it?" she asked.

He flinched—*snip-snip*—"No, ma'am," he said.

The sun was bright and, over the hedge beyond the strip of city, the ocean surf foamed and broke. Eddie kept his eyes on the green leaves that danced from the cutting blades. Miriam watched the boy. *Snip-snip.* "She had a green thumb, she surely did," remarked Miriam.

"Yes, ma'am," said Eddie, his shoulders hunched.

"I never saw such flowers—*snip-snip.* "Did you, Eddie?"

"No, ma'am."

"Did she ever talk to you, Eddie? I mean, when you and she were working together out there in the garden?"

Snip-snip. "She talked to the flowers kind of, that's all." He turned, his hands tight on the handles of the pruning shears, his eyes blue and worried as they pleaded through the forest on his face. "Mrs. Clark," he said, his voice softly cracked, "I just don't like to talk about Mrs. Morrison."

"Neither do I," said Miriam briskly. "But we were the only ones who knew her, you and I."

He turned back to the hedge. "Not me, ma'am. I didn't know her. I just worked for her, out there in the yard. I was never in the house. Not once. I didn't know her at all."

"Well, she was rather an unknowable woman, wasn't she?"

"Yeah, sure, I guess." *Snip-snip.* "But that was all right, Mrs. Clark. I didn't care. I just did my work. I did what she told me to do."

"I'm sure you did, Eddie." *Snip-snip.* "But didn't she talk at all? Not *ever?*"

"Well, like I said, she talked to the flowers some and told me what to do." *Snip-snip.*

"How about *besides* talking to the flowers and telling you what to do? Didn't she say *anything?*"

Snip-snip. "Hardly anything, ma'am. She told me what to do and when to come to work, like on Mondays and Wednesdays I was supposed to come. Fridays, too, but that was just for my pay."

Snip-snip. "Unless her garage door was open and her car was gone. Then I was supposed to come my next regular day." *Snip-snip.*

Miriam watched the boy while he snipped at the hedge, the leaf falls showering the lawn.

"She said that meant she was out of town."

"Where out of town?" asked Miriam softly. "Those once-a-month times when she took her car and left the garage open, where out of town did she go?"

"I don't know, ma'am." *Snip-snip.* "She just said she'd be back for my next regular day, as soon as she got back from Fairview." *Snip-snip.*

"*Fairview?*" cried Miriam. She grabbed Eddie's arm. "She said she went to Fairview?"

Eddie's startled eyes blinked. "I guess she did, ma'am."

"Look, Eddie, you finish the hedge and rake up, then yell through the back door, okay?"

"Sure, Mrs. Clark," said Eddie, glad to be left alone.

She got out the Road Atlas and, running her finger down the Fs, she found Fairview, Pop. 480, 11.17 E-4. She turned the pages to Map 11.17, found E, then 4 and the tiny dot off the freeway, faintly named Fairview, probably a farm community. Using a pencil point to approximate the scale in miles, she decided that this Fairview was about seventy miles inland.

"Mrs. Clark!" called Eddie through the back door.

She went out back, complimented him on his tip-top job, overpaid him outrageously and asked if he was sure Mrs. Morrison said nothing further about her out-of-town trips. Of that, he was certain, Eddie assured her, gazing at the riches in his hand.

"I will have more work for you, Eddie," said Miriam.

"Yes, ma'am," he responded with enthusiasm.

"So I'll call you as soon as I return from Fairview."

"What do you know about Fairview?" Miriam asked Nick.

"What's a fairview?"

"A town. A dot, really, on the map, about seventy miles away, off the inland freeway."

"Never heard of it. What do you want to know for?"

"It's where Mrs. Morrison used to go every month."

"Oh, for crying out loud!" He exclaimed.

"Eddie told me."

"Who's Eddie?"

"You know about Eddie. Eddie Hoffer, the kid that was questioned about the murder."

"Now you look here, Miriam. I told you to stay out of that mess across the street. Leave it alone. Don't even think about it."

V

She arrived in Fairview at a little after ten in the morning. The sun blazed, the air was filled with dust. She had mentally divided the population of 480 by four, using the statistic that the average family numbers four, to come up with 120 houses she would need to canvass in order to discover one where Mrs. Morrison might have visited once a month.

Fairview the community stretched far and flat with, here and there in the distance, a tree-shaded farmhouse. Workers, tiny hatted and kerchiefed figures, dotted the fields. Fairview the town, appeared to be one tree-lined street long. The Post Office was part of the grocery store. The doctor's office was in the drugstore building. There were a grain elevator, a feed store, grocery store and two churches. It was that kind of town. The houses rested, seemingly at random, along side roads, each quite isolated from the other, except for what

Miriam supposed were the field workers' homes, which were grouped together.

She found two *For Sale* signs that interested her. One before a tiny cottage dwarfed by a live oak, suggested she *Inquire at the drugstore.* The other, nailed to a peach tree in a small orchard, asked that she *Inquire at the P.O.*

She inquired, over a Coke, at the drugstore first and never did get to the P.O. The druggist was quite surprised. It was probably the first query he'd had in the seven years the house had been vacant.

"Since my mother died," he said. "It may need a little work done on it. Tell you what, I can run you out there at noon for a look-through. It's on a nice big lot, but since it's a little run down, I'll let it go cheap."

Miriam raised her hand to indicate that money was no object and asked about the neighbors. "That is most important," she explained earnestly, "the neighbors. I want to know who they are and what they're like and if they have much company. The thing is, I want quiet."

"Well, there aren't any real *near* neighbors and none of 'em have much company," said the druggist cooperatively. "They're *all* nice. Finest people around. The Gillicuddys live in that house at the bend of the road. Retired couple. Hardly get around much any more. Their sons come to see them once or twice a year, and that's about the extent of their company." Miriam checked off the Gillicuddys.

"On the other side, there's the Orvilles. Keep the house for a vacation place. They both work in L.A. Come out for a weekend now and then and in the summer for a while. When they do, they just hole in. Don't have anybody visiting them." Miriam checked off the Orvilles.

"The only other neighbor is Mrs. Ormsby across the road. Her house is back in that little grove of trees. A good woman, God-fearing, saddled with that orphan she took in after her husband was killed in World War II. Kind of a strange man, keeps to himself. Grows flowers."

Miriam jumped.

"Quiet people, both of them. You don't need to worry about things not being quiet, Mrs.—"

"Clark," supplied Miriam. "These people, the last ones, do they have much company? Visitors, I mean. Do many people come to see them?"

"No. Just some woman who comes pretty regular, stays the night and then she's gone. Been doing it for years—way back when my mother was alive. Look, Mrs, Clark, don't you want to wait here until I can get the key and take you out?"

"I'll be back," called Miriam over her shoulder.

She followed the two strips of concrete that formed the driveway, back to the grove and the little gray house. The slam of her car door was startling in the warm silence. The lawn, well-kept, sprouted clumps of tall blooming flowers, feathered fresh and green.

She stepped to the porch, lifted the door knocker and let it tap gently. She heard no sound. She tapped again and waited. Then once more. She was about to go around to the back when the door opened and a small elderly woman wearing glasses stood there in severe silence. She appeared so frail that Miriam wanted to reach out and support the tiny body, robed in yellow, accentuating the jaundiced tone of her skin.

"Yes?" she said at last.

"Oh! Well, are you Mrs. Ormsby?"

"I am."

"Well . . ." Miriam poured forth, in staccato embarrassment, the improbable tale of her interest in the house across the road and her desire to meet her neighbors. The woman didn't believe a word of it. She smiled thinly and started to close the door. "Mrs. Ormsby! Does Mrs. Morrison visit you?"

The door opened again. "Why?" she asked.

Miriam drew a deep breath. "Because she is dead, Mrs. Ormsby, and I am trying to find her relatives or friends."

The woman clung to the door and Miriam had the unaccountable impression that she clung not for support but with relief. "You have found a relative," she said, "but not a friend. How did my sister die?"

Miriam stood in silent shock for long moments until the woman jogged her to speech. "Well?"

"She was killed, Mrs. Ormsby. Murdered."

The woman opened the door wide and Miriam entered a house cluttered with religious artifacts. She seated herself uncomfortably in a straightback chair while Mrs. Ormsby sat stiffly on a hard sofa, carefully folding the robe over her knees, and placing slippered feet side by side.

"What happened and how?" she asked calmly. "I know why it happened and who did it. What I want to know now is what and how." Miriam drew in her breath, questions tumbling in her mind, but holding them before the autocratic, saffron face before her.

"Mrs. Morrison was killed a week ago Friday in her home," she said. Mrs. Ormsby nodded without expression while Miriam carefully and finically offered the sparse details including the extensive and outdated wardrobe, the library of nostalgia and the Adele Vanderveer clippings. She added Eddie Hoffer's precarious position and his belated and hazy recall of the Fairview name.

"Her son killed her," spoke Mrs. Ormsby.

"I beg your pardon?" asked Miriam politely.

"Her son. He lives here with me."

Without moving her head, Miriam cast her glance apprehensively about the room.

"He is probably out in his cottage. It used to be a plant shed where his father, my husband, worked long ago."

"My *God!*" breathed Miriam.

Mrs. Ormsby glared in reprimand and launched into an emotional tirade against a "Jezebel sister who painted her face and took on an outlandish name and entered the gates of a celluloid Babylon." Miriam's mouth dropped open as she listened to the "good sister's" tale of the "bad sister's" perfidy, canonized by theological quotations and colored with allegorical homilies. Even as she listened, she could not believe what she heard.

"*She* had the pretty clothes, the platinum hair, the dancing lessons and parties—and the men who gave her those things." Mrs. Ormsby paused for an instant of deep and irate breathing. "She called herself a starlet. A harlot is what she was. The way of the wicked is an abomination unto the Lord!"

Miriam wrapped her arms tight around her breast, feeling cold in the warmth of the house.

"I tried to lead her into the paths of righteousness. I prayed and I failed. She that refuseth instruction, despiseth her soul."

With that malediction spoken, Mrs. Ormsby's face softened as she told of her own marriage. "He was a good man, poor and struggling. We came here, the land was cheap, it was a time of depression. I helped him build the house and the greenhouse beyond and the outbuildings. I helped him build up the place into a nursery. I helped him with his flowers." She paused with the memory for a long, soft second, and then she said flatly. "And into this Garden of Eden came the serpent and it was defiled."

"My God!" gasped Miriam, without reprimand.

"Delia came. This was in forty-one, toward the last of forty-one, before Pearl Harbor. I hadn't seen her for years. She was nervous and tired and wanted a place to rest and I couldn't turn her out. It was a warm and beautiful winter. The cyclamen, dahlias, chrysanthemums and tigridia were all coming into bloom. She helped my husband in the gardens and rode with him in the truck when he took the flowers to market. I had hope for her then. I thought the good-ness of the land might come into her soul and the decency of this life might turn her back on the other. But she left."

Miriam remembered the newsprint photo of a dollface with stud-ied curls and bowed lips and was able, at last, to fit the woman gardener with the girl who dreamed of glamor.

"And she didn't return until the next spring, already bulging with child. My husband was overseas then, and I was alone. She came weeping, needing to hide, saying she would be ruined if her condi-tion was found out. But she was already ruined, for the sin was in her body."

Miriam wondered if this stern fundamentalist, this rigid zealot, had even the slightest awareness of the presently altered moral code, and looking at her, decided that—no matter—her own would remain steadfast.

"I delivered her of a son the day I was notified of my husband's death."

"Oh!" Without conscious impulse, Miriam reached out with a comforting gesture, which was ignored.

"I didn't know my husband was the father of my sister's illegiti-mate son until she left him with me. Then she told me." Mrs. Ormsby retreated into her martyred past before she outlined the future she had prepared for her husband's son and his mother. "I raised him to know that he would carry the sin of his birth until the day he died. I watched him grow, a bastard I hated, into the image of my husband whom I loved. Do you know what that is like?" Mrs. Ormsby leaned forward, seemingly aware, for the first time, that she had a listener.

Miriam shook her head dumbly.

The fierceness suddenly left the woman. "I wouldn't allow his mother to see him until he became a man—a man like my husband whom she loved for such a short time. That was after she was finished with the movies, or the movies were finished with her, and she had married Mr. Morrison, old enough and rich enough for her to wait for him to die. By then her bastard son was grown and I let her know that she could come out and look at him."

Miriam stared at the woman, feeling the hatred and the anguish of the years close her in—understanding, almost understanding with a shudder.

"So," said Mrs. Ormsby conversationally, "she comes to look at him once a month, regularly. That is," she corrected herself, "she *did* come to look at him once a month until he killed her."

Miriam turned her face away and pressed a finger against her lips.

"He is very withdrawn, a recluse, a hermit, almost an ascetic. He reads his Bible, tends his flowers and trucks them in to market, and I don't think he even sees her when she comes. I told her I would kill her if she let him know who she was. I didn't want to kill her. I wanted him to do the killing for it was her sin, not mine. And it wasn't time until now. I am sick—terminal—and I was afraid it was almost too late.

"I told him again what his mother was, and then I told him who she was and where to find her. And when the truck was gone so long on Friday, not his day to go to market, I supposed that he had done what he had to do." She folded her hands sedately in her yellow lap. "The wicked," she said, "is driven away in her wickedness, but the righteous hath hope in her death."

Whatever that means, thought Miriam, standing on trembling legs.

She let herself out, breathing deep of the sticky August air, finding it good.

With an apprehensive glance around the side of the house toward the back, green and dark, she stepped into her car and backed it up over the twin cement strips and turned toward town.

She would call Lieutenant Lila Albright and let her know that Adele Vanderveer and the relatives of Mrs. Delia Morrison had been found.

"My God!" she exclaimed aloud with no one to reprimand her.

Then she would call Nick and tell him she might be late in getting home, and why. He would shout through the phone: "I *told* you to mind your own business." She would hang up on him.

The calls had to be made, so she drove to the drugstore where there was a telephone booth and an eager druggist who thought she wanted to buy his property.

Old pro Lawrence Treat, early in 1976, was elected president of Mystery Writers of America, *an honor he richly deserves. Treat created the modern police-procedural story more than thirty years ago. Here he tries his hand at something entirely different—with memorable results.*

LAWRENCE TREAT
The Candle Flame

In all the times I've seen her I think she never smiled. Or showed anger.

She arrived at the back door on that hot sultry day when everybody with any sense was cooling off at the lake. She was wearing a long red velvet skirt that swept a broad swath in the sandy path to the cottage. Her embroidered bodice was a fine example of nomadic art, and her flowing costume could have held three of her. It seemed impossible that her frail flat-chested body could support the weight of that heavy velvet and those strings of beads.

"Yes?" I said. "You wanted something?"

For the few seconds before she replied, she gazed at me, and even now it is hard to describe her eyes. They were blue, they were white, they were colorless, and they seemed unable to blink or change expression. They were a child's eyes—porcelain eyes, with no appearance of depth.

"I heard you were looking for somebody to clean house," she said.

"Right. But my wife is down at the lake. She'll be back around six."

"Could I see the house first?" she said.

"Sure. My studio's separate. I take care of it myself, so there's just the living room-kitchen that you're looking at and a couple of small bedrooms. Not very much. It's nothing but a summer shack."

"I know," she said. She moved forward and appeared to study the room. "When were you born?" she asked.

It was a peculiar question, and later it occurred to me that it was even more peculiar that I answered it. "Nineteen thirty," I said.

"No. I mean what date?"

"October," I said. "The fourteenth."

"Libra," she said. Then she walked forward and touched the paperweight on my desk. "That's why you have the opal," she said. "It's your birthstone. And your wife? When was she born?"

"Same month as I was, but on the seventh."

"I'm a Virgo," she said, "so there won't be any problem. Just so you're not Scorpio."

She seemed about to leave, but before making up her mind she took a last look at the room and saw the sketch I'd made that morning. It was a quick drawing, only half finished, of a young girl. She picked it up and gazed at it rapturously.

"Oh, I *like* that!" she exclaimed. "It's *me!*" And she clasped it to her meager bosom. "May I borrow it? I have to be with it for a while."

"Of course," I said, flattered by her enthusiasm and watching her hug it, carrying it as she would a sleeping infant.

She seemed embarrassed, and she turned and looked at me with those pale, innocent eyes.

"I have to go to The Area," she said, as if she hated the necessity of explaining, "but you don't have to take me there unless you want to."

"Glad to," I said. "No trouble at all." And I felt noble and virtuous at giving her a ride.

I don't know when people first started calling that grassy peninsula "The Area." It had acquired the name long before Gerda and I had started coming to the lake, and by immemorial custom it was reserved for nude bathing. Nobody was sure who owned it. I tried once to check the title on the tax records and found that theoretically it didn't even exist. Perhaps that was why the police, otherwise so strict in petty law enforcement, stayed away from The Area.

When I returned to the house, Gerda was changing from her bathing suit, and I told her about the apparition that was due to work for us.

"What's her name?" Gerda asked.

"Amanda Pyle. She has strange, light-colored eyes, and her hair is blond-red, something like a pink grapefruit."

"What a romantic image!" Gerda said.

I had to go to town shortly before six, and when I returned to the house I saw Martin Fuller's beat-up bug parked nearby. I recognized his car by the variety of oversized flower decals that decorated its pockmarked hide. I pulled up alongside.

"Hi," I said. "What are you doing here?"

"Waiting for Amanda," he answered. "It seems she's decided to work for you."

"We certainly need her. Ever since Gerda hurt her arm, she's been desperate for somebody to help out."

"That's why Amanda came," Martin said.

That stopped me. Gerda needs someone, and Amanda divines or intuits or telepathizes, and comes to the rescue. Which was ridiculous.

"Oh," I said. "You mean somebody told Amanda about Gerda's arm and that she needed a housecleaner?"

"Well," Martin said. "I suppose so."

I felt stupid and wanted to apologize or change the subject and get back to normal. "Been waiting long?" I said.

"Ten or fifteen minutes."

"Why not have a swim with me?" I said. "I'm going to have a quick dip before dinner."

"I can't swim," Martin said.

"You? A big guy like you? How come?"

Martin gave me a sheepish grin. "Makes me unique," he said. "Everybody else swims, I don't." Then, becoming serious, he said, "When I was a kid I almost drowned, and I've been scared of the water ever since."

"Don't worry," I said. "You'll get over that. Maybe Amanda can manage it."

"I guess she will, eventually," he said. Which was a commonplace remark, and yet at the time I had the feeling that Martin meant she'd perform some kind of hocus-pocus, that she'd tell him he was no longer afraid of the water and could swim, and her saying so would make it so.

"Mmm. Well, I'd better bring my packages in."

Gerda told me later on that Amanda had walked into the house, tilted her head to one side while she studied Gerda, and announced that it was all right for her to work for Gerda.

"Just like that?" I said. "She told you she was going to work for you? She didn't wait to be asked?"

"I wanted somebody and she looked clean, so why wouldn't I give her a try?"

"Just like that?" I said again.

"Well, she said I had the right vibes—vibrations, I guess—so we went on to other things."

They were on the "other things" when I arrived. They were discussing when it was best to eat fiddleback ferns and whether purslane should be creamed or merely sautéed. It was clear that they were kindred souls, even to the point of finance.

I heard the bargain being made. Amanda was about to leave when Gerda mentioned money. "I forgot to ask you how much you want.

I suppose three dollars an hour, like everybody else."

Amanda objected. "Oh, no. I couldn't take more than two. Two is Yin and Yang, and three would be triad."

Gerda looked surprised, but she recovered quickly. "Oh, yes," she said. "That will be all right."

I quote the exact conversation, to prove that there was nothing sinister. Nothing.

I was in my studio the following morning when Amanda arrived, and I didn't see her until I came into the house for my second cup of coffee. She was standing at the sink. Despite the bright sunlight a lighted candle was burning on either side of her. She was using my favorite eggcups as holders, and she was slowly washing a coffee cup in a basin of water. Later on, when Gerda and I redid the dishes, she told me Amanda had put a white lily in the basin instead of soapsuds.

"It was quite beautiful," Gerda said.

At the time, however, I was overwhelmed by the sight of Amanda and her candles. "What!" I exclaimed. "What the——"

But Gerda put her finger to her lips and murmured a "Shh!" Amanda appeared not to hear. I think she was in a trance.

At lunch, after Amanda had left, I asked Gerda how things had worked out. "Well," Gerda said, "she did about ten cents' worth of work. Not much more."

"Did you complain?"

"In a way. She said she'd do better next time."

She did. Or at least Martin did. He brought her to the house and came in with her. "Martin is going to help me," Amanda announced. "It won't cost extra, he'll do a couple of things."

What he did was wash the kitchen floor, run the vacuum cleaner, sweep and clean the porch, and shake out the rugs.

"Twenty dollars' worth of work, easily," Gerda told me.

The next time, however, Amanda came alone. Perhaps in apology for her incompetence, she presented us with a loaf of health bread that she'd baked.

At almost every visit she brought something wild that she'd made or gathered, and she spent the first half hour or so, at our expense, telling Gerda how to prepare it. As the result, I found myself drinking sumac tea, eating pigweed or lamb's-quarters, and having wild sorrel salads and soups. Once Amanda arrived with a basket of mushrooms, and Gerda and I were shocked to see a couple of amanitas mixed in with some edible species.

"Amanda!" Gerda said. "Throw them out. Those white ones— they're a deadly poison."

"I know," Amanda said serenely. "I wasn't going to eat those. White is wrong."

"Amanitas," Gerda said sternly, "are poisonous."

"I'm careful," Amanda said, "and I know where to look. The ones that grow in circles are good to eat, and so are the ones that grow in clusters, but when they're alone and dressed in white they represent pride and vanity. I wouldn't dream of eating them."

"That's nonsense," Gerda said firmly. "Inedible ones can also grow in circles and clusters. That's no way to identify. You have to know a mushroom the way you know an aster or a rose."

Amanda didn't answer, and I'm not even sure she listened.

After a few weeks Gerda's arm had regained its normal strength, but it was not in her nature to fire anybody, particularly someone like Amanda.

"We're friends," Gerda said. "She tells me all kinds of things. How she came to the lake, for instance. She was in a commune, and she was on her way to town one day when Martin's name popped into her mind. She knew him from some yoga classes that they'd both gone to, and they'd kept up with each other in a vague sort of way. When she got back to the commune, she found out that Martin had phoned her, so she called him and he said to come up here. Naturally she did."

"Naturally," I said.

She worked for us on Mondays and Fridays. Sometimes she brought Martin, and when she did he polished up the house until it was spic and span. Otherwise she left behind her a faint scent of incense, a couple of burnt-out candles, and a stack of dishes to be rewashed. We were therefore surprised to see her arrive one Tuesday morning.

"Bob's coming," she said, "and I need money to buy him a present. Shall I start in the bathroom?"

"That will be fine," Gerda said. "Who's Bob?"

Amanda went to the refrigerator and took out an egg and some of her barley bread for breakfast. "He's very special," she said. "He's coming from California and I have to fix the room for him."

"What about Martin?" Gerda asked.

"Oh, Martin will understand. Bob's special, you see. He's been to India and he studied under the Master." From the way she spoke you could tell that Master was spelled with a capital M. "Bob has Power." And that was spelled with a capital P.

"Amanda," Gerda said, "I don't like to interfere, but I'm a little older than you are, and I'd like to give you some advice. Martin's been sweet to you, he's helped you and he's been a good friend and you have certain obligations toward him, so it's not fair to push him out and take somebody else, just like that."

"I'm not pushing him out," Amanda said. "I wouldn't dream of such a thing."

"Do they know each other?" Gerda said.

"They know each other through me. I think of both of them at the same time, and in utter harmony."

"But when they see each other, maybe there won't be quite that much harmony. Thinking doesn't always make things so."

Amanda turned slowly and fixed Gerda with her pale eyes. "I'd do anything that either of them asked me to," she said. "We're unity. We're not external, we're internal." Then she ate the egg and barley bread.

Later, after she'd meditated in the bathroom and then left with her $4 and breakfast on us, I teed off on Gerda.

"That little chit conned us," I said. "What did she do for her four dollars? What does she think we are?"

"She thinks we're lost in desire. She's a little sorry for us, and she uses us."

"I don't like to be used. I'm not a usee."

"Neither am I, but I'm learning things. Peter, what do you know about communes and long-hairs and acid freaks? What do you know about Amanda's young world?"

"I know plenty about her generation. First it went in for love and then it was acid and then the Jesus freaks and now I guess it's something else. These kids are looking for something. Sure. They haven't found it and I don't think they're on the right track, but they're having a hell of a good time and I'm glad they are, because by and by they'll settle down and have children and be good citizens and read the classics, just like you and me."

"You're old-fashioned," Gerda said, "and you're jealous of people like Amanda, and so am I. I envy Amanda and her two men, although I don't think it will work out, and that's why I said what I did. But deep down, Peter, I hope she gives it a try."

"If she does," I said, "it's going to be murder for one of them."

"Literally?"

"Of course not. They're gentle people. Amanda is one of the kindest and gentlest people I've ever met. But look at the way she leads Martin around. And us."

"You're sarcastic," Gerda said, "but wait and see."

"Martin's too nice a guy to be led around, and one of these days he'll see what's happening and he'll turn on her."

"And do what?" Gerda said. "Beat her up? Walk out on her? What?"

"I don't know. All I'm saying is that there's a limit. She puts things over on people, she does it all the time. Take yourself, for instance —has she ever really cleaned this place? Has she ever done a decent morning's work?"

"If she had," Gerda said, with her usual illogic, "my arm wouldn't have gotten better so fast. It's as if I had to cover up for her and my sprained arm was no excuse, so it had to get better and it did. All the things I've learned from her!" Gerda started laughing. "She's so pathetic that you feel sorry for her and you never realize what you've done until it's all over. Peter, how many pictures have you given her?"

"None," I said, grinning, "but she took two."

To nobody's surprise, neither mine nor Gerda's, Amanda failed to show up on her next cleaning day. "I guess that's the end of that," Gerda said. "No more groundnuts or crowberries, and no more barley bread. From now on we'll have to go to the corner store and buy our food like everybody else."

"But we can't let her go," I said. "I'm too damn curious about what's happening with Martin and Amanda and this Bob guy. How about going down to The Area and looking for them?"

It was a long time since Gerda and I had been there, and the initial impact was strange, almost shocking. The flat, grassy area was covered with dogs and naked bodies, small dogs and big dogs and thin bodies and fat bodies, lounging, sunning themselves, talking, or doing nothing. Two or three long-hairs were doing yoga exercises, and a small group was intent on watching a chess game. Some children were playing in the couple of feet of sand that had been imported long ago in an attempt to make a beach.

We found our threesome easily enough. They were lying in a circle, with their feet touching each other at the center. Martin, big and powerful, an athlete in perfect condition; Amanda, like a slender stick of flesh; and Bob, an undernourished little spider, all hair, hairy body and bushy beard with a stubby little nose poking out of it as if coming up for air. When I spoke, they sat up.

Amanda made a feint at introducing us. "This is Bob," she said.

"I've heard of you," I said.

Bob's squeaky voice surprised me. "Many have," he said.

Gerda tried to break the embarrassment by discussing edible wild plants with Amanda, but Bob's treble cut her off.

"Let's not talk about food," he said. "This is our day of fasting."

"Amanda fasting?" Gerda said. "She needs all the nourishment she can get. Just look at her."

"Her nourishment is of the spirit," Bob said. "She has a calm center."

I coughed. Gerda said, "Well, well!" Martin looked uncomfortable, and then pandemonium broke loose in the form of a dog fight.

They were big dogs, a German shepherd and a Doberman pinscher, and they battled in a snarling whirlwind of fury. Everybody near them jumped and ran off shrieking, except for a couple of brave young guys, probably the owners, who tried gingerly and ineffectually to separate them.

I grabbed Gerda's hand, ready, in case the tornado came our way, to pull her behind me in a gesture of protection. Bob, however, climbed to his feet, rising slowly, using some trick of elongating himself so that he seemed tall, despite the fact that he barely topped my shoulder. I was amazed to see him walk deliberately toward that whirling ball of canine destruction.

He was nude and unprotected against claws and teeth, while a pair of enraged animals were snapping and biting at each other and anybody near them. But Bob walked straight up to them, held out his hands, and said something no one could hear. Maybe he spoke, maybe he whistled, or maybe he exuded some power of silencing. In any case, the dogs stopped abruptly, withdrew, then faced each other growling. Bob held out his two hands and each of the dogs crept up to him, tails between their legs, and licked his outstretched fingers.

For a moment there was silence. Then you could hear the rising babble of astonishment, and a few sentences carried to where we stood—words of admiration, almost of awe.

Bob paid no attention to anyone. He said something to the dogs in a low voice, and they did not follow as he returned to us.

"That was wonderful," Gerda said. "What did you say to them?"

Bob didn't deign to reply. He reached out for Amanda's hand. "Let's go for a dip," he said.

She followed obediently, and we watched them walk toward the water, walking slowly until they reached the edge, where they seemed to explode and go splashing in. Martin gazed at them sadly.

"Does he do that kind of thing often?" I said. "Pull miracles, that is?"

"No, that's the first time I've seen anything like that."

"It's going to be tough on you," I said. "From now on he's a hero, whereas you——" I didn't finish the sentence.

"He's not a hero," Martin said. "You need an awful lot of ego to be a hero."

"You think he has none?" I said. "I think he has nothing but."

Martin shrugged. I felt that he agreed with me, but was afraid to say so. The subject seemed to be unpleasant to him, so I switched.

"Why don't you learn how to swim?" I said. "You're a good athlete, it ought to be easy for you."

"Amanda said she'd teach me when she thinks I'm ready for it."

"You'll be ready as soon as you try," I said. "How can *she* know when you're ready?"

"Don't," Martin said.

Don't talk about it any more? Don't destroy my confidence in Amanda and her way of life? Don't make problems for me? Don't —what?

We saw the three of them in town later that week. They were barefoot. Amanda was walking in the center, and her light cloak was thrown around both her escorts. It circled Bob's narrow shoulders and made him and Amanda as one, but on Martin's side the cloak was too short and too small to cover him, so it hung precariously from Martin's midriff and threatened to fall off at every step.

"Yin and Yang," I said to Gerda, "and three would be triad. I wonder whether she'd work for three bucks an hour now, if you offered it."

"Martin will leave her," Gerda said. "He has too much sense not to. He'll find himself a good healthy wench to love him, and he'll love her in turn."

"Sure," I said. "To the end of his days."

We were wrong.

The first we heard of the event was from one of our neighbors, who phoned to find out if we knew. Gerda answered the phone, and the shock in her voice made me gasp.

"What!" she exclaimed. "Martin? Oh, no! Not Martin. What happened?" She listened for a minute or so, then put the phone down gently. "Martin drowned," she said to me. "He went rowing with Amanda, and he fell out of the boat and drowned."

"But he was so scared of the water," I said. "What made him go? And how do you fall out of a boat? Only fools stand up, and Martin was no fool."

"You think not?" Gerda said. "You kept saying he was. Remember?"

The full account appeared in the local paper. It said that Martin Fuller, 22 years old and a part-time carpenter, had been drowned in a tragic accident. According to Miss Amanda Pyle, who had been with him, he had stood up in the boat, for reasons she was unable to explain. He either lost his balance or became dizzy, and he toppled and knocked over the oars in his fall.

Mr. Fuller, the story continued, weighed about 200 pounds and

Miss Pyle barely half of that. It was obviously beyond her strength to dive in and rescue him, and it was all she could do to paddle the boat with her hands and reach the floating oars. By that time it was too late for her to do anything to help Mr. Fuller. She rowed ashore and notified the first people she saw, who called the police. The body was recovered several hours later.

Amanda came to work for us the following Thursday. She seemed calm and collected, and at first she made no mention of the tragedy. She had a wreath of daisies in her hair. She removed the wreath ceremoniously and placed it on one of the two towels she took from the linen closet. She took the other towel into the bathroom, and presently we heard the shower going.

"What the hell is she doing in there?" I said to Gerda.

"Apparently she's taking a shower," Gerda said acidly. "But don't ask her any questions for a while. If she doesn't tell me anything, I'll ask later on."

"I don't like it," I said. "The least she ought to do is look sad and tell us about Martin. But she's so calm and quiet."

"Wait and see," Gerda said.

I waited patiently while Amanda came out of the bathroom, found two candles, and set them up on either side of the sink. She put them in my eggcups, as she always did, then lit the candles and went through her usual vague motions of washing. This time, however, it was all too much for me to take, and I marched over to the sink and blew out the candles.

"In case you're wondering why I did that," I said, "those are my eggcups, and I like to use them as such."

"I'm sorry," Amanda said meekly. "But when you're with a candle flame, you are the candle flame."

"What does that mean?" I asked.

"I hoped you'd understand," she said. "You're upset about Martin, aren't you?"

"You bet I am."

"You don't have to be," she said. "He's no longer lost in the darkness. He's part of us now."

Gerda interrupted what might have become a rather nasty and probably futile interrogation by me. "Amanda," she said gently, "tell us what happened."

"It was wonderful," Amanda said. "Martin finally conquered his fear of water, and with it he conquered all fear. He *asked* me to go rowing with him, and when we were in the center of the lake he said he was no longer afraid of the water, and he stood up in the boat and he was smiling. When he swayed, I tried to reach out to support him and keep him from falling, but there was a force between us. There was an energy that kept me from reaching out, and suddenly I knew that his time had come, this was his karma, and I was privileged to be there at the time. I was so happy!"

"Happy?" I exclaimed. "When he's dead?"

"You don't understand," Amanda said. "You're like the police. They didn't understand either. They kept asking me whether I'd pushed him."

"Did you?" I said.

"I can't stay here when people keep thinking that. Don't you see, Martin and I were one. For a wonderful instant we were joined as can only rarely happen between people. We found ourselves in a perfect circle."

"And now you're leaving The Area?" I said.

"Yes."

"With Bob?"

"Oh, no. With a friend of mine. You don't know him, but he's Gemini, and Bob, while he's wonderful, he's Pisces. So you see, Bob couldn't go with me."

"Well, I hope it works out," I said, "and that the tragedy—"

"Please, don't call it a tragedy. It was the way of life, it was good that it happened and good that it happened with me. Some other people might have tried to interfere." Her pale eyes gazed upward, where police and other unbelievers like myself couldn't possibly reach her.

"Tell me just one thing more," I said. "Why did he stand up?"

"Because I wanted him to."

"Oh," I said.

I watched Amanda cross the room and take the daisy wreath from the towel on which she'd placed it when she'd come in. She adjusted the wreath carefully and then she left, with her long velvet skirt trailing along the path. She did not look back.

As soon as she was out of sight, I walked over to the towel and examined it. Her wreath had left a faint, lightcolored ring that seemed to give off tiny shafts of light.

"It looks like a halo," I said, dumfounded.

Gerda smiled. "Yes," she said. "Didn't you see her draw it?"

"Sure," I said sarcastically. Then I bent over and touched the wet towel, and the yellow pollen came off on my fingers.

"Halo?" I said. "Halo?"

Good short stories about the Mafia are rare. This is a very good one, even though the word "Mafia" is never mentioned.

FRANK SISK
The Fly Swatter

Twice a day nearly every day Sr. Giampietro Saccovino, *l'Americano ricco* as the Portofinese referred to him, descended from his villa in the pine-shrouded foothills above the Via Roma and refreshed himself for a while at a table on the *piazza* outside the Trattoria Navicello.

He came first in the morning not long after the *carabiniere* had unpadlocked the heavy chain that stretched across the narrow road at the town's entrance from one stone post to another—about 7:30. He came again late in the afternoon, a few hours before sunset. Generally he was alone, although there were those rare occasions when he might be accompanied by a woman—one of a number who visited the villa with some degree of regularity; women who, in the eyes of the parochial natives, looked suspiciously like high-priced *sgualdrine* down from Genova. The *Signore* nevertheless was adjudged *il gentiluomo,* for man is not born to be a saint.

Besides, Sr. Saccovino tipped most handsomely all who served him.

Also he wore shimmering silk suits of a conservative cut. The third finger of his left hand shone with a stone worth perhaps two million lire or more. Another fortune was represented by the ruby-studded clasp formed like a scimitar that adorned a succession of hand-painted *cravatte.* Then there was the thin gold watch, not much larger than a Communion wafer, which told not only the hour down to the split of a second but the day of the week as well. Not to be overlooked either was the slender pen of (some said) platinum that the *Signore* employed with a smile and a flourish to sign the presented chits, never failing to write down that generous gratuity. Then—the pearl-handled fly swatter.

This fly swatter was final proof, if ever such proof were needed, that Sr. Saccovino was not only a rich American gentleman but *eccentrico* in the bargain, and this could be the very best kind to have around.

He entered Portofino toward the middle of March on board the yacht Santa Costanza. The *marinai* who operate the taxi craft in the harbor quickly learned that he had chartered the yacht at Bastia in Corse and had sailed here by way of Livorno and La Spezia.

Five boat-taxi and three mule-cart trips were required to transport the *Signore*'s luggage from the yacht, which soon thereafter raised anchor, to the villa that had been unoccupied since the previous spring when the owner, a crusty old, port-drinking *inglés,* had succumbed to *il colpo apopletico* while watching, as was his diurnal wont, the evening sun sink like a big orange into the Ligurian Sea.

Sr. Saccovino made his first exploratory visits to the quayside a few days after settling in. Flies being scarce at this time of the year, he came armed only with his warm engaging smile and his soft but authoritative voice. His *"Buon giorno,"* his *"Buona sera,"* his *"Venga qua, per piacere,"* his *"Mille grazie,"* were all uttered without the trace of a foreign accent. When he ordered *lasagna al pesto* (a regional manifestation of squared pasta covered with a green sauce in which basil is prominent, and sprinkled with grated goat cheese and crushed pine nuts), he obviously knew exactly what to expect.

These pleasant aspects of the man, combined with the dignified swaths of gray in his sleek black hair and the corded wrinkles in his mastiff-like face, earned him immediately a certain homage from the townspeople.

The pearl-handled fly swatter didn't appear until the last days of May. By then the *mosce* were growing bold and bothersome. While strolling from shop to stall and along the quays, the *Signore* carried the fly swatter as inconspicuously as possible. Often as not he concealed the greater part of the beautiful handle up the sleeve of his jacket in the fashion of a professional knife thrower, but whenever he sat at a table he always laid it out in plain view on the cloth to the right of the place setting, ready for instant use, and he could use it with remarkable accuracy.

Each morning the *Signore* broke his fast with the same nourishment—*caffé ristretto.* warm rolls with sweet butter and tart marmalade, a bottle of mineral water, more *caffé ristretto.* Mercia was usually the *cameriera* at his table and she batted her brown eyes outlandishly as she served him. She was a plump young widow with two small children.

In the evening, when he consumed a bottle of white wine with perhaps *pasta con frutti di mare,* he was most respectfully attended by a gaunt middle-aged bachelor named Silvestro, whose voice and mien were as funereal as an undertaker's at the obsequies.

During the noontime repast in the *trattoria*'s aromatic kitchen these two—Mercia and Silvestro—were forever dissecting and analyzing every nuance of Sr. Saccovino's utterances and behavior. The following colloquy, typical in mood, occurred one day in July:

"This morning the *Signore* praised the cool breeze coming in from the harbor."

"Last evening he spoke well of it too."

"Did he dine alone?"

"As if you didn't already know, Mercia."

"What did she look like?"

"Her hair was as black as a raven's wing . . ."

"You have a poet's tongue, Silvestro."

". . . Her eyelids were tinted green. A tiny black star occupied her left cheekbone. Her skin was the color of fresh cream. She possessed a pair of *mammelle* the like of which you see on—"

"Ah, one of that type again."

"What else?"

"What else indeed. He is a man with blood in his veins. His nature is affectionate."

"Last evening he ordered two bottles of *Cinque Terre* and permitted the lady to drink a bottle and a half."

"He is an abstemious man. His name is a gross misnomer. What did he eat?"

"Fish soup with an extra pinch of basil. Squid simmered in oil and garlic. Anchovies and capers in lemon juice. Bearded mussels in mustard. Pasta with clam sauce. Wild strawberries in brandy."

"The food of love."

"I must say he appeared to be wonderfully prepared for the lady by the time she had finished the last of the wine."

"I can well believe it. Did he kill many flies?"

"Only three in my presence. The lady was a powerful distraction."

"And the gratuity, it was generous?"

"More than generous. Eight thousand *lire.*"

"So it goes. This morning he presented the *carabiniere* with two long cigars and bought a dozen lace handkerchiefs from old Camilla."

"The dark hours of night rewarded him."

"Over coffee he inquired after my *bambini* by name."

"He is a most courteous gentleman."

"He asked why I do not marry again."

"How do you reply to such a question?"

"To the *Signore* I said that a good man is not to be found in the market as readily as a good fish."

"Alas, that is the truth."

"And he answered—Do you wish to hear what the *Signore* said to that, Silvestro?"

"I think so."

"He said that many a sweet-fleshed fish is overlooked because it is thought to be not fat enough or young enough."

"That also is true."

" 'Such a fine fish is Silvestro,' he said."

"He actually said that, Mercia?"

"I swear on the cross."

"Ah."

"He spoke in jest, of course."

"Of course."

"Then with his platinum pen he wrote out a gratuity of thirty-five hundred *lire* on a chit of half that sum. A night of love is a wonderful experience, Silvestro."

Toward the latter part of September—*sabato, settembre ventisimo primo,* as it would be remembered locally—the Hairy Tourist arrived in a rented Fiat just as the *carabiniere* was making fast the chain across the Via Roma. The time was 10:04 A.M.

"What's the big idea?" the Hairy Tourist asked as the *carabiniere* snapped shut the padlock. "I want to drive this heap into town." He spoke abominable Italian with an atrocious foreign accent.

"No motor vehicle is allowed in the town, *signor,*" said the *carabiniere,* whose name was Umberto. "Except between the hours of seven and ten o'clock in the morning. And then we allow only those vehicles authorized to make deliveries of essential commodities."

"What the hell kind of a town is this anyway?"

"An old town, *signor.* A peaceful town. A town as yet unblessed by the fumes of *benzina.*"

"Okay, admiral. Where do I park the heap?"—using the word *mucchio.*

"You may park the *mucchio* where the *mucca* grazes," Umberto said, pleased at the way he had worked a cow into the conversation.

It was Sr. Daddario, manager of the Hotel Nazionale, who dubbed this man the Hairy Tourist. The proffered passport identified him as Henry A. Scotti of St. Louis, Missouri, U.S.A., but Sr. Daddario was more impressed by the bushy black eyebrows, the sweeping black mustachios, the dense black beard, and the flowing black hair that fell nearly to his shoulders.

"You are fortunate, *signor,*" Daddario said. "Because of a late cancellation we have a single room available."

"I'll take it," the Hairy Tourist said, setting his luggage, an airlines flight bag, on the counter as he signed in.

"On the other hand, you are not so fortunate. This room is available for three days only."

"That's all right with me, captain. I'll be checking out early tomorrow morning."

"In that case, *signor,* you must pay in advance."

The room, a small one as are all the rooms in the Hotel Nazionale, was situated on the second floor and overlooked the town square. The Hairy Tourist remained in it just long enough to drop the flight bag on the bed and then he was outside wandering around the town and asking questions of everyone about everything.

Where is the Church of San Martino? Who lives in the Castello Brown? Are there dolphins in these waters? Where is the Church of St. George? Is the fishing good outside the harbor? How cold does it get here in the winter? How old are some of these old arches? Do many tourists come here? Where do most of the tourists come from? Are there any Americans in town now? Has Sr. Giampietro Saccovino been living here long? Where does he live? When he dines here in town does he dine alone? How many miles is it to Rome? How much is a kilometer?

Sr. Saccovino strolled down from his villa an hour before sunset, graciously greeting all whom he met on the way, and finally settled down at a table outside the Trattoria Navicello. The chair he sat in, his favorite, afforded him a view of the harbor, with its flotilla of pleasure craft, impeded only by an occasional passerby. He enjoyed the warm glittering look of the water at this time of day.

Silvestro materialized at his side with a mournful *"Buona sera"* and *"Desidera, signor?"*

The *Signore* ordered a bottle of *Cinque Terre* and the antipasto and placed the pearl-handled fly swatter on the table. The flies of September are obnoxious and hardy. In a moment one of the creatures buzzed past his ear and settled on the corner of a folded napkin. The *Signore*'s veined right hand moved stealthily toward the pearl handle, grasped it firmly, lifted it slightly, slapped it down unerringly.

The crumpled fly left a spot of black blood on the white napkin. Using the rubber palm of the swatter, the *Signore* meticulously shoved the small corpse off the table onto the cobbles.

"This I had to see with my own two eyes," twanged an American voice close by. "Old J. P. Sacco killin' flies for his kicks."

The *Signore* raised his eyes from the spot of blood and saw the

Hairy Tourist standing where Silvestro normally stood, with what appeared to be an exultant grin breaking its way through the hirsuteness. The *Signore*'s eyes grew suddenly slitted but his voice, when he spoke, was toned to its usual softness. *"Buona sera, signor. A que ora c'è l'omicidio?"*

"Let's talk United States," the Hairy Tourist said.

"As you wish," said the *Signore*. "Since you probably plan to stay a while, take a seat."

The Hairy Tourist, sitting in a chair that placed his back to the harbor, said, "You got a very quaint scene here, J.P."

"It's restful."

"I guess. A man could rest in peace here. Forever."

"There are worse things. What is your name?"

"What's the diff? We ain't gonna know each other long enough to get acquainted."

"We're already acquainted," the *Signore* said, lifting the swatter and striking down a fly in midair. "You're acquainted with me by sight and reputation. I'm acquainted with you because I've known a dozen of your kind."

"It takes one to know one," the Hairy Tourist said.

"Don't equate me with yourself, young man. I never did a thing in my life for just money alone."

"Oh yeah."

Silvestro arrived with the wine and cast a look of sad inquiry at the newcomer.

"Bene, grazie, Silvestro," the *Signore* said. *"Un altro bicchiere, per favore."* To the Hairy Tourist: "What will you drink?"

"What's good enough for you is good enough for me."

"Would you care for an antipasto?"

"Why not?"

The *Signore* gave instructions to Silvestro, who left for a moment and returned with another glass. He poured a dram for the *Signore*'s taste of approval and then filled the Hairy Tourist's glass to the brim.

"Can this ginzo understand English?" the Hairy Tourist asked after Silvestro's departure.

"No more than ten or twelve simple words," the *Signore* replied, his attention on a fly that had landed a few inches from the tip of his fork.

Taking a swallow of wine, the Hairy Tourist watched the *Signore* slap the insect fatally and flick it from the table. "What's all this business with the fancy fly swatter?" he asked.

"Swatting flies is second nature to me," the *Signore* said. "The first money I ever made was paid to me for swatting flies."

"You're tryin' to put me on, J. P."

"Not at all."

"This is Cutter Moran you're talkin' to."

The *Signore* took a thoughtful sip of the wine. "I knew a Cutie Moran back in the old days."

"None other than my old man."

"You don't say. Like father like son. As I remember, Cutie got too cute for his own good. And suddenly he wasn't around anymore."

"Just like you, J. P. Suddenly you weren't around no more and one hell of a lot of bread went with you."

"I took my retirement fund, Cutter. That's all."

"I ain't interested in the details, man. All I'm gettin' paid for is findin' you and finishin' you."

"How did you find me, by the way?"

"It wasn't easy."

Silvestro served the antipasto and asked whether there would be anything else. The *Signore* thanked Silvestro and promised to signal when further service was required. Silvestro bowed somberly and left.

The Hairy Tourist fingered a slice of red *peperoncino* from the dish in front of him and popped it into the whiskery opening in his face. "One thing's for sure, J.P.," he said, chewing, "you got off the beaten track when you picked this burg. They don't even let cars inside. Wow, these peppers are hot!" He downed a big draft of wine. "Now, if you'd gone to Rome or Naples, we got connections there and could've dug you out in a couple a weeks. In fact that's where I was goin' first, to Rome, but then I decided I better see an uncle a mine in Corsica I hadn't seen in four or five years, a nice old guy retired like you but clean, and that's where the old coincidence come in. I'm in a waterfront joint outside Bastia a couple nights ago and I get talkin' baseball with this cat speaks United States pretty good and it turns out he goes to sea whenever a job turns up, except he ain't been to sea since way last spring when he gets a berth on a yacht chartered by a rich American named Saccovino, this cat says —Jampeetro Saccovino—and I think to myself, I wonder. Plain dumb luck, but here I am, two days later drinkin' wine with old J. P. Sacco himself."

"Do your employers in St. Louis know about this dumb luck?" the *Signore* asked, laying another fly low.

"Not yet. Until I seen you in person I wasn't a hundred percent sure you'd be the same cat who chartered that yacht. Besides, I hate to use the phones in this damn country. I don't trust the damn phones, you know what I mean."

"And quite right too, Cutter."

Beads of perspiration began to form on the bare area of the Hairy Tourist's face, that space between the bushy eyebrows and the low bangs. "That pepper was *hot.*" From the lapel pocket of his jacket he flicked a handkerchief embroidered with a blue *M* and patted his brow. "Do you eat these damn peppers as a regular thing?"

"Yes," the *Signore* said. "I find they sharpen my wits."

"Like swalleyin' a lighted match."

"Well, you've got to be properly dressed to eat these peppers."

"Oh, sure you do."

"That turtleneck sweater you're wearing, for instance, and the tweed jacket. Absolutely no good for anyone who plans to eat a few red peppers."

"Yeah, you gotta be naked to eat them."

The *Signore* chuckled. "It might help at that, yes it might. But I can promise you one thing, Cutter, you'll definitely be more comfortable without that heavy wig and those phony whiskers."

The Hairy Tourist registered confoundment, at least to the degree that it was able to seep through the camouflage, and then tried to cover it up by pouring more wine into his own glass. Finally he said, "A real sharpie, ain't you? They told me that about you—a real sharp cookie. Don't ever rate him low, they said. He's got a sharp eye for a lot a little things nobody else notices. That's why he lives so long. He keeps an eye open for the——"

The *Signore*'s swatter took toll of another fly.

"Flies they failed to mention. Little things like flies. What's this fix you got on flies, man? You act like a cat with a bad habit."

"It's an old habit anyway," the *Signore* said. "I've already told you that."

"Yeah, you made money at it. Tell me more."

"Are you really interested, Cutter?"

"Until the sun goes down, J. P., you're my main interest in life."

"That's very flattering, Cutter. *Silvestro!*"

"Keep it cool, man."

"That's why I'm ordering more wine."

"Whatever you do, you talk United States."

"That wouldn't be cool at all, Cutter. I always converse with Silvestro in Italian."

"Then keep it short. My old lady was Italiano and I capeesh and don't you forget it."

Silvestro materialized and leaned deferentially toward Sr. Saccovino, who ordered another bottle of wine and two plates of lasagna al pesto. The Hairy Tourist followed every word with the big-eyed concentration of a bloodhound.

"My first flies," the *Signore* said as Silvestro withdrew, "I was eight or nine at the time, a small boy, small for my age, my father already dead, my dear mother forced to work long hours in sweatshops . . . Are you sure you want to hear this, Cutter?"

"With violins it would be better, but keep talkin'."

"My mother had a younger brother Isacco—Ike to all who knew him—and somehow he got enough money together to rent a small shop in our neighborhood. Much later I was able to guess where the money came from. Anyway, for sale in Ike's shop were olive oil, cheeses, prosciutto, sardines, salami, tomato paste, figs, mushrooms, peppers hotter than even these in this antipasto, braciole—"

"Skip the Little Italy part, man, and get to the flies. That's the part I'm interested in. How you started out makin' money by killin' flies."

"Of course. Well, my uncle's inventory attracted flies in the warm weather. And although this inventory was merely a front for his real stock-in-trade, he had a fussy prejudice against—"

"You mean he was like hustlin' somethin' else out of the back room there, I guess. Right, man?"

"That's right, Cutter. This was during the time of the Eighteenth Amendment. Ever hear of it?"

"Sure, the no-booze bust."

"Right again. Uncle Ike didn't sell enough Italian food to pay the rent. He moved what was known in those days as hooch. Still, he had a certain number of food customers, old-country people who came in for a pound of provolone or something like that, and he honored them by keeping the front of the store neat and clean. No flies allowed. He let me hang out there after school and on Saturdays for the express purpose of keeping the place free of flies. I used a rolled-up newspaper to kill them and earned a penny a corpse. At the end of a good day I often collected as much as . . ."

While the *Signore* was talking Silvestro served the lasagna and more wine and the sun slipped into the shimmering sea and violet shadows crept rapidly over the pines on the uplands behind the town. Soon the darkness lay everywhere outside the meager light from the old-fashioned streetlamps and the boats moored in the harbor.

The Hairy Tourist washed down the last morsel with the last of the wine. "I feel so good right now," he said, "that I almost might grab the check right off the waiter."

"Don't strain yourself," the *Signore* said. "I have a weekly account here."

"This could be the week it don't get paid." The Hairy Tourist chortled mirthlessly in his beard.

"That depends on how well you do your job."

"I ain't flubbed a job yet, J. P."

"Silvestro!"

The Hairy Tourist, sobering, leaned across the table. "Watch yourself with the waiter, man. One word outta line and I'll put a shiv in your gut so fast you won't have time to say *scusa.*"

"Don't worry, Cutter. I have due respect for any man with a name like yours." The *Signore* took the proffered tray from Silvestro and signed the chit with his renowned pen, adding a fat gratuity.

"Mille grazie, signor," Silvestro said.

"Prego, Silvestro," the *Signore* said benignly.

"Buona notte, signor."

"Arrivederci, Silvestro."

A few minutes later the *Signore* and the Hairy Tourist passed from the town square side by side. The Signore was carrying the fly swatter, pearl handle up, under his right arm, much in the manner of an NCO with a baton on parade. The Hairy Tourist was smoking a cigarette silently, all talked out.

As they proceeded around one of the stone posts that held the chain across the Via Roma, the *Signore* said conversationally, "Did you come by car?"

"Yeah, that's right."

"Where did you park it?"

"You'll see soon enough."

"You plan to give me a ride?"

"Just a short one."

Out in the darkness, away from the lights of the town, a thousand stars became visible around a nearly full moon. In a moment the *Signore*'s searching eyes caught a metallic glint ahead on the side of the road—a steel wheel disc.

"Do you have another cigarette?" he asked.

"Sure do," the Hairy Tourist said.

"I could use one."

"Okay, but no tricks." The Hairy Tourist took a pack of cigarettes from one pocket of his tweed jacket and a switchblade knife from the other. "Just in case," he said, snapping out the business end of the knife.

With his left hand the *Signore* pulled a cigarette from the pack. "Do you have a match?"

"You want me to spit for you too?" Returning the cigarette pack to his pocket, the Hairy Tourist came up with a butane lighter. "Here you are, man," he said, clicking a blue flame into life. "Enjoy it. You got time for maybe five good drags."

The *Signore* was standing ramrod straight, a few inches shorter than his companion. He still held the fly swatter tucked under his arm like a baton. As the Hairy Tourist leaned forward to touch the cigarette in the *Signore*'s mouth with the shimmying flame, the *Signore*'s left hand went swiftly to the pearl handle and gave it a double twist. There was a vibrating sound—*piiing-giing-giing*—and the lighter shook convulsively.

"Aaah gug ach," the Hairy Tourist said, dropping the switchblade and reaching for his throat. In a few seconds he got down on his knees and in another few seconds he prostrated himself at the *Signore*'s feet.

After rolling the body over on its back, the *Signore* squatted beside it and began to remove the wig, the eyebrows, the beard, the moustache. The face thus revealed struck a chord of memory. Cutie Moran all over again, twenty years later, with a few minor variations. Still stupid, still inept. Like father like son.

He raked the nearby ground with his fingers until he located the butane lighter. Then with the lighter's help he explored the throatal region until he found what he was looking for—the tip of a narrow stainless steel shaft protruding a tiny fraction of an inch from the folds of the turtleneck sweater. With a pair of jeweler's pliers taken from the pocket of his silk coat he grasped the tip of the shaft and gently pulled, presently extracting a needle six inches long. He wrapped it carefully in the monogrammed handkerchief which he took from the breast pocket of the dead man's jacket and set it on the ground next to the fly swatter for reloading at a later time. He stripped off the jacket and went through the pockets. Wallet, money, traveler's checks, *two* passports.

The first passport, containing a photograph of the Hairy Tourist, identified him as Henry A. Scotti of St. Louis, Missouri; the second, depicting a living likeness of the hairless corpse, was issued to Charles Moran, also of St. Louis.

"*Addio,* Enrico," the *Signore* muttered. "*Addio,* Carlo."

He spread the tweed jacket on the ground. Onto its lining he dropped the passports and the switchblade. The turtleneck sweater followed. Next went the slacks, in the hip pocket of which he found the car keys. When the corpse was stark naked he dragged it several yards off the road and propped it in a sitting position with its back against a boulder.

He made a bundle of the tweed jacket by tying its arms together. He carried the bundle to the car—a rented Fiat, he noticed—and locked it in the trunk. He climbed into the driver's seat and drove the car in the direction of Paraggi until he reached a place where the road hung recklessly over the Golfo Marconi. He got out of the car, its motor idling, and walked it with some effort to the brink of doom. As it began its irreversible tilt he lit the butane lighter and tossed it into the front seat. Then he began the longish walk—three kilometers, at least—back to the villa, reloading the pearl-handled fly swatter en route.

The next day was *domenica,* God's day, but the Portofinese weren't talking about God. The main subject of conversation was the discovery of the nude body of an unidentified man on the Via Roma outside the town. The man was generally assumed to have been an Italian because of the tattoo on the left forearm—a serpent (evil) climbing a cross (good). Though not yet officially determined, the cause of death was attributed by Umberto the *carabiniere,* who had seen such things, to a fishbone's lodgment sidewise in the man's gullet. Nobody seemed to wonder why a naked stranger would be eating bony fish out there at night.

A minor topic of conversation that same morning concerned the fact that Henry A. Scotti had departed unseen from the Hotel Nazionale without taking along his airlines flight bag which contained, according to the manager, Sr. Daddario, a safety razor, a package of razor blades, an aerosol can of shaving cream and a bottle of lime-scented lotion.

"Why should such a hairy devil carry around articles like these?" Sr. Daddario was fond of asking whenever the subject arose, which was not often.

On this same day Sr. Saccovino killed 27 flies.

This is Gerald Tomlinson's first appearance in this annual collection, but we predict it won't be his last. This story should appeal to librarians everywhere . . .

GERALD TOMLINSON
Miss Ferguson versus JM

Elsie Ferguson, a spinster with gold-rimmed granny glasses, had been a library clerk in Elm City for forty-three years. She knew the Dewey Decimal System down to the fourth digit after the period. She knew the card catalogue from *A, A Novel* to *Zylstra, Henry.*

Despite her expertise neither library books nor catalogue numbers were her true forte. Names and faces were. She had a photographic memory for people.

Whenever a person brought books to the circulation desk at the Elm City Library, Miss Ferguson would close her eyes for a moment, match the face with a name in her files, smile over the top of the gray book-charging machine, and say, "It's nice to see you again, Mr.——, Mrs.——, or Miss——" and fill in the name.

But if the borrowers' names and faces were a challenge to Miss Ferguson, their reading habits bored her to blasphemy. The average reader carried away books that to Miss Ferguson seemed as dull as baseball and as mindless as bowling: mysteries, historical romances, Gothic novels, celebrity biographies, science fiction.

There was one exception. Miss Ferguson loved books on coin collecting. She had spent most of her life and most of her small income in building a collection of United States coins. It was a tiny collection compared with the great ones—the Smithsonian's or the American Numismatic Society's—but it was strong on early American Large Cents.

Miss Ferguson did not belong to the Tionega Valley Coin Club, and she avoided coin shows. She seldom exhibited her collection, but instead kept much of it stored in a vault of the First Tionega Canal Bank.

The quality of her collection was well known, however, and she had recently lent three of her rarest Large Cents, two 1793s and an 1804, to the Calvert Coin Museum in Baltimore.

Miss Ferguson was both a collector and a student of numismatics. On early American Large Cents she was one of the three or four living experts. She had written articles on the subject for *The Numismatist,* one of which had been published as a book and stood, to her satisfaction, in section 737.4 of the Elm City Library.

Once every couple of years she and her hobby were the subject of a feature column and a photograph or two in the local newspaper.

Coins fascinated her. So did books on coins. But she did not mix business with pleasure. At the library she watched people come and go, fed cards into the book-charging machine, and thought little about either coins or books.

Yet this people-watching was less a sociable exercise than an intellectual one, as Miss Ferguson knew. She said hello to more people in a day than most people did in a month, but still she was a loner, a dedicated loner. She had no close friends, no social life, and had never tried to have any. She cherished privacy. She had been followed by neither suitors nor trouble, and not for one moment in her sixty-five years had she thought seriously about marriage.

The names-and-faces ritual was simply a game she had made up to lighten the long leaden hours at the library. It was a form of escape. She did not consider it an especially praiseworthy pastime. She always tried to be honest with herself about her motives, not to lie to herself the way some people did.

The memory game had begun, she remembered, forty years before when she learned that the then Postmaster General, James Farley, could pair off 50,000 names with 50,000 faces. She was impressed. She knew almost no borrowers by name in those early days. Now, four decades later, she figured her repertoire at 10,000 names and faces.

Although no one interested her very much personally, some people interested her more than others. There was one great hulk of a man in particular: Mr. Joseph Moldavi, a tall, swarthy gentleman, black-bearded like Ivan the Terrible, a man whose choice of books caused Miss Ferguson to look twice at the borrower, and to wonder.

He was a strikingly handsome man, this Mr. Moldavi, a point that Miss Ferguson noted at first with more disdain than delight. Looks, like books, were suspect. Anyway, the small black mole on his left cheek marred his appearance; it looked to her like an ugly embedded insect. But it did give her a mnemonic hook on which to hang the name Moldavi: mole–Moldavi.

After a while, given her gift for observation, she could not help noticing how his reading habits matched—and matched alarmingly —what had been happening in Elm City.

Side by side with the usual street construction, schoolbudget defeats, and political corruption, Elm City was having a series of big-money burglaries. In the past two years there had been five spectacular thefts—an Elm City crime wave that coincided exactly, Miss Ferguson noted, with Mr. Moldavi's career as a borrower at the library.

First there had been three jewelry store burglaries, clever night-time heists with no clues and no suspects. The jewels were on the premises one day and gone the next. These events had followed hard on the heels of Mr. Moldavi's three-month concentration on books about gems and minerals.

Next there had been two art thefts. The Blauberg Art Gallery had lost two Ben Shahns in one night, the only two valuable paintings in the Blauberg collection. Less than six months later Langdon College found itself missing a Schneider Esch portrait of Mark Twain valued at $20,000. These two thefts had coincided with Mr. Moldavi's persistent enchantment with books on art.

Each of these five thefts had required expert knowledge, according to the Elm City Chief of Police, Thomas McEachern, a morose man with a gray crewcut and five nagging reasons to be morose. Only the best items in each place had been taken. And all the thefts had been executed, he said, by the same thoroughgoing professionals, men or women who knew jewels, art, locks, alarm systems, and enough else to stay out of suspicion and prison.

Miss Ferguson did not see herself as a detective. But there it was: Mr. Moldavi, the self-taught expert, the suave, bookish thief. Black beard, black mole, black money. He had stopped borrowing books on art after the Esch robbery, and for the past two months he had been charging out armloads of books about wine.

This new interest puzzled Miss Ferguson. Jewels were understandable. So were paintings. But wine?

No one enjoyed a glass of white table wine more than Miss Ferguson. But her Sunday evening sauternes or riesling's cost only $2 or $3 a bottle, not much more than the bottled spring water she drank on weekdays. She had never supposed that sauternes could be in a class with sapphires and Shahns.

Miss Ferguson, her suspicions aroused, decided to test her theory, to research the wine market on her lunch hour. The best place to investigate, she knew, was Parrish's Wine Cellar, a downtown landmark for three generations, a small shop on Charles Street with wide plank flooring and the smell of cheese. Even a teetotaler with a taste for TV dinners knew that Parrish's was the finest store in Elm City for wine, liquor, and cheese.

She drove to Parrish's in her rusted-out, mauve Dodge, arriving a little after noon. She dropped a nickle in the meter out front, paused under the zebra-striped awning, and considered her strategy.

Inside the store Miss Ferguson addressed herself to a ruddy face behind a white goatee. "It's nice to see you again, Mr. Parrish," she said. She recognized him because he occasionally took out books on woodworking or some equally dreary subject. "I'd like to see your most expensive bottle of wine."

Alex Parrish smiled across the counter at her—a bit patronizingly, she thought. Probably he recognized her as a novice at wines. But he nodded and said. "Certainly. You realize, of course, that in order to see that particular bottle, we will have to go down into the cellar."

She looked at him steadily over her bifocals, not quite sure what he meant.

"Well," he explained, "I really can't afford to disturb a fine old Bordeaux unless you wish to purchase it." She looked innocent, questioning. "You usually buy a domestic riesling, don't you, Miss——?"

"Ferguson." She felt herself blushing. "Yes, I do." She was surprised that he remembered her. "But if it's not asking too much, Mr. Parrish, I would like to see your most expensive bottle today. A gift——"

"Of course, Miss Ferguson. Please step this way."

She was astonished at the extent of the Parrish wine cellar. A dozen ceiling-high racks stretched the length of a long room, and the racks were filled with thousands upon thousands of bottles.

Mr. Parrish led Miss Ferguson to the far side of the cellar where, under a hanging fluorescent fixture, he pointed toward a bottle with a slight covering of dust. "There it is." Then, observing her disappointed expression, he shrugged his narrow shoulders and slowly, carefully drew out the bottle, using both hands, and tilted it ever so slightly to show her the label.

She could not read French and did not know the cryptography of wine labels, but she could see *Chateau Lafite-Rothschild* and *1945.*

He smiled at her. "Eight hundred dollars," he said simply, but in a reverent tone of voice.

Miss Ferguson gulped. She cleared her throat. "That's a bit more than I expected. Do you have any bottles for—well, maybe fifty dollars?"

The proprietor of the Wine Cellar chuckled as if he might have anticipated this sudden shattering of the dream. "Certainly, Miss Ferguson. Dozens, perhaps hundreds. In fact, many of them are Lafites such as this one. But not"—he paused and raised his eyes—"not the legendary '45."

"My goodness."

"Would you care to see a less expensive year from that Chateau? Or perhaps a Latour or a Margaux?"

"Thank you, Mr. Parrish, I do appreciate your courtesy. But perhaps I'd better think about it some more. May I come back another day?"

"By all means."

He returned the bottle to its resting place, and Miss Ferguson, in a state of mild shock, drove back to the Elm City Library.

That afternoon Mr. Moldavi returned five books on wine, pushing them firmly across the polished oak counter. Yes, indeed, he was a fine figure of a man. He strode down the dark tunnel into the stacks with that disturbing *macho* manner of his, a stride that both enchanted and annoyed her. He returned a few minutes later with four new books about wine.

Miss Ferguson met him at the book-charging machine, closed her eyes for an instant so as not to change her mnemonic routine— heavens, she knew *him* all right—then smiled nervously and said, "It's nice to see you again, Mr. Moldavi." She had been rehearsing a question to ask him about Chateau Lafite. Did she dare? "May I ask——?"

"Yes?" Mr. Moldavi smiled, displaying a costly set of capped teeth. "What can I do for you?" His voice was warm and ingratiating, an actor's or a prophet's voice. He made it sound as if he had been eagerly waiting for the moment he might be allowed to talk to her.

Miss Ferguson's heart jumped. This was a bit too heady. "Nothing." She bit her lip, steadied her shaking hand, and hurriedly punched the date cards. Mr. Moldavi watched her through cobalt-blue eyes.

As soon as he had left, she chided herself for her silly show of emotion. After a few minutes she crossed to a file of membership applications and took out Joseph Moldavi's card. According to the information on it he lived at 23 Strathmore Drive, West Elm City. His telephone number was 382–5968. His employer was Consolidated Prefabricated Homes, where he was a supervisor.

His reference—a line on the card required of all applicants but seldom checked—was Harvey Galton of 19 River Knolls, Northwood. Telephone 602–1948.

Miss Ferguson hastened to the telephone and dialed 602–1948. Mr. Galton. Her breath came in short puffs as she waited. Investigative work was stimulating, but it was not really in her line. A woman's voice answered. "Yeah?"

"Hello. Mrs. Galton?"

"Right on, dearie." The voice was fuzzy. "Except now I'm remarried. The name is Bowman."

"Oh, I see." Miss Ferguson frowned. "I'm calling from the Elm City Library, Mrs. Bowman. My name is Elsie Ferguson. We have received an application for a library card from a Mr. Joseph Moldavi. I would like to verify your husband's—that is, your ex-husband's—acquaintance with him."

"Hold on. Moldy-who? What are you talking about, hon?"

"Joseph Moldavi. Did your husband know him?"

There was a muffled curse on the other end of the line, aimed at either a pet or a child underfoot, followed by a noisy swallow. "Harvey Galton knew zip. Now he knows angleworms. He's dead."

"Oh, I'm sorry."

"I'm not. He was a loser from the word go. You know any losers?"

Miss Ferguson stared into the black holes of the mouthpiece. "I beg your pardon?"

"Don't beg, dearie. Never beg." A long pause; then Mrs. Bowman said, "Marvelous Harv, as I used to call him, was killed in a bank holdup in Albany two years ago."

"Oh, how terrible."

"Yeah, terrible. You said it, terrible. He had a satchel full of cash that never got past the State Street curb."

Miss Ferguson gasped. "He was holding up the bank?"

A high laugh rattled across the wire. "You're too much, hon! Where're you from anyway, the Little Sisters of Mercy, Seven Miles Outside the City of Jerusalem?"

"No. I mean—" Miss Ferguson stopped to think, trying to put her meager facts in order. Then she gambled for the second or possibly the third time in her life. "Mrs. Bowman, could you tell me if one of the other men in the bank holdup was a Mr. Moldavi? Joseph Moldavi?"

"Who's this guy Moldy you keep bringing up? I never heard of him. Wait a minute." Miss Ferguson heard the clink of ice against glass in the background. A moment later Mrs. Bowman's voice returned. "There was no Moldy in the gang, dearie. How about Larry Kincaid? Would he do? He got shot along with Harv. Died a couple of days later at Albany Hospital."

"I'm afraid not. Moldavi is the name."

"Well, call 'em like you see 'em, hon. I'll tell you what I know. There was one other guy on the bank job. Brad Eaton, who's now in Dannemora. Oh, yeah, there was also the lamebrain who planned it. Joe Masseno, the so-called genius of the operation. You get that? Joe the Genius." She snorted. "Some genius. But he backed out before they went to Albany—said the plan still needed work. It sure did. Huh, I guess maybe Masseno *did* have more brains than the rest of them."

"Joe Masseno? He was the one who planned it?"

"You deaf?"

"I'm sorry. And you say he backed out before they went to Albany?"

"Deaf as a fence post."

"Mrs. Bowman, could you tell me what Joe Masseno looked like?"

"Never saw him, hon. Never saw anybody except Harv. Only saw *him* about twice a month. Just heard him talk about the rest of the meatheads. Joe the Genius. *He* knew the score, Harv used to say. Yeah, he knew the score all right. The score was cops three, crooks nothing." She hiccupped.

"Thank you very much, Mrs. Bowman."

"Don't mention it, hon. A day's work for a day's pay, I always say. What do you always say?"

Miss Ferguson said nothing.

"Well, cheers then!"

"Yes."

"Roger and out!"

With a scowl Miss Ferguson lowered the receiver to its cradle. She immediately dialed 382–5968, the Moldavi number. She knew pretty much what to expect. When the answering voice droned, "The number you have dialed is not in service—" she smiled and hung up.

Joe Masseno. Initials: JM. She leafed idly through the M's in the Elm City phone book, not expecting a miracle. People with aliases were slippery and hard to find, she supposed, this being her first experience with aliases. There was no Joe Masseno listed in the directory.

But there was a Joseph Malloy, and suddenly Miss Ferguson's mnemonic system clicked into gear. JM. Somehow, for some reason, the name Joseph Malloy meant something. For the first time in forty years her names-and-faces repertoire came up against a genuine, practical problem. She leaned back in her chair, excited by the sudden associations, and thought hard, concentrated, racked her memory, conjuring up mental images, grasping at mnemonic hooks.

Mallow, marshmallow, white skin, toasted marshmallow, brown, brown, not a name, brown marks, scars, the double *l*s, parallel scars on one cheek. Malloy, Malloy, that was it. Joseph Malloy. She knew him. She squinted to clear up the haze of time. Thirty, thirty-five years ago, he had borrowed books at least a dozen times. The young

Joseph Malloy, a high school kid, basketball injury to his face, bad teeth, tall—that was him.

Joseph Malloy was Joseph Moldavi as a young man. Thirty or more years ago. No question about it. Why hadn't she seen it before? And Joseph Malloy—she supposed that must be his real name—now lived at 278 Foster Avenue, Elm City. She whistled.

She ignored the phone number. The name and address were enough. They were like Large Cents from heaven, precious and hers alone. She had to see Joseph Malloy in person.

That evening after work Miss Ferguson began a new day-by-day routine. From the Elm City Library she swung her rusted-out Dodge north on Wycherly Boulevard for two miles, then east on Foster Avenue, a modest residential street. She drove slowly past 278, a white Cape Cod with dark blue shutters, a tidy and cheerful house. She peered and blinked, like a sparrow hawk hunting an insect.

For about a month she saw nothing. Just a quiet house and sometimes a nondescript car. Then, unexpectedly, on a dark muggy Thursday, with her Dodge clattering and the heat indicator touching red, she saw him—Joseph Malloy, Joseph Moldavi, one and the same—and Joseph Masseno, too, she assumed—mowing the lawn, sweating in a T-shirt, muscles bulging, tall body leaning into the curved handle of his power mower, glaring at her Dodge, unaware of the fate closing in on him like gray storm clouds over the Tionega River.

Miss Ferguson now knew all she needed to know. But what was she to do with it? Inform the police?

She considered the possibility. Mr. Moldavi-Malloy-Masseno would be arrested and convicted, she was sure of it. He would be sentenced to a long prison term.

And if Miss Ferguson gave the police an anonymous telephone tip, got him arrested that way, which seemed the safest course, there would be no chance of the trapped man blaming his arrest on her and perhaps later taking revenge.

But there were two problems. One: Miss Ferguson did not believe in prisons. She hated the idea of locking up human beings like cattle. She thought prisons were pestholes, breeding grounds for more crime, teeming swamps of brutality and nameless perversions.

The second problem was more personal. She had come to admire Joseph Moldavi and had finally come to realize it. Exactly why, she didn't know, but she admired him a great deal. He was a suave gentleman, handsome, yes, handsome despite the mole, a wide reader, a man of action, a scholar of sorts, surely not a common thug.

The police—oh, dear, she knew the police by reputation. They would not treat their captive like a gentleman and a scholar. They would treat him like a criminal, like a found victim. Chief of Police McEachern obviously hated Mr. Moldavi already, without even knowing him, to judge by the Chief's comments to reporters.

No, Mr. Moldavi could not expect justice in Elm City. He would be demeaned, manhandled, confined, his talents scorned, and then he would be shunted off to prison, perhaps for the rest of his life. Miss Ferguson could meet him again, if at all, only behind bars, or at the morgue, or at the funeral.

No. It must not happen that way.

The next night, in the solitude of her small apartment, with the air conditioner whirring and the bright faces of a Norman Rockwell print beaming down on her, she sat at her Underwood portable and typed out a message on plain, untraceable 3x5 notepaper.

> Dear Mr. Malloy,
>   Do not try to rob Parrish's Wine Cellar. The police have been informed of your plans. Mr. Parrish has been given your description and is armed. You are in grave danger in Elm City. You must move away. Please, for your own safety, leave town.
>   An Admirer

She typed his name and address on the blank white envelope, pasted a stamp on it upside down, and made a special trip to the post office to mail it.

Three nights later, when she had worked up the nerve to drive past his house, she found it vacant, tidy but cheerless, a For Rent sign on the lawn.

Mr. Malloy-Moldavi-Masseno had left town, or gone underground. Parrish's Wine Cellar would not be burglarized. Miss Ferguson had succeeded where the Elm City police had failed.

She felt no sense of triumph. A tear trickled down her cheek. If she had been a more emotional woman, she would have drowned her sorrow in a pool of tears, then or later, for that was how she felt about her recent acts and their consequences.

An end to snooping, she vowed. For weeks afterward she concentrated on her coin collection, thankful more than ever for it. At the bank and in her apartment she studied the many faces of the ageless and aloof Miss Liberty, the unsleeping beauty of numismatics, whose copper profile glowed in low relief and whose eyes stared unblinking, unseeing, toward the edge of her tiny universe. Almost as penance she lent another of her precious possessions, a mint 1799 Large Cent, to the Calvert Coin Museum in Baltimore.

Mr. Moldavi was gone. Out of Elm City and out of her life. Forever, she supposed.

For three years.

It was late August when he reappeared, and at first Miss Ferguson did not recognize him. The mole was gone. The beard was gone. He had lost weight. His hair was longer and lighter in color. He wore a pencil-thin moustache, as if trying to impersonate the devil or Vincent Price.

He was carrying a black overnight bag.

As he entered the library, he glanced sharply around, alert but calm. He fixed his attention on the circulation desk and walked toward Miss Ferguson.

At the desk he leaned down, placed his black bag on the floor, and unzipped it with a flourish. He removed a green corked bottle, which he set on the oak counter in front of her.

Her heart jumped to her throat, and she stammered, "Hello. It's nice to see you again, Mr.——"

"Mohrmann," he said, flashing his ivory grin. "It's nice to see *you* again, Miss Ferguson. I brought you a little present—a bottle of wine from an excellent shop on Charles Street. Chateau Margaux '47. I hope you enjoy it."

"But——"

He leaned an elbow on the desk. Miss Ferguson backed away, a chill icing her spine. He continued to smile. "How did I learn your identity? Is that what you're wondering?" He ran a forefinger along his mustache. "It's elementary, my dear. I have a memory for cars —for makes and models and colors and years and dents and licenses. The same kind of memory you must have for names and faces. It's useful in my line of work."

Miss Ferguson had an intense urge to run away, to get to a phone, to call the police. Mr. Moldavi was no longer an object of her concern, he was an instant enemy. She wanted to move but couldn't. Her heart pierced by betrayal, she stood motionless.

"Now, you, Miss Ferguson, you drive an eleven-year-old Dodge Charger, unless you've gotten rid of it. It's reddish violet, rusted out, with a broken left taillight—which is probably fixed by now— and license number 398–KLV." He spread his arms wide, palms up, as if to make light of his talent. Joe the Genius.

She spoke haltingly, her thin voice trilling like a schoolgirl's in spite of her efforts to control it. "But why me, Mr—? Why are you bothering with me?"

He pretended patience. "My dear lady, when a car goes creeping past my house night after night for two or three weeks, I pay attention to it. I find out who's driving it, and why. Your license number told me who—I have sources for that kind of information—and your charming note told me why."

She felt frightened and ridiculous at the same time. She summoned up her courage. She wanted him gone. "You were foolish to come back, Mr.—The police——"

Mr. Malloy-Moldavi-Masseno-Mohrmann smiled at her with no trace of humor. "I'm just passing through. I can work in whatever city I choose. I'm here for a goodbye look at my secret admirer, nothing more. The museum yesterday was my fourth and last target in Baltimore. I'm moving west."

Miss Ferguson said nothing. She felt a sinking sensation deep within her, touching her soul.

"Yes, I've come from there this morning," he said in an even voice, following her thoughts. His cobalt-blue eyes, the handsome eyes of doom, stared straight into hers. There was no liking in them, only mockery. "Since I won't be going back, Miss Ferguson, could you please mail these books to the Enoch Pratt Free Library in Baltimore for me? I wouldn't want them to be overdue."

He reached into his overnight bag again, and handed her, one by one, five books on coin collecting.

James Holding's tale of political kidnapping in South America is as timely as today's headlines—with an extra plot twist that would do justice to Borges.

JAMES HOLDING
The Fund-Raisers

The security guard at the door of the Ministry of Justice bid him a pleasant good night as he emerged from the gloomy corridors of government into the glories of a South American sunset. A wash of golden flame behind flamingo clouds stained the western sky.

Outside the Ministry gates he stood for a moment, his head thrown back, feeling the drift of evening breeze against his cheek, enjoying the gentle riot of sunset colors, seeing the illuminated cross on the mountaintop begin to glow. Then he lit the thin cigar that was his invariable companion on his daily walk from his office to his home.

Ramón Ribera, praised by colleagues and adversaries alike for his brilliant management of the legal and judicial red tape that plagues all governments, was an important official and, as such, was eligible for a car and a driver to transport him about the city. Yet he preferred to walk the distance to his home each evening, insisting smilingly that he believed in the efficacy of exercise for the deskbound, and that stretching one's legs after a hard day's work was not only salutary but essential.

On this particular evening he glanced at his wristwatch, turned his back on the sunset that painted the sky, and set off briskly for his home near the university.

He was a man below medium height yet of powerful physique. This meager stature, combined with his dark complexion, black eyes and great strength, made him look more Indian than Spanish. Indeed, he often jokingly confided to his friends that he could trace his ancestry on his mother's side back to a princess at the royal court of Atahualpa, last and greatest of the Inca rulers.

Now, striding through the darkening streets of the city, he acknowledged in kind the smiles and frequent verbal greetings of those passersby who recognized him as a celebrity of sorts. He felt pleasantly stimulated by their recognition and by the popularity it implied. So he proceeded almost gaily, savoring the rare quality of the evening as it hesitated halfway between daylight and darkness. The streetlights came on, although not yet needed. Ribera looked again at his wristwatch.

He was approaching the central plaza, walking at the outer edge of the sidewalk, when it happened.

There was no warning, no unusual sight or sound to alert him. He was unaware of the small mud-spattered car that paralleled his course in the street just behind him, matching its pace to his. The twilight crowds went energetically about their business; a policeman at the intersection fifty yards away directed traffic with motions of his white-gloved hands.

In the middle of a step, Ribera saw this familiar street scene suddenly freeze into shocked immobility, saw it become as thoroughly paralyzed—although only for a moment—as though the crowd had unexpectedly glimpsed a Gorgon's head and been instantly turned to stone.

It was no Gorgon's head, however, that suspended movement in that busy street. It was a sudden snarling burst of automatic machine-gun fire. The shots ripped the peaceful evening air to shreds, reverberated in whipping shrill echoes between the buildings lining the avenue.

It was in the single moment of shock and surprise that followed these shots—at whom had they been fired? from where? by whom? —when all was confusion, bewilderment, fear, that the thing was done; smoothly, without a wasted motion, without a word.

The car which had been paralleling Ribera's course drew in to the curb, pulled up with a squeal of brakes abreast of him. The rear door nearest Ribera popped open. Out sprang two men in stocking masks, grotesque and menacing figures from a mechanical jack-in-the-box.

They bracketed Ribera between them, seized his arms in a painful, unbreakable grip, and in what seemed less than a heartbeat of time, flung him into the rear seat of the muddy car, followed him in, scrambling, diving, any which way, and somehow, in the resultant flurry of arms, legs and thrashing bodies, somebody had managed to pull shut the car door with a crash.

The crash of the closing car door was lost in the sound of yet another burst of gunfire, this one more prolonged and minatory than the first. It erupted from the front window of the car, just as the vehicle spurted forward under high acceleration. With a screech of rubber on cobblestones, it sped past the thunderstruck traffic policeman whose upraised hand all unconsciously cleared its way of traffic. By the time the officer realized what was happening, the kidnappers of Ramón Ribera, Minister of Justice, were eight blocks away and already transferring their prisoner from the muddy car to another, thoughtfully stationed beforehand on their escape route to implement their escape and to confuse the pursuit.

Ramón Ribera was not aware of the transfer. He had been rendered unconscious several minutes earlier by the professionally administered blow of a blackjack just before his captors removed their masks.

When he returned to full awareness, he opened his eyes on inky darkness, pervasive, impenetrable. He knew a moment of panic, thinking confusedly that the sharp pain in his head, surging back and forth like a clock pendulum marking the anguished seconds, might have blinded him. Yet it was far more likely, wasn't it, that the unexpected blow to his head, recalled now fuzzily, had done something to his optic nerves?

No, not that, either, for he wasn't blind. As his eyes became accustomed to the gloom, he could make out a faint square, high up, of lesser blackness than the surrounding dark. A window? Yes. Because now, framed by the window, he could see stars blinking in a distant sky. From somewhere nearby came the smell and night sounds of penned llamas. His exploring hands told him he was lying on a woolly skin on a packed mud floor.

Gradually, the exquisite pain in his head moderated. He sat up, swallowed with dry throat to hold back nausea, and rose slowly to his feet. Swaying unsteadily, he remembered his cigar lighter, got it out of his pocket and snapped it into flame.

Holding it above his head, he saw four walls of sun-dried adobe bricks, a patchwork door of packing-case lumber hung on leather hinges, and the single small window he had already noticed. No chairs, no table, no shelves; the squalid room was without furnishings of any kind save for an earthenware jar of water at his feet beside the llama-skin rug on which he had been lying, and in a corner, a rusty five-gallon petrol can with its top removed. This gasoline can, he thought grimly, was perhaps a special luxury provided for him as a government official used to indoor toilet facilities. His prison, he concluded, was an isolated herdsman's hut, somewhere within a few hours' travel of the city; in the mountains, perhaps, or more likely, along the desert border where it sometimes rained only once in twenty years.

Ribera tilted the water jar to his parched lips, feeling an almost
intolerable sense of outrage at his captors. Bitterly he resented that
unnecessary blow which had knocked him senseless last night. Had
he offered the slightest resistance during the kidnapping? Had he
so much as opened his mouth to scream for help? Had he made a
single motion toward escape? No. So why did they think it necessary
to knock him senseless? His brain, of course, supplied the answer
but in his anger he refused to accept it.

After drinking a few mouthfuls of the brackish water in the jar he
found the strength to stagger to the packing-case door. He pushed
against it. It was immovable, as he had expected. He shook it and
called, "Hello! Hello! Is anybody there?" The words came out as
a hoarse croak.

Unexpectedly he was answered, although in no distinguishable
words. From just outside the door came a strange gobbling sound,
reminiscent of an animal in pain, but it was a human voice, he
decided—wordless and formless, but still human. So, a man without
a palate? Without a tongue? A mute, perhaps? In any case, Ribera's
repeated calls brought no further response. He heard sounds of
movement in the llama pen, nothing else.

Ribera shrugged, searched his pockets for the small bottle of
tranquilizers he always carried, and finding it, washed down two of
the tablets with another gulp of water from the earthenware jar.
Then he lay down on his llama skin and composed himself to wait
until morning.

Unable to sleep, his thoughts turned immediately to the man
almost certainly responsible for his present predicament, a revolutionary whose proper name he did not even know. Their only meeting was still quite clear in his memory.

After a tiring acrimonious day at the Ministry, he had been drinking a preprandial pisco sour alone in his library while the cook
prepared dinner and his wife talked interminably on the telephone
in their bedroom abovestairs.

All at once a sound at the library window drew his eyes that way,
and he was astonished to see the figure of a man standing quietly
outside the window in the thickening dark and indicating by sign
language that he would like to come into Ribera's study.

Ribera hesitated, trying to make out the stranger's face, which was
in shadow. Then he rose from his chair, moved to the window and
opened it a few inches. "Who are you?" he asked querulously out
of his long day's ill humor. "And what are you doing in my garden?"

The man laid a finger across his lips, cautioning silence. In a
whisper he answered, "I am El Pico. May I come in?"

"Decidedly not," Ribera said, and made to slam the window shut when he noticed that the stranger had a gun in his hand. The muzzle was tilted, almost casually, upward toward Ribera's face.

"I intend you no harm," the man whispered. "Let me in. It is a matter of business."

Ribera was not a timid man. "I transact business at my office," he said coolly. "See me there tomorrow if your business is urgent."

The revolver made an infinitesimal movement, somehow more menacing than a spoken threat. Ribera shrugged, opened the window wide, and stepped back.

El Pico slid noiselessly inside. He closed the window behind him. Without being bidden, he sat down in a chair beside the inlaid table on which Ribera's half-finished drink rested. His revolver disappeared with a flickering gesture. He smiled broadly at the Minister. "There," he said, reaching out a hand to Ribera's drink, "that's better." He sipped, watching with amusement Ribera's flush of annoyance.

"Who are you?" Ribera demanded through his teeth.

"I told you. El Pico." He was dirty, raggedly dressed and smelled bad. He waited arrogantly.

"I want your real name."

"El Pico is how I am known. Can we talk here without being overheard?"

Ribera nodded.

"No hidden microphones?" An evil grin.

"This is my home. There is no surveillance here."

"Teodoro sent me," El Pico said.

"Teodoro?"

"Yes, You know him, don't you? He's a fund-raiser, like me. And like you, too, Señor Ribera." His voice underlined the "señor" with malice.

Ribera regarded his visitor with cold eyes and said, "You have the advantage of me. I know of no one named Teodoro. Nor have I ever heard of—what did you call them?—the fund-raisers."

El Pico insisted, "Teodoro. Perhaps you know him better as La Garra. But you know him. And you know the fund-raisers too, being one of us, in a way. So we begin again. Teodoro sent me."

"Teodoro or La Garra . . . I never heard of him." Ribera gave a short explosive laugh and went on sarcastically: "La Garra, the claw! El Pico, the beak! Are these fund-raisers of yours a society of bird-watchers?"

The moment he asked this derisive question, Ribera regretted it. For an indescribably savage expression flitted across El Pico's face in a warning more persuasive than his revolver, which suddenly reappeared in his hand. El Pico said flatly, "I have a message from Teodoro for you. Here. Take it. Read it." He passed a tightly-rolled slip of paper across the table to Ribera. The Minister, still standing, reluctantly unrolled it. His visitor meanwhile drained the last of the pisco sour and smacked his lips in rude appreciation.

An almost indecipherable scrawl:

> *Minister Ribera: this is a good friend. He wants legal advice on a business transaction. You may want to help him.*
>
> *Teodoro*

Ribera handed the note back to El Pico. "All right. So you know a man named Teodoro and he recommends you to me. That doesn't mean *I* know *him.*"

"Will you stop beating about the bush? To hear you talk, a man would think your association with Teodoro was dishonest . . . or even treasonous." He assumed an expression of finicky distaste.

Ribera said, "Leave. Or must I call the servants to throw you out?"

El Pico gave him a sour look. "That would be most unwise. I ask you again, you don't know Teodoro?"

"Never heard of him."

"You know nothing of a group known as the fund-raisers, headed by this same Teodoro?"

"Nothing whatever."

"And the names La Garra and El Pico mean nothing to you?"

"Parts of a bird, that's all."

"Parts of what bird?"

"Any bird," said Ribera. "You bore me. You are a babbling fool." He reached for a bellpull on the wall.

El Pico slapped himself on the forehead. "I *am* a fool!" he exclaimed in a mock-chastened voice. "I have forgotten the most important thing of all!" He paused, then went on, "Look here, Señor Minister, does this refresh your memory?"

He placed the green tail feather of a parrot beside the empty glass on the inlaid table.

Ribera looked at it for a long moment, then dropped his hand from the bellpull and came to sit in a chair across from El Pico. He was smiling broadly. "A charade?" he said. "You withheld the feather purposely to test me?"

"Of course. I am here on very serious business. I needed to be absolutely sure of your discretion. Though the Society of the Parrot grows stronger every day, we still must move with reasonable caution." He slanted a sly look at Ribera. "Especially those who are not actually *of* the Society, but merely profit from its fund-raising activities."

Ribera nodded, his eyes hooded.

El Pico went on earnestly, "Because you have helped us, Señor Minister, you shall not be forgotten when we come to power. Now . . . we need your help again."

"To raise more funds?" Ribera folded his hands on the tabletop, a businessman discussing terms.

"What else? The time of revolutionary action approaches. And the Society is still short of certain necessities that only money can buy. Weapons, of course. Transport we can depend on. Communications equipment. Many things." He brightened. "But we are almost ready. This will be our final fund-raising. And the biggest yet."

Ribera said with impressive deliberation, "I am a public official, an important one. You realize that to finance undertakings of a revolutionary party sworn to overthrow the government I serve, is a very dangerous thing."

"Understood." El Pico was impatient. "Yet the danger to you has been outweighed always, has it not, by your ten percent share of the funds we raise?"

Ribera nodded, his eyes far away, imagining the fat current balance in his bankbook, swollen into comfortable plumpness by his bankrolling activities for the Society of the Parrot. "Yes, that is true," he said slowly. He mentally reviewed the kidnappings of wealthy citizens, the bank robberies, the bombings of government property, the foreign exchange coups he had secretly financed for the Society over the years. And now, why not? One final bold venture to cap it all?

"You said, 'the biggest yet,' did you not, El Pico?" he inquired carefully.

"Correct." The revolutionary grinned wolfishly. "And because it is such a big operation, we will need generous financing from you to plan it, to prepare the means, to take care of necessary bribes."

"How much?" Ribera asked.

"Fifty thousand."

Ribera's face betrayed nothing. "And how much do you hope to raise?"

"We'll ask for at least ten million sols," El Pico replied quietly.

"Ten million!" Ribera was startled. "You'll never get it!"

"We'll get it. I, El Pico, the Beak of the Parrot, tell you so!" He thumped his chest with one thumb and his eyes narrowed. "Have you got fifty thousand?"

Ribera said, "I can get it—if I like the sound of your fund-raising project. What is it?"

El Pico leaned back in his chair and crossed his legs. "Another kidnapping."

Ribera was incredulous. "Who in this country is rich enough to pay a ransom of ten million sols?"

"The government," El Pico said viciously. "With all respect, Minister, your stinking capitalist government. We plan to kidnap a government official this time."

Suspecting the truth, Ribera asked, "Who?"

"You," El Pico said. He laughed.

On his smelly llama skin, Ribera smiled into the darkness of the herdsman's hut. His must be a dramatic kidnapping, El Pico had insisted. Done with enough panache to maximize its impact—to convince citizens and government alike that the Society of the Parrot meant business. They would snatch the Minister from the very midst of a crowd on a public street, El Pico said, under the very eyes of the stupid police. Then who, after such a coup, could possibly doubt the power, the cleverness, the determination of the revolutionary leaders?

Who, indeed, Ribera had agreed. He knew quite well that he would be ransomed, just as he knew that El Pico's followers were naive in the extreme if they expected their draggle-tail revolution ever to succeed in overthrowing the present government; his government.

So here he was, a willing kidnap victim with a ten percent interest in his own ransom. That uncalled-for blow on the head still rankled, but when you looked at it sensibly, it was a small price to pay, admittedly, for one million sols; and at no great risk either to himself or his government. I suppose, thought Ramón Ribera on the edge of sleep, El Pico will arrive with news in the morning.

He was mistaken.

It was not until four days later that El Pico made an appearance at the herdsman's hut to bring him the news.

Meanwhile the mute guard outside the door, gobbling meaningless words at him and keeping him carefully covered with a villainous-looking machine pistol, brought him a wooden bowl of hot stew three times a day, and refilled his water jar when he requested it. Ribera chose not to inquire too closely into the ingredients of the stew, yet it proved nourishing enough for all that.

Aside from the visits of his jailer, he was as solitary as Robinson Crusoe on his island. The hours were unbelievably heavy-footed and as they dragged slowly past, Ribera's patience wore thinner and thinner. He mentally composed a scathing reprimand for El Pico on the matter, but when at last he heard a car drive up outside, and recognized El Pico's voice addressing a cheerful greeting to the gobbling guard, he was so relieved that he forgot his anger. When El Pico entered the hut through the packing-case door, Ribera stood in the middle of the mud floor and actually smiled a welcome.

"What news?" he asked eagerly. "Did they pay the ransom?"

El Pico nodded with ill-concealed triumph. "Paid up like little lambs!" he said. He squinted his eyes at Ribera. "Does it not make you proud to know that you are worth so much to your colleagues? They put up no argument."

"I knew they'd pay," Ribera said, "or I should never have consented to this venture." Nevertheless, he sighed with vast relief. "So let's get back to the city," he said briskly. "I want to be free of this dreadful place as soon as possible."

"At once." There was an odd note of embarrassment in El Pico's voice. He made the flickering motion that Ribera remembered from their former meeting and produced the same black revolver from his clothing. He stepped back a pace and pointed the gun at Ribera's forehead.

Ribera stared at the gun muzzle in stunned amazement. "If the fund-raising was a success," he began, "I fail utterly to understand—"

El Pico interrupted him. "We have the money, true, paid before we made a second demand, which your stinking government rejected."

"Second demand?"

"Yes. That the government release immediately seventeen members of the Society of the Parrot now being held in government prisons for political crimes. Do you understand?"

Ribera understood, but he shook his head, suddenly as powerless to speak as his gobbling guard beyond the door.

"Release our comrades from prison, we demanded!" El Pico declaimed rhetorically. "Or Ramón Ribera, your Minister of Justice, who is in our hands, will pay the price!" He gestured with the revolver. "I am sorry, Minister, but your life is not worth *that* much to your colleagues, apparently. They have refused to release our comrades."

Ribera found his tongue. "Well, then, since you have the money —ten million sols!—you can let me go, can't you? You will have a friend at court to work with you again." He looked down at the revolver. "There is surely no need to kill me?"

El Pico shrugged. "You understand how it is, Señor Minister," he said. "We can't let the people of this country believe that the Parrot doesn't keep its promises." With the air of a man delivering an apology, he shot Ribera through the left eye.

Outside, the sudden sharp report made the llamas in their pen stir restlessly for a few moments, hissing and stamping their hooves. Then they were quiet again.

Henry T. Parry publishes very little. I've seen only one or two stories a year by him since he first appeared in EQMM *in 1965. But each of his stories has a way of remaining in the reader's memory long afterward—as with this tale of a twelve-year-old boy's first experience with murder.*

HENRY T. PARRY
Love Story

Paul Busher kicked me squarely in the rear end and I overbalanced and fell headfirst into the trash barrel.

"I knew I'd catch one of you kids spreadin' that trash all over the alley," he said after he yanked me out and set me on my feet.

My newspapers had slipped out of the strap and when I stooped over to pick them up I was real careful not to get too close to Paul. The *Public Ledgers,* the *North Americans,* the one *Journal of Commerce* for Eckert Bros., wholesale grocery, and *The New York Times* for Dr. Sharer. The *Times* was lying in a patch of motor oil and I hated to think of Miss Elizabeth Sharer opening the paper maybe at breakfast and finding the first page all greasy. I wouldn't have cared if it had been one of my other customers on the route. Most of them were too fussy anyway.

If some kid had kicked me I would have been just about wild until I punched him in the nose or banged his head on the macadam to get even, because when somebody hits me I feel lowered and I burn all over. But there wasn't much chance of me punching Paul Busher or getting even with him because he was a big guy, maybe twenty-five or thirty years old. He played football at State for two years but then he had to come home because he couldn't keep up the courses. Anyway, that's what everybody said.

Busher had a lot of jobs around town, but he didn't keep any of them very long. Right now he was running Fatty Leffler's Poolroom and, everybody said, playing in the poker game that ran there from Saturday noon until Monday morning. It was the poolroom trash barrel that he'd caught me in, only I don't know why he was up that early unless it was that he hadn't been to bed yet. After I stocked up on my papers at Charley McCall's Stationery Store, I would go through the alley that ran behind the stores that fronted on Market

Street, behind Jones's Pharmacy, Pritchard's Togs for Men, Fatty Leffler's Poolroom, and the other places.

Paul used to park his Ford runabout in the alley behind the poolroom and a couple of times when I was starting out with my papers I'd see him asleep on the seat of the car, sometimes with a bottle of, I guess, whisky lying on the pavement. Why he didn't go home I can't say, because Mrs. Busher was a real nice lady. But I guess maybe he was ashamed for his folks to see him this way. Mrs. Busher was always saying how Paul was going to do this or that and better himself but nobody paid much attention any more.

Us kids who delivered papers—there were four of us for the whole town—we had kind of a trade secret and that was, when you were up early and walking through the streets and alleys, especially the alleys, before anybody else was awake, you had first whack at whatever had been left behind by whatever happened during the night. I suppose kids who live by the sea must have the same thing on the beaches after the tide goes out. Stuff people lose on the sidewalk walking home, or things people put out with the trash.

One time Whitey Nash, who has Route 1, found a radio that somebody had put out with the trash and he fixed it up so he could get KDKA. In the fall I used to pick up butternuts before the kids on the way to school got a chance at them. What I was looking for in Fatty Leffler's trash barrel were deposit bottles so I could get the money when I returned them. Once I found a pretty good deck of cards there, with only three cards missing.

You got kind of an important feeling, too. We lived at the top of Morgan's Hill and I used to walk down the hill around 5:15 in the morning and see the town in the valley just beginning to turn gray and sometimes with the street lights still on. I passed Dr. Sharer's driveway about halfway down the hill and the light on the big stone post made me think of a lighthouse and I used to think I was something like a guy who steers a ship while all the passengers are asleep, or a locomotive engineer on a long night-passenger run, or maybe one of those guys who fly the mail, guys who are trusted and who get kind of a reward by seeing things other people never get to see, or maybe seeing them differently because they are awake and working when everybody else is asleep.

One of the things I didn't like so much about delivering the papers so early was that I hardly ever got to see Miss Elizabeth Sharer. I used to walk up the driveway and stick the paper between the porch banisters and hope she'd come out to get it. But it was always so early that nobody was awake, though once or twice I'd meet Dr. Sharer just as he was coming back from a night call.

Miss Elizabeth Sharer was a real swell girl and I liked her a lot. Sometimes when I was coming home from school she'd be working in the flower garden near the street, and she'd stop and talk over the hedge and ask me about school and what I was reading. She gave me the names of lots of swell books and when they didn't have them in the town library she would lend them from her father's library. The Sharers had one room—I guess it used to be the dining room —with the walls all covered with books.

She was real pretty, too, with dark hair and dark eyes, and her skin was kind of pink. Some days she had kind of an excited manner and asked me a lot of questions and seemed awfully happy, and other times she'd be kind of depressed and mopey. But she was always nice to me and listened when I talked to her about what I thought and what I was going to do. She never laughed at me the way my sister Helen does.

If I ever was going to get married—and I don't think I ever will —I would have liked to marry Miss Elizabeth Sharer. But I guess you have to be twenty-one to get married and that was nine years away, and by that time Miss Elizabeth Sharer would be thirty or forty or something, anyway too old to get married. But I'd think about her a whole lot, how dark and pretty and kind she was. I never liked to hear anyone else talk about her, even when they were saying something good, which mostly they were, and that didn't happen too often in our town.

Miss Elizabeth Sharer was kind of like my ideal. I knew I would never get to know anybody else as fine as Miss Elizabeth Sharer. One time my sister Helen said Beth Sharer was stuck up and I got mad at her, and then she said it sounded to her like I had a big crush on her. Mom told Helen to hush up and no wonder she wasn't married herself, with a tongue like that.

One morning when I had just wedged the *Times* between the banisters on Dr. Sharer's porch, Miss Elizabeth Sharer came out. She seemed kind of keyed-up and excited and her face had that rosy color that made her look beautiful. She asked would I do her a favor. I hoped it would be something big where I could show off, not something like would I stop in at Jones's Pharmacy with a prescription. Because there wasn't anything she asked, anything, that I wouldn't do.

But all I could get out was: "Yeah, Miss Elizabeth. Sure."

"But you'll have to keep it a secret. Now don't promise unless you're really going to keep it a secret. Not ever tell anybody anything. Ever. Just something you and I know about."

I wanted to tell her they could put me on one of those stretching machines they used in the Middle Ages, or in one of those rooms where the walls come together on you like in that story by Edgar A. Poe, but I mumbled something about not ever telling.

"You know the alley downtown behind Jones's Pharmacy and Fatty Leffler's Poolroom and those places?"

"I go through it every morning on my paper route," I told her.

"Well, on the wall of the Leffler Building there's a metal box with telephone wires coming out of it. It has a lid with a hinge. Every morning I want you to open that box and take out any envelope that's in there and bring it along with you on your route and put it in the screw-cap jar in the flowerbed near the street. Bury the jar in the mulch. And any envelopes you find in the jar, you take them down with you early the next morning and put them in the telephone box on Leffler's back wall. Do you have that straight, Johnny? And don't let anyone see you."

"Yeah, Miss Elizabeth, I got it. Envelopes in the telephone box I put in the jar. Envelopes in the jar I put in the telephone box. Early in the morning."

"That's right. But remember, it's our secret, yours and mine. Now, how are you fixed for movie money?"

She picked up her handbag from the porch floor and it sagged open with some junk spilling out. A round gold case rolled under the railing and fell into the shrubbery. I crawled under the bushes and got it and I noticed that it had some words engraved on the outside, but I didn't like to read them standing right there in front of her.

"Thank you, Johnny," she said and put it into her bag. "Daddy brought me that compact from White Springs last year. They were giving them out as souvenirs for the ladies at the convention. Now what about that movie money?"

"Gee, thanks just the same, Miss Elizabeth," I said, "but I couldn't take anything. I walk by both those places every day."

"You're sure now?" She looked at me and her eyes were kind of questioning and smiling at the same time, as if she had set up some kind of a problem for me by offering me money and was interested to see what I would do about it, to see whether I would take the money.

"No, I'm sure. I don't mind doing it."

What I wanted to add was "for you," but I wasn't brave enough or sure enough to say it, even though I knew she wouldn't laugh at me.

That was how it started. I didn't know then who would be picking up the messages I left in the telephone box, but I found out soon enough.

I was lying on the swing on the side porch, reading. The sitting-

room window was open and Mom was talking on the telephone to
Aunt Annie. Mom always talks loud on the phone. Aunt Annie used
to live just down the hill from us until she moved to the other side
of town, but you'd think it was to China or something because she
still wanted to know all the news from our neighborhood.

I wasn't paying any attention to what they were talking about until
it seeped into my head that they were talking about Miss Elizabeth
Sharer.

"Oh, Doc's busy as usual," Mom was saying. "And they say that
Elizabeth has just plain lost her head over that Paul Busher. Doc's
put his foot down and says she's to have nothing to do with him.
Can't say I blame him, not after that Blaney girl. You know."

Then she went on to say more about how she thought Doc was
wrong to have ever sent Elizabeth away to what's-its-name Hall
instead of letting her finish high school with the other kids, and how
hard it must be on Doc what with Ellie Sharer being in that mental
hospital all these years, ever since Elizabeth was ten.

"Poor Elizabeth," Mom said, "I don't see what there is for her
around here. Just withering on the vine, she is."

A couple of mornings later I found out that no matter what her
father was telling her, Miss Elizabeth Sharer was meeting Paul
Busher. And those notes I was carrying between the telephone box
and the screw-cap jar must have been to set up the times and places.

I was coming down the hill on my way to get my papers and I
had just passed Dr. Sharer's place when I saw a Ford coming up the
hill. It wasn't too light yet but the car didn't have any headlights on.
It stopped a couple of hundred feet down the hill from where I was
and backed around to face downhill. I saw Miss Elizabeth Sharer get
out of the car and come up the hill toward her house.

I knew she wouldn't want to be seen, so I slipped behind the
hedge and she went by just three or four feet from where I was
standing, and she was humming to herself. I waited, to give her time
to get to her house, then started on down the hill. The Ford was
gone. It had coasted down the hill without having the engine turned
on. It was Paul Busher's Ford all right. I had seen it sitting in the
alley behind Leffler's Poolroom about a hundred times.

That was the first time. Over the summer I must have seen Miss
Elizabeth Sharer about ten times coming home just as it was getting
light. And as she went by where I was standing behind that hedge
I could hear her humming to herself, and once or twice she was
saying words that sounded like poetry. I was happy to see her happy
and at the same time I was jealous over why she was happy. And I
was right in the middle, carrying messages but not supposed to
know who was taking them out of that telephone wire box.

Then two things happened. I noticed that there wasn't nearly as many messages for me to take out of the telephone box to put into the screw-cap jar as there was going the other way. And I was glad. The other thing was when Dr. Sharer told off Paul Busher.

I went into Fatty Leffler's Poolroom to buy a bottle of soda. I wasn't allowed in there but I thought I would be acting more like the big guys if I could hang around there for a while. So I used the soda as an excuse and I tried to make it last as long as I could.

Paul Busher was shooting some pool and had just said, "Nine ball in the corner pocket" or something like that, and he was bent over the table sliding the cue stick back and forth on the back of his left hand and getting ready to shoot when Dr. Sharer walks in and taps him on the shoulder.

"Busher," he said, "I want you to stop seeing my daughter. I will only tell you this once. If you don't stop I shall take the necessary steps."

Paul straightened up and looked down at him and picked up the chalk and chalked his cue. He looked Dr. Sharer right in the eye— Paul was chewing a matchstick and he slid it from one side of his mouth to the other, then back again—and said, "Doc, when she gets as tired of it as I'm gettin', maybe she'll stop seein' me."

Paul turned his back on Dr. Sharer and sank the nine ball. Dr. Sharer turned white and walked out, without saying or doing anything. I felt something bad was about to happen, that there was some kind of dangerous fumes in the air between the two men. I was scared because I'd never seen grown men face each other before in a kind of hate and violence that seemed stronger than they were, and I felt that I had seen something that I had better stay away from.

Perk Smith, who is the biggest liar I know, said his brother told him that a couple of days later the boys in the poolroom began making remarks to Paul about him and Miss Elizabeth Sharer and that Paul didn't say anything, he just smiled. I picked a fight with Perk and he gave me a black eye. I had a lot of fights around the end of the summer over one thing or another and I guess I lost more than half of them.

About a week later, a week when I carried a message every day from Miss Elizabeth Sharer's screw-cap jar to Paul Busher's telephone box but none the other way, I was on my way down the hill to pick up my papers at Charley McCall's when I saw Miss Elizabeth Sharer come walking fast up the hill. There wasn't any Ford around this time. As usual, I knew she wouldn't want anyone to see her, so I ducked behind the hedge until she went by and turned into her driveway.

When she came by I could hear her crying, not big open-mouthed bawls the way kids cry, but in low moans and sobs like the hurt was so deep there was almost no way of crying about it. I wanted to go after her and do or say something that would make her stop crying, but I was helpless. What could a kid like me say or do that would be of any help to a great lady like Miss Elizabeth Sharer?

I picked up my papers at Charley McCall's and was going through the alley behind the poolroom when I noticed that Paul Busher's Ford, that was parked there like always, had a leak. I squatted down and looked under the engine but saw that the leak was farther back, probably in the gas tank. I straightened up and went around to the side of the car and there was Paul Busher curled up on the seat just like I'd seen him so many times before.

But this time the rubber mat on the floor was covered with blood and there was blood slowly dripping down through the floorboards onto the macadam. This time there wasn't any whisky bottle on the macadam either.

I hugged my papers to my chest with both arms and started to run back to Charley McCall's. On the way I had to stop to throw up because of what I had seen and because maybe they would think I had something to do with it on account I found it first. Lots of people think Charley McCall is a fuddy-duddy, but when I told him what I had seen he moved plenty fast. He picked up the phone and when Netta Eisley down at the exchange answered, he told her to get Dr. Sharer right away.

"Doc ain't home, Charley," I could hear Netta say in that flat, tinny voice you can hear coming out of a telephone receiver. "He's been away all week at some meeting."

"All right. All right. Get me Doc Simmons then. And as soon as he hangs up, get me the police. I believe it's Jim Bowers' turn to be on duty this week."

It didn't take long before a crowd of people, mostly half dressed, began gathering behind Leffler's Poolroom, because once Netta Eisley gets a piece of news the first thing she does is call her mother and from then on it's public property. I hung around the edge of the crowd, not wanting to see Paul Busher again. The people up front kept repeating and passing back what Doc Simmons and Jimmy Bowers were saying.

"Didja hear that? Hear what Doc says? He's dead. Paul's dead. Doc says whoever did it had a knife as sharp as a scalpel."

After they took Paul's body away, and then towed the Ford away, and the crowd had thinned out, Charley McCall said, "Johnny, you look kind of white. You want I should get somebody else to take your route this morning?"

But I told him I could deliver the papers all right and I set off on my route, thinking maybe I had already hung around that place too long.

When I turned into Dr. Sharer's driveway, the house was quiet and shady, and the garden was wet and fresh-smelling and clean and private behind the hedges, and I kept thinking how different it was from the oil and blood on the macadam behind Leffler's Poolroom. I didn't see anybody around when I put the *Times* between the porch banisters, but as I turned to go back down the driveway, Miss Elizabeth Sharer came out and stood at the top of the porch steps.

She was still dressed the way I had seen her when she came up the hill. Her face seemed like the skin had shrunk and her eyes were darker than ever. She picked up the paper and stood holding it as if she didn't know what to do next or whether she should speak to me. I couldn't be sure she even knew I was there.

I waited at the foot of the steps, looking up at her and thinking that whatever I had done, it wasn't enough for someone as beautiful and kind as Miss Elizabeth Sharer. I wanted to speak to her and tell her, but instead I turned around and ran down the driveway to the street.

At the flowerbed I stopped and pointed down a couple of times to where the glass jar was buried. When I was sure that she saw where I was pointing, I started running up the hill toward home.

Because what I put in the glass jar was what I found that morning on the macadam under Paul Busher's Ford. It was lying in a pool of blood, and blood had dripped on top of it. It was the round gold powder-and-mirror thing, engraved *State Medical Association—White Springs—August 1923.*

The reason I was running up the hill was because I didn't want to be around when she opened the jar and found the note I had put there. I'd be ashamed to be where she could see me when she read the note, because what I wrote was:

> Dear Miss Elizabeth Sharer:
> I love you.
> > Respectfully yours,
>
> > John Price
> > Paper boy—Route 2.

Bill Pronzini's nameless, pulp-collecting private eye has appeared in three novels and several short stories to date. More about him when you finish reading this latest adventure.

BILL PRONZINI
Private Eye Blues

Sunday Morning Coming Down . . .

That's the title of a sad popular song by Kris Kristofferson, about a man with no wife and no children and nowhere to go and very little to look forward to on a quiet Sunday morning. On this quiet Sunday morning I was that man. Nowhere to go and very little to look forward to.

I carried a cup of coffee into the living room of my flat in San Francisco's Pacific Heights. It was a pretty nice day out, cloudless, a little windy. The part of the Bay I could see from my front windows was a rippled green and dotted with sailboats, like a bas-relief map with a lot of small white flags pinned to it.

I moved over to the tier of bookshelves that covered one wall, where most of my six-thousand-odd detective and mystery pulp magazines were arranged. I ran my fingers over some of the spines: *Black Mask, Dime Detective, Clues, Detective Fiction Weekly, Detective Story.* I had started collecting them in 1947, and that meant almost three decades of my life were on those shelves—nearly three-fifths of the time I had been on this earth—and next Friday, I would be fifty years old.

I took one of the *Black Mask*s down and looked at the cover: Chandler, Whitfield, Nebel, Babcock—old friends that once I could have passed a quiet Sunday with, that would have lifted me out of most any depressed mood I might happen to be in—but not this Sunday. . . .

The telephone rang.

I keep the thing in the bedroom, and I went in there and caught up the receiver. It was Eberhardt, a sobersided lieutenant of detectives and probably my closest friend for about the same number of years as I had been collecting the pulps.

"Hello, hot stuff," he said. "Get you out of bed?"

"No. I've been up for hours."

"You're getting to be an early bird in your old age."

"Yeah."

"Listen, how's for a little cribbage and a lot of beer this after-noon? Dana and the kids are off to Sausalito for the day."

"I don't think so, Eb," I said. "I'm not in the beer-and-cribbage mood."

"You sound like you're in a mood, period."

"I guess I am, a little."

"Private eye blues, huh?"

"Yeah—private eye blues."

He made chuckling sounds. "Wouldn't happen to have anything to do with your fiftieth coming up, would it? Hell, fifty's the prime of life. I ought to know, tiger, I been there two years now."

"Sure."

"Well, you change your mind about the beer, at least, come on over. I'll save you a can."

We rang off, and I went back to the living room and finished my coffee and tried not to think about anything. I might as well have tried not to breathe. I got up and paced around for a while, aimlessly.

Sunday morning coming down . . .

Abruptly, the old consumptive cough started up. So I sat down again, handkerchief to my mouth, and listened to the dry, brittle sounds echo hollowly through the empty flat. Cigarettes—damned cigarettes! An average of two packs a day for thirty-five years, thirty-five out of fifty. More than a half-million cigarettes. More than ten million lungsful of tobacco smoke. . . .

Knock it off, I told myself sharply. What's the use in that kind of thinking? Once more I got to my feet—all I seemed to be doing this morning was standing up and sitting down. Well, I had to get out of there, that was all, before I became claustrophobic. Go some-where, do something. A long solitary drive, maybe; I just did not want to see Eberhardt or anybody else.

I put on an old corduroy jacket, left the flat and picked up my car. The closest direction out of the city was north, and so I drove across the Golden Gate Bridge and straight up Highway 101. Some two hours later, in redwood country a few miles north of Cloverdale, I swung off toward the coast—and eventually, past two o'clock, I reached Highway One and turned south again.

There, the sun was invisible above a high-riding bank of fog, and you could smell the sharp, clean odor of the sea; traffic was only sporadic. The breakers hammering endlessly against the shoreline began to have a magnetic attraction, and near Anchor Bay I pulled off onto a bluff. I left my car in the deserted parking area, found a path leading down to an equally deserted beach.

I walked along the beach, watching the waves unfold, listening to their rhythmic roar and to the sound of gulls, wheeling unseen somewhere in the mist. It was a lonely place, but the loneliness was part of its appeal; a good spot for me on this Sunday.

The cold began to get to me after half an hour or so, and the cough started again. I came back up the path, and when I reached the bluff I saw that another vehicle had pulled into the parking area —a dusty, green pickup truck with a small, dusty camper attached to the bed. It listed a little to the left in back, and the reason for that was evident enough: the tire there was flat. Nearby, motionless except for wind-tossed hair and clothing, two men and a girl stood looking at the tire, like figures in some sort of alfresco exhibit.

I started in their direction, the direction of my car. The crunching sound of my steps carried above the whisper of the surf, and the three of them glanced up. They did some shifting of position that I didn't pay much attention to, and exchanged a few words; then they stepped away from the pickup and approached me, walking in long, matching strides like marchers in a parade. We all stopped, a few feet apart, along the driver's side of my car.

"Hi," one of the men said. He was in his early twenties, the same approximate age as the other two, and he had longish red hair and a droopy moustache, wore a poplin windbreaker, blue jeans and chukka boots. He looked nervous, his smile nothing more than a forced stretching of his lips.

Both the other guy and the girl seemed to be just as nervous. His hair was dark, cut much shorter than the redhead's, and he had a dark, squarish face; his outfit consisted of slacks, a plaid lumberman's jacket and brown loafers. She was plain, thin-lipped, pale, wearing a long, heavy car coat and a green bandanna tied forward around her head like a monk's cowl. Chestnut-colored hair fell across her shoulders. All three of them had their hands buried in their pockets.

I nodded and said, "Hi."

"We've had a flat," the redhead said.

"So I see."

"We haven't got a jack."

"Oh. Well, I've got one. You're welcome to use it."

"Thanks."

I hesitated, frowning a little. You get feelings sometimes, when you've been a cop in one form or another most of your life, and you learn to trust them. I had one of those feelings now, and it said something was wrong here—very wrong. Their nervousness was part of it, but there was also a heavy, palpable tension among the three of them: people caught up in some sort of volatile and perhaps dangerous drama. Maybe it was none of my business, but the cop's instinct, the cop's innate curiosity, would not allow me to ignore the feeling of wrongness.

I said, "It's a good thing I happened to be here. There doesn't seem to be much traffic in these parts today."

The redhead took his left hand out of his pocket and pressed diffident fingers against his moustache. "Yeah," he said, "a good thing."

The girl snuffled a little from the cold, produced a handkerchief, snapped it open, and blew her nose; her eyes were focused straight ahead.

The dark-haired guy shifted his feet, and his eyes were furtive. He drew the flaps of his jacket in across his stomach. "Pretty cold out here," he said pointedly.

I glanced over at the pickup; it had Oregon license plates. "Going far?"

"Uh . . . Bodega Bay."

"You on vacation?"

"More or less."

"Must be a little cramped, the three of you in that camper."

"We like it cramped," the redhead said. His voice had gone up an octave or two. "How about your jack, OK?"

I got my keys out and stepped back around the car and opened the trunk. The three of them stayed where they were, watching me. They don't belong together, I thought abruptly, not those three— and that, too, was part of the feeling of wrongness. The redhead was the mod type, with his long hair and moustache, and the dark one had a more conservative look. Did that mean anything? One *could* be an interloper, the unwanted third wheel—though in a situation that may have had a lot more meaning than the average kind of two's-company-three's-a-crowd thing. If that was it, which one? The girl had not looked at one guy more than the other; her eyes, crinkled against the wind, were still focused straight ahead.

I unhooked the jack and took it out and closed the trunk again. When I returned to them I said, "Maybe I'd better set this up for you. It's trickier to operate than most."

"We can manage," the dark guy said.

"Just the same . . ."

I took the jack over to the rear of the pickup; the spare tire was propped against the bumper. There were little windows in each of the camper doors, one of them draped in rough cloth and the other one clear. I glanced inside through the clear window. There were storage cupboards, a small table with bunk-type benches on two sides, a ladder that led up to sleeping facilities above the cab; all of it neat and clean, with everything put away or tied down that might roll around when they were in motion.

The three of them came over and formed another half-circle, the girl in the middle this time. I got down in a crouch and slid the jack under the axle and fiddled with it, getting it in place. As soon as I began to work the handle, both the redhead and the dark-haired one pitched in to help. Nothing passed between any of them that I could see.

It took us fifteen minutes to change the tire. I tried several times to make conversation, small talk that might give me a clue as to what was going on among them, which of them didn't belong, but they weren't having any. The boys gave me occasional monosyllables, and the girl, snuffling, did not say anything at all.

When I had worked the handle to lower the truck onto all four tires again and pulled the jack out from underneath, I said, "Well, there you go. You'd better get that flat repaired at the first station you come to. You don't want to be driving around without a spare."

"We'll do that," the dark guy said.

I gave them a let's-bridge-the-generation-gap smile. "You wouldn't happen to have a beer or a soft drink or something inside, would you? Manual labor always makes me thirsty."

The redhead looked at the girl, then at the dark-haired one, and began to fidget. "Sorry—nothing at all."

"We'd better get moving," the dark guy said, and he picked up the flat and slid it into the metal holder attached to the undercarriage, locked it down. Then the three of them went immediately to the driver's door.

I did not want to let them go, but there was no way I could think of to keep them there. Following, I watched the redhead open the door and climb in. That gave me a good look inside the cab, but there wasn't much to see; nothing there that shouldn't be there, nothing at all on the seat or on the little shelf behind the seat, or on the dashboard or on the passenger-side floorboards. The girl got in second, and that made the dark one the driver. He swung the door shut, started the engine.

"Take it easy," I said, and lifted my hand. None of them looked at me. The pickup jerked forward, a little too fast, tires spraying gravel, and pulled out onto Highway One. It went away to the south, gathering speed.

I stood watching until they were out of sight. Then I went back to my car and got inside and started her up and put the heater on high. So now what? Drive back to San Francisco, forget about this little incident—that was the simplest thing to do—but I could not get it out of my head. One of those kids, or maybe even more than one, did not belong. The more I thought about it, the more I felt I ought to know which of them it was. More importantly, there was that aura of tension and anxiety all three had projected.

I had no real cause or right to play detective, but I did have a duty to my conscience and to the vested interests of others, and I did have a strong disinclination to return to my empty, quiet flat. So, all right. So I would do some of what I had been doing in one form or another, for bread and butter, the past thirty-one years.

I put the car in gear and drove out and south on the highway. It took me four miles to catch sight of them. They were moving along at a good clip, maybe ten over the speed limit but within the boundaries of safety. I adjusted my speed to match theirs, with several hundred yards between us. It was not the best time of day for a shagging operation—coming on toward dusk—and the thick, drifting fog cut visibility to a minimum; but the pickup's lights were on and I could track it well enough by the diffused red flickers of the tail lamps.

We went straight down the coast, through Stewart's Point and past Fort Ross. There was still not much traffic, but enough so that we weren't the only two vehicles on the road. The fog got progressively heavier, took on the consistency of a misty drizzle and forced me to switch on the windshield wipers. Daylight faded into the long, cold shadows of night. When we reached Jenner, at the mouth of the Russian River, it was full dark.

A few miles farther on, the pickup came into Bodega Bay and went right on through without slowing. So that made the dark-haired one a liar about their ultimate destination. I wondered just where it was they were really headed, and asked myself how far I was prepared to follow them. I decided all the way, until they stopped somewhere, until I satisfied myself one way or another about the nature of their relationship with each other. If that meant following them into tomorrow, even into another state—OK. I had no cases pending, nothing on my hands and too much on my mind; and work, purposeful or purposeless, was the only real antidote I knew for self-pity and depression.

Valley Ford, Tomales, Point Reyes . . . the pickup did not alter its speed. We were maybe thirty miles from the Golden Gate Bridge then, and I was running low on gas; I had enough to get me into San Francisco but not much farther than that.

The problem of stopping to refuel turned out to be academic. Just south of Olema Village the pickup slowed considerably, and I saw its brake lights flash. Then it swung off onto a secondary road to the west, toward the Point Reyes National Seashore.

When I got to the intersection a couple of minutes later, my headlamps picked up a sign with a black-painted arrow and the words *Public Campground, 3 Miles.* So maybe they were going to stop here for the night, or for supper anyway. I debated the wisdom of running dark. The fog was thinner along here, curling tendrils moving rapidly in a sharp, gusty wind, and you could see jagged patches of sky, like pieces in an astronomical jigsaw puzzle. Visibility was fairly good, and there did not figure to be much traffic on the secondary road, and I did not want to alert them. I switched off the lights, turned onto the road, and drove along at less than twenty.

The terrain had a rumpled look because this area was a major San Andreas fault zone. I passed a little "sag pond" where run-off water had collected in depressions created by past earthquakes. Exactly three miles in, close to the ocean—I could hear again the whisper of combers—the campground appeared on the left. Backed in against high sand dunes westward, and ringed by pine and fir to the east and south, it was a small state-maintained facility with wooden outhouses, and stone barbecues, and trash receptacles placed in reminder every few yards.

The pickup was there, lights still on, pulled back near the trees on the far edge of the grounds.

I saw it on a long diagonal, partially screened by the evergreens. Instead of driving abreast of the entrance and beyond, where they might see or hear me, I took my car immediately onto the berm and cut off the engine. Ten seconds later, the pickup's lights went out.

I sat motionless behind the wheel, trying to decide what to do next, but the mind is a funny thing: all the way here I had been unable to clarify the reasons why I felt one or more of those three didn't belong, and now that I was thinking about something else, memory cells went click, click, click, and all at once I knew just what had been bothering me—three little isolated things that, put together, told me exactly which of them did not belong. I felt myself frowning. I still had no idea what the situation itself was, but what I had just perceived made the whole thing all the more strange and compelling.

I reached up, took the plastic dome off the interior light and unscrewed the bulb, then I got out of the car, went across the road. The wind, blowing hard and cold, had sharp little teeth in it that bit at the exposed skin on my face and hands. Overhead, wisps of fog fled through the darkness like chilled fingers seeking warmth.

Moving slowly, cautiously, I entered the trees and made my way to the south, roughly parallel to where the pickup was parked. Beyond the second of two deadfalls I had a glimpse of it through the wind-bent boughs, maybe forty yards away. The cab was dark and seemed to be empty; faint light shone at the rear of the camper, faint enough to tell me that both door windows were now draped.

I crossed toward the pickup, stopped to listen when I was less than ten yards from it and hidden in shadow along the bole of a bishop pine. There was nothing to hear except the cry of the wind and the faint murmuring of surf in the distance. I stared in at the cab. Empty, all right. Then I studied the ground along the near side of the pickup: no gravel, just earth and needles that would muffle the slow tread of footsteps.

One pace at a time, I went from the pine to the side of the pickup. Near the end of the camper I stopped and leaned in close and pressed my ear against the cold metal, put my right index finger in the other ear to shut out the wind. At first, for a full thirty seconds, there were faint sounds of movement inside but no conversation. Then, muffled but distinguishable, one of them spoke—the one who didn't belong.

"Hurry up with those sandwiches."

"I'm almost finished," another voice said timorously.

"And I'm damned hungry—but I don't want to sit around here any longer than we have to. You understand?"

"It's a public campground. The State Park people won't bother us, if that's what—"

"Shut up! I told both of you before, no comments and no trouble if you don't want a bullet in the head. Do I have to tell you again?"

"No."

"Then keep your mouth closed and get those sandwiches ready. We got a lot of driving left to do before we get to Mexico."

That exchange told me as much as I needed to know about the situation, and it was worse than I had expected. Kidnapping, probably, and God knew what other felonies. It was time to take myself out of it, to file a report with the closest Highway Patrol office— Olema or Point Reyes. You can take private detection just so far, and then you're a fool unless you turn things over to a public law-enforcement agency. I pulled back, half-turned, and started to retreat into the trees.

In that moment, the way things happen sometimes—unexpectedly, coincidentally, so that there's no way you can foresee them or guard against them—the wind gusted sharply and blew a limb from one of the deadfalls nearby, sent it banging loudly against the metal side of the camper.

From inside, in immediate response, there was an abrupt scraping and a crashing of something upended. I was still backing away, but it was too late then for running. The camper's doors rattled open and one of them came lurching out and into my vision, saw me and shouted, "Hold it, you! Hold it!" In one extended hand was something long and black, something that could only be a gun. I held it.

The figure was the one who didn't belong, of course—and the one who didn't belong was the girl.

Only he wasn't a girl.

He stood there with his feet spread, crouching slightly, holding the gun in both hands: nervous, scared, dangerous. He was not wearing the wig or the bandanna now; his hair was clipped close to his scalp, and it was light-colored, almost white in the darkness. Except for his pale, girlish face, his hairless hands—physical quirks of nature—there was nothing at all effeminate about him.

"Move up this way," he said.

I hesitated, and then I did what he told me. He backed away quickly, into position to cover both me and the rear of the camper. When I was three long strides from him I stopped, and I could see the other two standing between the open doors, silhouetted in the light from inside. They were motionless, eyes flicking between me and the one holding the gun.

"What the hell?" the guy with the gun said. He had recognized me. "You followed us."

I did not say anything.

"Why? Who are you, man?"

I watched him for a moment, then, stretching the truth a little because I wanted to see his reaction, I said, "I'm a cop."

He didn't like that. A tic started up on the left side of his mouth and he made a swaying motion with the gun, as if he could not quite keep his hands steady. He wasn't at all chary about using the weapon, I was pretty sure of that—on me or on the two scared kids by the camper. You get so you can gauge the depths of a man, how far he'll go, what he's capable of; this one was capable of murder, all right, and in his agitated state it would not take much to push him into it.

He said finally, "That's your problem," and made a sound that might have been a grunt or a skittish laugh. "You don't seem surprised that I'm not a female."

"No."

"What put you onto me?"

"Three things," I said flatly. "One was the way you blew your nose back there on the parking area. You took your handkerchief out and snapped it open in front of you; that's a man's gesture, not a woman's. Second thing is the way you walk. Long strides, hard strides—masculine movements, same as the other two kids. Third thing, you weren't carrying a purse or a handbag, and there wasn't one inside the camper or cab. I never knew a girl yet who didn't have some kind of handbag within easy reach at all times."

He rubbed the back of his free hand across his nose. "I'll have to watch those things from now on," he said. "You're pretty sharp, old man."

Old man, I thought. I said, "Yeah, pretty sharp."

The redheaded kid said, "What are you going to do?" in a shaky voice.

The guy with the gun did not answer immediately; he was staring intently at me, mouth still twitching. I watched him think it over, making up his mind. Finally he said to the other two, "You got rope or anything inside there?"

"Some clothesline," the dark one answered.

"Get it. We'll tie the cop up and take him with us."

Anger started up inside me. You let him tie you up, I told myself, you stand a good chance of dying that way, helpless; you and those two kids, dead by the side of the road somewhere. I said, "Why not shoot me right here and be done with it? Here or someplace else, what difference does it make?"

His face darkened. "Shut up, you!"

I took a measured step toward him.

"Stand still!" He made a convulsive stabbing motion with the gun. "I'm warning you, old man, I'm shooting if you don't stop."

"Sure you are," I said, and jumped him.

The gun went off a foot in front of my face.

Flame and powder seared my skin, half-blinded me, and I felt the heat of the bullet past my right cheek. The roar of the shot was deafening, but I got my left hand on his wrist, coming in close to him, and twisted the arm away before he could fire again. I hit him twice with my right—short, hard blows to the stomach and chest. Breath spilled out of his mouth, and he staggered, off balance. I kicked his legs out from under him, wrenched the gun free as he fell and then went down on top of him. When I hit him again, on the lower jaw, I felt him go limp. He was out of it.

I pulled back on one knee, stood up holding the gun laxly at my side. My cheek was sore and inflamed, and my eyes stung, watered, but that was all the damage I'd suffered. Except for a liquidy feeling in my legs, I did not seem to have any belated reaction to what I had just done.

The redhead and the dark guy moved forward jerkily, the way people will after a full release of tension; their faces, stark and white, were animated with a kind of deliverance.

"OK," I said to them, "you'd better get that clothesline now."

We used my car to deliver the one who didn't belong, whose name turned out to be Cullen, to the Highway Patrol office in Point Reyes. On the way, the other two—Tony Piper and Ed Holmberg—gave me an account of what had been for them a twelve-hour ordeal.

They were students at Linfield College in McMinnville, Oregon, and they had set out from there early this morning for a two-day camping trip along the Rogue River. However, near Coos Bay they had made the mistake of stopping to offer a ride to what they thought was a girl hitchhiker. Cullen pulled the gun immediately and forced them to drive down the coast into California. He wanted to go to Mexico, he'd told them, and because he did not know how to drive himself, they were elected to be his chauffeurs all the way.

He had also told them that he'd escaped from the local county jail, where he had been held on one count of armed robbery and two of attempted murder after an abortive savings-and-loan holdup. Following his escape, with a statewide alert out on him, he had broken into an empty house looking for clothing and money. The house apparently belonged to a spinster, since there hadn't been any male clothing around, but there had been a couple of wigs and plenty of female apparel of Cullen's size. That was when he had gotten the idea to disguise himself as a woman.

When we arrived at the Highway Patrol office, Cullen was still unconscious. Piper and Holmberg told their story again to an officer named Maxfield, the man in charge. I gave a terse account of my part in it, but they insisted on embellishing that, making me out, in their gratitude, to be some sort of hero.

Maxfield and I were alone in his private office when I showed him the photostat of my license. He gave me a cynically amused smile. "A private eye, huh? Well, the way you disarmed Cullen was private eye stuff, all right. Just like on TV."

"Sure," I said wearily. "Just like on TV."

"You've got a lot of guts, that's all I can say."

"No, I don't have a lot of guts. I've never done anything like that before in my life. I just couldn't let those kids be hurt, if I could help it. Cullen might have killed them, sooner or later, and they've got plenty of living left to do."

"He almost killed *you*, my friend," Maxfield said.

"I didn't much care about that. Just the kids."

"The selfless op, right?"

"Wrong."

"Then why didn't you care what happened to you?"

I did not say anything for a time. Then, because I had kept it inside me long enough: "All right, I'll tell you. In fact, you'll be the first person I've been able to tell. My best friend doesn't even know."

"Know what?"

I went over to the window and looked out so I would not have to face Maxfield's reaction. "Unless something of a minor miracle takes place, the doctors give me maybe eighteen months to live," I said. "I've got terminal lung cancer."

EDITOR'S NOTE

You have just read a story which concludes with the approaching death of its series protagonist. Coincidentally, the biggest mystery news of 1975 was the death of Agatha Christie's master detective Hercule Poirot in her novel Curtain. *The news was featured on the front page of* The New York Times, *and the book quickly climbed to the top of the best-seller lists. Poirot thus joined Ellery Queen's Drury Lane (whose demise was oddly similiar) and Nicholas Freeling's Van der Valk among the small band of deceased detectives. (At least three other series characters—Doyle's Sherlock Holmes, Hornung's Raffles, and Stribling's Dr. Poggioli—died but were later resurrected by their authors.) At the time Bill Pronzini published the story you have just read, he fully expected it to be the last about his nameless private eye. But by year's end he was having second thoughts.*

Isaac Asimov, leading science-fiction writer and prolific essayist on just about every subject under the sun (and including the sun), has long had close ties to the mystery field. He has published three detective novels, two of them about Elijah Baley and his robot-assistant R. Daneel Olivaw, and two volumes of mystery short stories: ASIMOV'S MYSTERIES *(1968) and* TALES OF THE BLACK WIDOWERS *(1974). This story, one of the year's best short-shorts, is certain to find a place in his next collection.*

ISAAC ASIMOV
The Little Things

Mrs. Clara Bernstein was somewhat past fifty and the temperature outside was somewhat past ninety. The air conditioning was working, but though it removed the fact of heat it didn't remove the *idea* of heat.

Mrs. Hester Gold, who was visiting the 21st floor from her own place in 4-C, said, "It's cooler down on my floor." She was over fifty, too, and had blond hair that didn't remove a single year from her age.

Clara said, "It's the little things, really. I can stand the heat. It's the dripping I can't stand. Don't you hear it?"

"No," said Hester, "but I know what you mean. My boy, Joe, has a button off his blazer. Seventy-two dollars, and without the button it's nothing. A fancy brass button on the sleeve and he doesn't have it to sew back on."

"So what's the problem? Take one off the other sleeve also."

"Not the same. The blazer just won't look good. If a button is loose, don't wait, get it sewed. Twenty-two years old and he still doesn't understand. He goes off, he doesn't tell me when he'll be back——"

Clara said impatiently. "Listen. How can you say you don't hear the dripping? Come with me to the bathroom. If I tell you it's dripping, it's dripping."

Hester followed and assumed an attitude of listening. In the silence it could be heard—drip—drip—drip—

Clara said, "Like water torture. You hear it all night. Three nights now."

Hester adjusted her large faintly tinted glasses, as though that would make her hear better, and cocked her head. She said, "Probably the shower dripping upstairs, in 22-G. It's Mrs. Maclaren's place. I know her. Listen, she's a good-hearted person. Knock on her door and tell her. She won't bite your head off."

Clara said, "I'm not afraid of her. I banged on her door five times already. No one answers. I phoned her. No one answers."

"So she's away," said Hester. "It's summertime. People go away."

"And if she's away for the whole summer, do I have to listen to the dripping a whole summer?"

"Tell the super."

"That idiot. He doesn't have the key to her special lock and he won't break in for a drip. Besides, she's not away. I know her automobile and it's downstairs in the garage right now."

Hester said uneasily: "She could go away in someone else's car."

Clara sniffed. "That I'm sure of. *Mrs.* Maclaren."

Hester frowned, "So she's divorced. It's not so terrible. And she's still maybe thirty—thirty-five—and she dresses fancy. Also not so terrible."

"If you want my opinion, Hester," said Clara, "what she's doing up there I wouldn't like to say. I hear things."

"What do you hear?"

"Footsteps. Sounds. Listen, she's right above and I know where her bedroom is."

Hester said tartly, "Don't be so old-fashioned. What she does is her business."

"All right. But she uses the bathroom a lot, so why does she leave it dripping? I wish she *would* answer the door. I'll bet anything she's got a décor in her apartment like a French I-don't-know-what."

"You're wrong, if you want to know. You're plain wrong. She's got regular furniture and lots of houseplants."

"And how do you know that?"

Hester looked uncomfortable. "I water the plants when she's not home. She's a single woman. She goes on trips, so I help her out."

"Oh? Then you would *know* if she was out of town. Did she tell you she'd be out of town?"

"No, she didn't."

Clara leaned back and folded her arms. "And you have the keys to her place then?"

Hester said, "Yes, but I can't just go in."

"Why not? She could be away. So you have to water her plants."

"She didn't tell me to."

Clara said, "For all you know she's sick in bed and can't answer the door."

"She'd have to be pretty sick not to use the phone when it's right near the bed."

"Maybe she had a heart attack. Listen, maybe she's dead and that's why she doesn't shut off the drip."

"She's a young woman. She wouldn't have a heart attack."

"You can't be sure. With the life she lives—maybe a boyfriend killed her. We've *got* to go in."

"That's breaking and entering," said Hester.

"With a *key?* If she's away you can't leave the plants to die. You water them and I'll shut off the drip. What harm?—And if she's dead, do you want her to lay there till who knows when?"

"She's not dead," said Hester, but she went downstairs to the fourth floor for Mrs. Maclaren's keys.

"No one in the hall," whispered Clara. "Anyone could break in anywhere anytime."

"Sh," whispered Hester. "What if she's inside and says 'Who's there'?"

"So say you came to water the plants and I'll ask her to shut off the drip."

The key to one lock and then the key to the other turned smoothly and with only the tiniest click at the end. Hester took a deep breath and opened the door a crack. She knocked.

"There's no answer," whispered Clara impatiently. She pushed the door wide open. "The air conditioner isn't even on. It's legitimate. You want to water the plants."

The door closed behind them. Clara said. "It smells stuffy, in here. Feels like a damp oven."

They walked softly down the corridor. Empty utility room on the right, empty bathroom—

Clara looked in. "No drip. It's in the master bedroom."

At the end of the corridor there was the living room on the left, with its plants.

"They need water," said Clara. "I'll go into the master bath—" She opened the bedroom door and stopped. No motion. No sound. Her mouth opened wide.

Hester was at her side. The smell was stifling. "What——"

"Oh, my God," said Clara, but without breath to scream.

The bed coverings were in total disarray. Mrs. Maclaren's head lolled off the bed, her long brown hair brushing the floor, her neck bruised, one arm dangling on the floor, hand open, palm up.

"The police," said Clara. "We've got to call the police."

Hester, gasping, moved forward.

"You musn't touch anything," said Clara.

The glint of brass in the open hand—

Hester had found her son's missing button.

The idea of Dr. Sam Johnson as a great detective and Boswell as his Watson is an attractive one, and Lillian de la Torre has been proving since 1943 that the idea works quite well. Reading her wonderful pastiches can give one as clear an insight into the life of Johnson's England as Boswell himself provided.

LILLIAN DE LA TORRE
The Bedlam Bam

AUTHOR'S NOTE: *When James Boswell first met Dr. Sam Johnson, in 1763, it was still a fashionable amusement to visit Bethlehem (pronounced Bedlam) Hospital and laugh at the lunatics; and the two friends once made such an excursion, though certainly not to laugh.*

Artists (notably Hogarth) and writers have transmitted to us their impressions of the lot of a madman in a society which still acted as if it thought a madman needed the Devil beaten out of him.

What would be the plight of a sane man mistakenly confined, and how could he regain his liberty? "The Bedlam Bam" answers this question . . .

(as told by James Boswell, May, 1768)

"To find my Tom o' Bedlam ten thousand miles I'll travel," chanted the ballad singer in a thin, rusty screech, lustily seconded by the wail of the dirt-encrusted baby in her shawl.

"Mad Maudlin goes with dirty toes to save her shoes from gravel,
Yet will I sing bonny mad boys, Bedlam boys are bonny,
They still go bare and live by air . . ."

All along the fence that separated Bedlam Hospital from the tree-lined walks of Moorfields, ill-printed broadsides fluttered in the breeze, loudly urged upon the public by a cacophony of ballad sellers. As I flinched at the din, a hand plucked my sleeve, and a voice twittered:

"Poor Tom o' Bedlam! Tom's a-cold!"

I turned to view a tatterdemalion figure, out at elbow and knee, out at toe and heel, out of breech, with spiky hair on end and clawlike hand extended. As I fumbled for a copper, my wise companion restrained me.

"Let be, Mr. Boswell, the man's a fraud. No Bedlamite has leave to beg these days; they are all withinside. Come along."

Leaving the mock madman to mutter a dispirited curse, we passed through Bedlam gate and approached the noble edifice, so like a palace without, so grim within—as I, a visitor from North Britain, was soon to learn.

Behold us then mounting the step to the entrance pavilion. If "great wits are sure to madness near allied," as the poet has it, then what shall be said of that ill-assorted pair?—Dr. Sam: Johnson, the Great Cham of Literature, portly of mien and rugged of countenance, with myself, his young friend and chronicler, James Boswell, advocate, of Scotland, swarthy of complexion and low of stature beside him. Believing London to be the full tide of human existence, he had carried me, that day in May 1768, to see one of the city's strangest sights, Bedlam Hospital, the abode of the frantick and the melancholy mad.

Entering the pavilion, we beheld before us the Penny Gates, attended by a burly porter in blue coat and cap, wearing with importance a silver badge almost as wide as a plate, and holding his silver-tipped staff of office. Beside the flesh and blood figure stood two painted wooden effigies holding jugs, representing gypsies, a he and a she. Though the woman was ugly, we put our pennies into her jug, and heard them rattle down; whereupon the porter passed us in, and we ascended to the upper gallery.

As we came out on the landing, our senses were assailed by a rank stench and a babel of noise, a hum of many voices talking, with an accompaniment of screech and howl that stood my hair on end.

A second blue-gowned attendant passed us through the iron bars of the barrier, and we stood in the long gallery of the men's ward. Around us milled madmen and their visitors in a dense throng, the while vendors shouldered their way through the crush dispensing nuts, fruits, and cheesecakes, and tap-boys rushed pots of beer, though contraband, to the thirsty, whether mad or sane.

Along the wide gallery, tall windows let in the north light. Opposite them were ranged the madmen's cells, each with its heavy door pierced with a little barred Judas window. Some doors were shut; but most were open to afford the inmates air. I peeped in the first one with a shudder. A small, unglazed window high up admitted a shaft of sunlight and a blast of cold spring air. For furnishings, there was only a wooden bedstead piled with straw, and a wooden bowl to eat from; unless you counted a heavy iron chain with a neck loop, stapled to the wall. No one was chained there, however; the fortunate occupant had "the liberty of the corridor," and perhaps stood at my elbow.

Others were not so fortunate. As we strolled forward, we saw through the open doors many a wretch in fetters, chained to the wall, and many a hopeless mope drearily staring.

"Here in Bedlam," remarked my philosophical friend, "tho' secluded from the world, yet we may see the world in microcosm. Here's Pride—"

I looked where he pointed. Through the open door of the next cell, I perceived one who in his disordered intellect imagined himself to be, perhaps, the Great Mogul. He sat on straw as on a throne, he wore his fetters like adornments, and his countenance bore the most ineffable look of self-satisfaction and consequence. For a crown he wore his chamber pot.

"A pride scarce justified," said I with a smile.

"For mortal man, pride is never justified. Here's Anger—"

The sound of blows rang through the corridor. In the neighboring cell, a red-faced lunatick was furiously beating the straw on his pallet.

"What do you, friend?" enquired a stander-by.

"I beat him for his cruelty!"

"Whom do you beat, sir?"

"The Butcher Duke of Cumberland. Take that! And that!"

"Madmen have long memories," remarked my friend with pity. "The cruelties of the '45 are gone by these twenty years."

The noise had stirred up the menagerie. Pandemonium burst forth. Those who were fettered clanked their chains. Those who were locked in shook the bars. Some howled like wolves. Keepers banging on doors added to the hullabaloo. My friend shuddered.

"God keep us out of such a place!"

"Amen!" said I.

The tumult abated, and we walked on through the throng. A little way along, my friend greeted an acquaintance:

"What, Lawyer Trevelyan, your servant, sir. Miss Cicely, yours. Be acquainted with my young friend Mr. Boswell, the Scotch lawyer, who visits London to see the sights with me."

As I bowed I took their measure. The lawyer was tall and sturdy, with little shrewd eyes in a long closed-up face. The girl was small and slim, modestly attired in dove gray. At her slender waist, in the old-fashioned way, she wore a dainty seamstress' hussif with a businesslike pair of scissors suspended on a ribband. Her small quiet face was gently framed by a cap and lappets of lawn. Meeting her candid amber gaze, I was glad I had adorned my person in my gold-laced scarlet coat.

"How do you go on, Mr. Trevelyan? And how does the good man, your uncle Silas, the Turkey merchant?"

"On his account, Dr. Johnson, we are come hither."

"What, is he confined here?"

"Alas, yes. Yonder he stands."

I looked where he pointed. The elder Mr. Trevelyan was a wiry, small personage, clad in respectable black. He had a thin countenance, his own white hair to his shoulders, bright black eyes, and a risible look. With a half smile, he listened to the tirade of a distrest fellow inmate, giving now and then a quick nod.

"He has no look of insanity," observed my friend.

"Perhaps not, sir. But the prank that brought him hither was not sane. You shall hear. Being touched with Mr. Wesley's *enthusiasm——*"

"Mr. Wesley is a good man."

"I do not deny it, sir. But my uncle has more zeal than prudence. He abandons his enterprises, and goes about to do good to the poor, in prisons and workhouses and I know not where."

"Call you this lunacy?"

"No, sir. Stay, you shall hear the story. Of a Sunday, sir, he gets up into the pulpit at St. Giles, just as the congregation is assembled. He wears a pair of large muslin wings to his shoulders, and 'Follow me, good people!' he cries, 'Follow me to Heaven!' Whereupon with jerks of his hands he flaps his wings, crows loudly, and prepares to launch himself from the lectern. But the beadle, a man of prompt address, pulls him back, and so he is hustled hither without more ado, and here he must stay lest he do himself a mischief. But never fret, Cicely, I have his affairs well in hand, by power of attorney and so on."

But Cicely had gone impulsively to the old gentleman.

"How do you, Uncle?"

"Why, my dear, very well. Reflect (smiling), 'tis only in Bedlam a man may speak his mind about kings and prelates without hindrance. And where else can a man find so many opportunities for comforting the afflicted?"

"Yet, dear uncle, it distresses me to see you among them."

"Be comforted, Cicely. 'Tis only a little while, and I shall be enlarged, I promise you. Your cousin Ned will see to it."

A wise wink accompanied this assurance. Cousin Ned sighed.

"All in good time, Cicely."

Since Cicely seemed minded to canvass the subject further, we bowed and retired. The morning was drawing to a close. I was glad to leave the whole scene of madness, and return to the world of the sane.

Nor would I willingly have renewed my visit so soon, had not the dove-gray girl come to us in distress and urgently carried us thither to visit her uncle.

What a change was there! Two weeks before, we had seen him fully cloathed and quite composed. Now as we peeped through the Judas window, we beheld him lying on straw in the chilly cell, his shirt in tatters, his white locks tangled, shackled and manacled to the floor.

"A violent case," said the burly mad-keeper. "I dare not unlock the door."

He dared after all, but only upon receipt of a considerable bribe, and upon condition that he stand by the door with staff in hand.

In a trice Miss Cicely was kneeling by her uncle's side, putting her own cloak about him.

"Alas, how do you, Uncle?"

The eyes he turned upon her were clear and sane.

"Why, very well, dear love," he said. "I have learned what I came here to learn, and more too," he added wryly.

"What have you learned, Uncle?"

"I have learned how the poor madmen here are abused, aye and beaten too, when their poor addled wits make them obstreperous. That staff (nodding towards the blue-coat by the door) is not only for show."

"Alack, Uncle, have you been beaten?"

"Beaten? Aye, and blistered, physicked, drenched with cold water, denied my books, deprived of pen, ink, and paper. And all for a transport of justifiable anger."

"Anger at what?" enquired Dr. Johnson.

"At my nephew."

"Why, Uncle, what has Ned done?"

"Ned has cozened me. You must know, Dr. Johnson, I am as well in my wits as you are—save for my ill judgment in trusting Ned. You see, sir, Mr. Wesley and his followers are barred from visiting New-gate Gaol—lest they corrupt the inmates, I suppose—and from Bedlam Hospital, lest they make them mad. Well, sir, being deter-mined to know how matters went on behind these doors when they are closed, I resolved to make myself an inmate. I gave Ned—more fool me—my power of attorney and a letter that should enlarge me when I so desired, and by enacting a little comedy, with muslin wings, I got myself brought hither; in full confidence that Ned would see me released when I chose."

"Well, sir?"

"Well, sir, when I gave Ned the word to produce my letter and release me, this Judas Iscariot looks me in the eye, and says he, 'What letter? The poor man is raving.' All came clear in a flash. Ned has no intention of enlarging me. Why should he, when he has my power of attorney, and may make ducks and drakes of my fortune at his pleasure? Nay, he is my heir. What are my chances, think you, of coming out of here alive? Do you wonder I was ready to throttle the scoundrel? But they pulled me from him, and I have been chained down ever since. The keepers are bribed, I suppose. To my expostulations they turn a deaf ear. If not for Cicely, my plight need never have been known."

"Alack, Dr. Johnson," cried Cicely, "now what's to be done?"

"Have no fear, my dear. When next the Governors of the hospital meet, they shall hear the story, and he'll be released, I warrant you."

That very Saturday at nine of the clock we presented ourselves in the Court Room of the hospital. This handsome chamber is located abovestairs in the central pavilion, a gracious room with large windows overlooking Moorfields, a ceiling of carven plaster, and painted coats of arms about the walls.

Here sat the Governors, a stately set of men in full-bottom wigs and wide-skirted coats. My eye picked out Dr. John Monro, head surgeon, a formidable figure with bushy eyebrows, a belligerent snub nose, a short upper lip over prominent dog-teeth, a vinous complexion, and a bulldog cast of countenance; for upon his say-so, in the end, depended our friend's freedom or incarceration.

Four of us came to speak for him that morning: James Boswell, lawyer, Dr. Johnson, his friend, and Miss Cicely, his kinswoman—and to strengthen our ranks, we brought a medical man, Dr. Robert Levett, Dr. Johnson's old friend, who for twenty years had dwelt in his house and attended him at need. He was a little fellow of grotesque and uncouth appearance, his knobby countenance half-concealed by a bushy full-bottom wig. He wore a voluminous rusty black coat, and old-fashioned square-toed shoes to his feet. Thus ceremoniously attired, he came with us to speak as a physician in support of Mr. Silas Trevelyan's sanity.

Then they brought him in, and my heart misgave me. Gaunt, ragged, in chains, with his white hair on end—was this man sane? At his benevolent greeting to us, however, and his respectful bow to the committee assembled, I took heart again. As the blue-coated warders ranged themselves beside him, for fear of some disorderly outbreak, the gentlemen seated along the dais scanned him intently, and he looked serenely back.

Footsteps hurrying up the stair announced yet another participant, and nephew Edward Trevelyan appeared precipitately in the wide doorway—heir, attorney, and nearest of kin to the supposed madman, all in one.

The proceedings began. Dr. Johnson was eloquent, Dr. Levett earnest and scientifick, Miss Cicely modest and low-spoken. I was furnished forth with legal instances. Our one difficulty was in explaining how, if he was sane, our friend had gotten himself into Bedlam in the first place. We dared not say, in effect, "He came in voluntarily, as a spy." We skirted the subject, and concentrated upon his present state of restored sanity.

"We have now," said Dr. Monro, "only to hear from Mr. Edward Trevelyan, the inmate's attorney and kinsman. Mr. Trevelyan?"

Cousin Ned unfolded his length, rolled up his little eyes, and spoke softly in a deep resonant voice:

"Grieved I am to say it," he began, "my friends over there mistake my poor uncle's condition. He can be sly and plausible, sirs, but with me, whom he trusts,"—Old Mr. Trevelyan stiffened, and Cicely put a dismayed hand to her mouth—"with me he speaks otherwise. His brain still swarms with lunatick fancies. He proposes to get upon the roof and with his wings elude them all, and a good job too, says he, for the Governor is a puppy that wants a cannister to his tail, and Dr. Monro is a cork-brained clunch—"

With a roar the uncle broke from his keepers and flung himself upon his nephew.

"Thou prevaricating pup! Thou lying leech! Thou Judas! Where is my letter that I gave thee for my safety?"

"The man is mad," growled Dr. Monro. "Take him away, and let him be close confined."

We four met again next morning for breakfast in Johnson's Court. We shared a loaf, and little Levett brewed pot after pot of tea, for which Dr. Johnson's capacity was vast.

"And now," pronounced Dr. Johnson, setting down his cup at last, "what's to be done next for our incarcerated friend, Mr. Silas Trevelyan? He cannot stay where he is. Chains and fetters would soon drive the sanest man mad."

"If we could persuade the keepers he is sane?" suggested Miss Cicely timidly.

"After Dr. Monro's verdict," said I, "how can we so? We can never get him away openly."

"Then we must bring him away covertly," said Dr. Johnson. "Can you not, Mr. Boswell, devise some bam that shall bamboozle the keepers and set Mr. Silas free?"

"Let me think. What do you say, sir, if we take a leaf from Shakespeare, and deliver our friend, like Falstaff, in a bucking-basket of foul linen?"

"Chain and all?"

"True, there's the chain."

"Take a leaf from *Romeo and Juliet,* and they'll undo the chain fast enough, I warrant you," mused little Levett.

Johnson frowned; then smiled: "We'll try it."

Accordingly we spent the best part of the day concerting our measures and assembling our properties. As the afternoon wore on, our physician was furnished forth with a bagful of flasks and vials, clean linen, and money to spend, and so departed for Bedlam to acquaint Mr. Silas with our plan, and put things in motion. We set our rendezvous there for midnight.

Punctually at midnight, we two, escorting Miss, drove up to Bedlam gate in a hackney coach. A cart followed us, with a large pine box for freight. Instructing our Jehus to stand, we rang the porter's bell. That functionary presently appeared, rubbing sleep from his eyes.

We soon saw that our precursor had opened the way for us by his authority as a medical man, plus, I doubt not, a judicious outlay of cash bribes. When we named our stricken friend, Mr. Silas Trevelyan, the fellow looked grave, passed us up the stair, and went yawning back to his hole.

At the barred gate on the landing, a second blue-coated warder was ready with the keys. They hung by a loop at his broad leather belt. As he selected and turned the right one, I scrutinized him narrowly, for upon his behavior depended, in part, the success of our scheme.

The fellow was tall and muscular, as befitted one who was often called upon to grapple with lunaticks. Little squinting eyes in a broad doughy face gave him a look more dogged than quick. True to his looks, he dogged us close as we entered the ward.

The long shadowy corridor was empty; the madmen had all been sequestered for the night. Eerie noises attested to their presence behind the locked doors: a snore and a snort here, a patter of prayer there, an occasional howl or screech of laughter that shocked the ear.

One door only was open, whence faint candlelight fell along the floor. Dr. Levett stood in the doorway.

"Be brave, my dear," said he to Cicely, taking her hand. "He is very far gone, and turning black. He has sent for you, only to give

you his last blessing. Stand back, fellow (to the mad-keeper), these
moments are sacred."

The warder, looking solemn, took up his stance by the door, and
we passed within. Our friend Mr. Silas lay on his straw pallet, his
eyes turned up in his head. Out of respect for his obviously mori-
bund condition, his chains had been removed.

As Dr. Levett advanced the candle and pushed back the tangled
locks, I saw the awful, leaden blackness of the skin. Had I not been
prepared for it, I should have been shocked. Even prepared, Miss
Cicely clung to my hand as she whispered:

"How do you, Uncle?"

The dark eyes came into focus upon her.

"Ill, ill, my dear," he breathed. "The lawyer—is he here?"

"I am here, sir."

"Then write my last will—quickly. To my niece—everything to my
niece."

His head dropped back. Dr. Levett held a draught to his lips. I
drew forth my tablets and wrote down his bequest the briefest way.
Faltering fingers signed it, and Dr. Johnson added his firm neat
signature as witness.

"Take it, Cicely," murmured the testator. She slipped it into her
bodice. "And," the failing voice continued, "may Heaven bless you.
I forgive—"

The voice died, the white head dropped back, the jaw fell. Dr.
Levett touched the slack wrist. Swiftly he closed the eyelids and
drew the sheet over the darkened face.

"Our friend is no more," he pronounced gravely.

"What, dead?" ejaculated the mad-keeper, starting forward.

"Stand back!" cried Dr. Levett. "On your life, stand back! Such
a death has not been these hundred years in England, for our friend
is dead of the Black Plague! Look at his face—"

He flicked back the sheet and momentarily by the pale light of the
candle revealed the blackened countenance; at which the mad-
keeper started back with an oath.

"Now hark'ee, my friend," began Dr. Johnson portentously, "be
guided by me: were this known, there would be rioting within these
walls; what keeper would be safe? Do you but keep silence, all shall
be decently done by us, his friends. He shall be gone by morning,
and the episode forgotten. Nor shall you be the loser," he added,
fingering his pocket suggestively.

The fellow was stupid, which suited us; but so stupid that precious
moments went past while we strove to make him see the supposed
seriousness of the situation. Not so another keeper, a dark-visaged

fellow with a squint who happened by. Hearing that Mr. Silas Trevelyan had but now died of the Black Death, he at once clapped a dirty
handkerchief to his nose, and clattered off down the stair.

The first fellow was still mumbling when Dr. Levett settled the
matter. He advanced the candle, clapped a hand to the fellow's face,
and cried out:

"What, friend! 'Tis too late! You have taken the infection! You
are all of a sweat, and turning black! (And so he was, glistening with
ink from Levett's hand.) A clyster! Only a clyster will save you now!
This way! To your own quarters!"

Speaking thus urgently, the physician steered the terrified fellow
in the direction of his lair in the attick. We were left to do the last
offices for the "dead," who lay motionless, looking more risible now
than ever.

The supposed corpse was neatly laid out, cocooned in his winding
sheet, when Dr. Levett appeared in the gallery alone, chuckling.

"A good strong enema—that will take care of the keeper," said
he with a grin. "He'll be busy for a while. Come, let us go."

"Go!" cried Dr. Johnson. "Without the keeper, how are we to
make our way through the barriers?"

"With his keys," said Levett, and produced them. "A clyster is a
powerfully distracting operation. 'Twas child's play to get at the
keys, though under his nose."

"Well done, Dr. Levett. Come, let us go."

Among us we made shift to carry the sheeted body through the
barred gate, down the wide stair, and out at the portal, which the
largest key unlocked, not without an alarming screech. A snore from
the porter's lodge gave us Godspeed. Dawn light was graying the
sky as we lifted our burden into the waiting cart. We eased the
sheeted figure into the pine coffin. I lowered the lid, and Dr. Johnson screwed it lightly down.

"—in case we encounter the curious. 'Tis but until we get clear
of the grounds," he reassured his friend in an undertone.

I noted with approval that underneath the bow of crape that
mournfully adorned the lid, auger holes had been bored to provide
the "corpse" air to breathe.

The carter, a scrawny pockmarked boy, was regarding our proceedings between alarm and superstitious awe.

"Is he dead? I'll have no part in it! Give me my money and get
him out of my cart!"

By paying a double fee, we managed to retain the cart; but the
carter took to his heels. I must perforce take the reins. Miss elected
to share my lot. She could not be persuaded to leave her uncle in

my hands, but sat herself determinedly upon his coffin. Dr. Johnson and Dr. Levett mounted the hackney coach without us.

We had wasted precious time. Before we could drive off, we were intercepted. Two fellows came up at the run. One wore the blue coat of a mad-keeper. I recognized the swarthy keeper who had sheered off so quickly. Now it became clear: the fellow was one of Ned's tools and had run off, not to shun infection, but to inform; for his companion was Ned.

"Alas, my uncle!" said the false, mellifluous voice. "Why was I not notified? As his heir—"

"We have performed the last offices," said Dr. Johnson coldly from the coach, "and you shall hear further. We'll not bandy words at Bedlam gate. Drive on, Mr. Boswell."

I drove on.

How it fell out I know not, but I missed my rendezvous in the leafy walks of Moorfields. It was not the coach that overtook me, but a pair of footpads coming suddenly out of the shadows.

"Stand and deliver!"

A weapon glinted, and a rough hand pulled me from the high seat.

"Stay, you mistake," I cried; "here is no treasure chest—"

But the two fellows were up and slapping the reins, and off they went, cart and coffin and Miss and all; and as I stood dumbfounded, there floated back to me the girl's despairing cry:

"Cousin Ned!"

Here was calamity indeed. I could think of no better plan than to bellow "Stop thief!" which I did with a will. Wheels crunched on gravel, and the coach drew up beside me. Little Levett reached a hand and pulled me inside.

When he had heard my story, Dr. Johnson looked utterly grave.

"What have we done? We have delivered our friend, out of Bedlam indeed, straight into the hands of his enemy!"

"And his heir!" exclaimed Dr. Levett.

"No, sir," I corrected him. "Recall, sir, that as part of the comedy of the 'death bed,' I made his will. 'Everything to my niece.' The girl is his heir."

"But does her venal cousin know that?"

"She knows it," said Levett wryly. "She need not lift a finger. She has only to let him be buried, and his fortune is hers."

"Great Heavens!" I cried. "That innocent face!"

"Innocent faces have masked murderous hearts before now," mused Dr. Johnson. "*Vide* Mary Blandy, *vide* your own Katharine Nairn."

"I'll never believe it," said I stoutly.

"Believe it or no, we must act to save him, and quickly."

"The more quickly," said Levett urgently, "that in too slavish imitation of *Romeo and Juliet,* I have made him helpless with a sleeping draught."

"Thus, then, the matter stands," Johnson summed up. "The lawyer thinks himself the heir. Perhaps he supposes he is in possession of his uncle's corpse. If so, he will bury him, thus rendering him a corpse indeed. Perhaps he has unscrewed the coffin lid and found a sleeping man. What is to hinder him from quietly doing away with him? Either way, he looks to inherit."

"And perhaps he is in concert with Miss; they'll bury him and split the swag," suggested Levett.

I shook my head vehemently.

"We must find him," said Dr. Johnson. "There is one hope yet. No one at all will inherit, if the old gentleman is not known to be dead. They cannot inter him secretly. Come, let us make inquiries. They all dwell together in a house in Jasper Street. To Jasper Street, coachman."

Jasper Street was nearby. There all was silent. No cart stood before the door, but as we stood knocking, a manservant trudged up. He stared.

"Han't you heard? I have just carried the news to our nearest friends. The master is dead of a mighty infection. They daren't keep him. His sermon will be preached as soon as may be, and so they'll put him hastily under ground."

"Where, friend?"

"At the parish church, where else, St. Giles, Cripplegate."

Without further parley we drove off in haste. As we turned into the street called London Wall, we heard the great bell of St. Giles begin to toll. A few moments more, and we were there. The east transept door was nearest, and we entered in haste. A charnel-house smell seemed to taint the dusky air. It emanated from the opened vault before the Trevelyan monument, where soon the deceased must be inhumed.

Was he deceased? Within that plain pine coffin forward in the aisle, sleeping or waking, did he still live? Could we bring him off alive from this peril we had put him in?

My eye sought the chief mourner where he sat in his forward pew. Nephew Ned wore a black mourning cloak, and made play with a large cambrick handkerchief. Miss was not beside him.

Then I saw her, kneeling at the coffin foot in her dove-gray gown, clinging with both hands to the edge. As I looked, the sexton tried to detach her from this unseemly pose, but she shook her head and clung.

From the pulpit the sermon was already flowing over us in a glutinous tide. The deceased was a mirror of all the works of mercy, visiting the sick, the imprisoned, the distracted, and now gone to his reward in the blessed hope of the resurrection.

"For verily he shall rise again——"

Miss Cicely stood up suddenly. A long creaking rasp set my teeth on edge as the coffin lid was slowly pushed up, and a sheeted figure rose to a sitting position.

The parson gabbled a prayer, ladies shrieked, and Lawyer Trevelyan uttered a most unseemly curse.

Helped by Cicely, the supposed corpse put back his cerements and bowed to the startled company.

"I thank you, Reverend," said Mr. Silas coolly, "for your good opinion, and you, my friends, for paying me my honors, tho' prematurely. 'Tis too long a tale, how I came hither thus. Suffice it to say, I am neither dead nor mad, and I desire you will all join me at my house to break fast in celebration. You, nephew, need not come. You'll hear from me later. But you, dear niece, give me your hand. Come, friends, let us go."

So saying, in his madman's rags as he was, wearing his winding-sheet like a cloak, handing Miss Cicely, he led the way down the center aisle. We fell in behind him, and so the strange procession came to the house in Jasper Street. There the dumbfounded servants served the old gentleman his own funeral baked meats (hastily fetched from the nearby tavern).

Only when the general company had dispersed did we learn the full story of those hours between the time the coffin was stolen by nephew Ned, and the time we found it lying in the church to be preached over.

"The rattling of the cart awoke me," said old Trevelyan, "for your sleeping draught, sir (to Dr. Levett), was not so very strong. When I heard my nephew's voice, I knew my situation was precarious indeed. I kept silence, only thanking Dr. Johnson for his foresight in screwing down the lid."

"What is screwed may be unscrewed," remarked Dr. Johnson, "that was the most of my concern."

"That it was not," said Mr. Silas, "we may thank this brave girl here. She sat upon the lid, and would not stir, and between seeming stubborn grief and the menace of infection, she kept her cousin at a distance. She never budged from my side. Only after Ned had left my coffin in the aisle and was gone to instruct the parson and the sexton, did I hear the screws turn in the lid."

"How, with what, then, Miss Cicely, did you make shift to turn them?" asked Dr. Johnson.

"The scissors of a hussif, sir, have more use than snipping thread. But, sir," she went on, with a smile that irradiated her quiet face, "I dared not lift the lid while my cousin ruled. I still clung tight to the coffin, hoping, sir (to Dr. Johnson), for your arrival to protect us. When I saw you in the doorway, I whispered, 'Now, Uncle——' and the rest you know."

"A very pretty resurrection scene," remarked my friend with a smile.

" 'Tis not every man," added Mr. Trevelyan, "that lives to hear his own eulogy preached. I am your debtor, sir (to Dr. Levett), for that privilege. To you, gentlemen three, I owe my liberty; and to you, dear Cicely, having fallen into Ned's hands, I am well assured I owe my life. I have made you my heir in a mummery, my dear: you shall be so in earnest."

John Lutz, another newcomer to these pages, is at his best with the sort of wildly humorous story that's typified here. I'm still laughing.

JOHN LUTZ
Mail Order

Angela lay quite still. I watched her sleep. About her blond-streaked locks wound the black lace contraption that was supposed to protect her hairdo as she slept. An elastic chin strap was relentlessly working to keep her double chin from growing. Dark eyeshades covered the upper part of her face to keep the morning sun from waking her prematurely. I knew that beneath the special thermo-weave blanket was an intricately designed sleeping bra the purpose of which was to preserve her bosomy uplift. At the foot of the bed a wire framework beneath the covers lifted them tentlike eighteen inches above the mattress to prevent them from causing pressure on the toes that would lead to ingrown toenails and later serious foot problems. Lying open across Angela's softly heaving chest was the latest Happy House mail-order catalogue, its colorful pages riffling gently in the soft breeze from the air-conditioning vent near the bed.

Angela was a mail-order maniac. Almost every day some item featured in one of dozens of catalogues we regularly received would find its way into our mailbox or onto our front porch, while the checking account struggled for survival.

I had talked to her, explained to her, argued violently with her. What was the use? Like many other women, her mail-order addiction was too strong for her. The miniature watermelon plants, the inflatable picnic plates, the battery-heated ice cream scoops, and countless similar mail-order items continued to pour into our household. Angela was incurable and I was slowly being driven mad.

The electric scent dispenser that emitted a pleasant-smelling antiseptic spray every fifteen minutes hissed at me from my dresser as I bent down to lift the Happy House catalogue from Angela's sleeping form. Through some cross-up in the mail due to our having moved three times during the past two and a half years, this Happy House catalogue that had arrived two weeks ago was the only one we'd received during that time.

I don't know if you've ever seen what happens when you haven't ordered from one of these catalogues for a long time, but they become quite adamant that you should continue to buy from them. This one contained a particularly strong though typical warning printed on the back cover with our family name typed in to make it seem more personal—or more ominous.

"Final warning:" it was very officially headed. *"It comes to our attention,* Mr. and Mrs. Crane, *that you haven't ordered from our catalogue for the past two years. This is to warn you that we must have an order of at least five dollars from the* Crane *family NOW in order to maintain your account. Remember,* Mr. and Mrs. Crane, *this is your last chance—it's up to you!"*

As I was lifting the catalogue lightly, the doorbell rang, and I lowered the open pages again onto Angela and crossed the room to climb into my pants. Almost midnight, I noticed with a glance at the imported, family-crest clock as I tried to locate my slippers. I didn't know who could be on the porch, but I hoped they'd refrain from punching the doorbell again before I could reach the door. Even through her special sleep-aid earplugs the sound of the loud bell might wake Angela. As I straightened and buckled my belt I almost struck my head on the portable TV aerial attachment that allowed clear, free reception in any weather, then I hurried from the bedroom and down the hall to the front door, my slipper soles padding noisily across the carpet.

Just as I reached the foyer the bell clanged again, and I angrily flipped the night latch and opened the door.

They were in uniform. One of them carried a flashlight that he shone onto a little note pad as if double-checking the address.

"Mr. Harold Crane?" the tall one asked. He was trim and broad shouldered, with clean, anonymous features and short-cropped hair. His partner with the flashlight was much shorter, heavyset, with a blank moon face and long blond hair that stuck out from beneath his high-peaked, black uniform cap. Their uniforms were completely black; they wore gloves and black leather jackets with insignia on the shoulders.

"I'm he," I said, rubbing my eyes. I'd been sleeping on the sofa before going into the bedroom and my mind was still sluggish.

"Come with us, please," the taller man said in a clipped, pleasant voice.

In the moonlight I saw the initials P.D. on the short man's shoulder patch. "Are you police . . . ? Come with you . . . ?"

Both men took me gently by the upper arms and I was led toward a small, dark-colored van parked at the curb in front of my lawn.

"Just cooperate, please," the round-faced blond one said, lagging behind for a moment to close the front door softly behind us.

"Now, wait a minute . . . !" But the van doors were open and I was pushed gently inside. The two men climbed in behind me and closed the doors. The tall one tapped on a partition with his gloved knuckles and the van pulled away.

"I'm not even dressed!" I objected. I was wearing only my pants, slippers, and pajama top.

Neither man answered me, or even looked directly at me, only sat on either side of me on the low bench as the van sped through the dark streets.

We drove for almost an hour, and gradually my eyes became accustomed to the dim light in the van. I studied the uniform of the man on my left. He wore two shoulder patches on his black leather jacket, one of them a red circle with the yellow P.D. initials that I'd noticed earlier, and below the circle a blue triangular patch containing a white cloud and the initials H.H. I studied the black square-toed boots, the brass studwork designs on their glossy outer sides. I didn't have to be told that the P.D. on the patches didn't stand for "Police Department" as had originally run through my sleep-filled mind. I wasn't sleepy now.

"A kidnapping?" I asked incredulously. "You must have the wrong victim."

No answer.

"You'll find out," I said. "It's a mistake . . ."

"No mistake, Mr. Crane," the tall one said without looking at me.

The van suddenly braked to a smooth halt.

I could hear the crunching of footsteps on gravel as the driver got out and walked to the rear of the van. The van was opened and I was led quickly into what looked like a motel room, though in the darkness it was hard to tell. The closing of the room's door cut short the high trilling of crickets. The van driver, whose features I had never clearly seen, stayed outside.

The inside of the room was neat and impersonal, clean and modern with a small kitchenette. I was led to the kitchenette table and both men forced me down into a chair. The tall one sat opposite me across the small table while the pudgy, blond one remained standing, uncomfortably close to me.

"I'm Walter," the tall man said. "My partner's name is Martin."

"And you're not police," I said, braving it out despite my fear. "Just who the hell are you?"

"Police . . . ?" Walter arched an eyebrow quizzically at me from across the table. "Oh, yes, the P.D. on our shoulder patches. That stands for 'Persuasion Department,' Mr. Crane. We're from Happy House."

"Happy House? The mail-order company?"

Walter nodded with a smile. There would have been a suavity about him but for the muscularity that lurked beneath the shoulders of his leather uniform jacket. "We're one of the biggest in the country."

"In the world," Martin corrected beside me.

"This is absurd!" I said with a nervous laugh that sounded forced.

Martin pulled a large suitcase from beneath the table and opened it on the floor.

"Our records show it's been almost two years since your last order, Mr. Crane," Walter said solemnly.

"Actually it's my wife . . ."

Walter raised a large, silencing hand. "Didn't you receive our final warning notice?"

"Warning . . . ?"

"Concerning the infrequency of your orders."

"He knows what you're talking about," Martin said impatiently.

"Yes," Walter agreed, "I think he does. What's been the problem, Mr. Crane?"

"No problem, really . . ."

"But a problem to Happy House, Mr. Crane," Walter politely pointed out. "You see, our object is for our organization and our customers to be happy with our merchandise. And if we don't sell to our customers that's not possible, is it?"

"Put that way, no . . ."

"Put simply," Walter said, "since Happy House has to make a profit through volume to be able to keep on offering quality merchandise at bargain prices, in a way each customer's happiness is directly related to each other customer's continuing willingness to order from us."

"In a sense, I suppose that's true . . ."

"Here, Mr. Crane." Walter placed a long sheet of finely typed white paper on the table before me.

I stared at him. "What's that?"

"An order blank," he answered.

"Since you've been hesitant to order from our catalogue," Martin said, "we thought you might be more enthusiastic if we showed you the actual merchandise." From the suitcase on the floor he drew a flat red plaster plaque and set it on the table.

"What is it?" I asked, looking at the black sticklike symbols on the plaque.

"Why, it's your name, Mr. Crane. Your name in Japanese. A real conversation piece."

"Perhaps you missed it in our catalog," Walter said. "Only nine ninety-nine."

"No, thanks," I said, and I didn't even see Walter's gloved hand until the backs of the knuckles struck me on the jaw. I rose half out of my chair in rage only to be forced back down by the unbelievable pain of Martin digging his fingers skillfully into jangling nerve endings in the side of my neck.

"Of course you don't *have* to order the plaque," Walter said, smiling and laying a ball-point pen before me.

I picked up the pen and checked the tiny box alongside the plaque's description on the order form. Martin's paralyzing grip on my neck was immediately loosened.

Martin bent again over the large suitcase and came up with a coiled red wire with tiny brass clips on each end. "Everyone needs one of these," he said.

"I bought the plaque with my name in Japanese," I pleaded.

Walter smiled at me and began to pound his right fist into the palm of his left hand.

"I'll take it," I said, "whatever it is."

"It's a Recepto-booster," Martin explained. "You hook one clamp onto the aerial of your transistor radio, the other end you clamp onto your ear. Your entire body becomes a huge antenna for your portable radio."

"Only five ninety-nine," Walter said. "Two for ten dollars."

"I'll take two," I said, checking the appropriate box on the order form—but not any too happily.

"I thought you'd be receptive to that." Walter smiled.

A gigantic red-handled scissors with one saw-toothed blade was placed on the table next. "Our Jumbo Magi-coated Lifetime All Purpose Garden Shears," Martin said. "The deluxe chrome-plated model. You can cut or saw, trim grass or hedges, snip through inch-thick branches. Never needs sharpening. Twenty-nine ninety-nine."

"Twenty-nine ninety-nine!"

Walter appeared hurt. "It's made of quality steel, Mr. Crane." The back of his hand lashed across my cheek and I was the one who was hurt. This time I did not try to rise. I checked the order form.

The gigantic scissors was followed by inflatable rubber shoes over three feet long for walking on lake surfaces, an electric sinus mask, a urinal-shaped stein bearing the words "For The World's Biggest Beer Drinker," tiny battery-operated windshield wipers for eyeglasses, fingertip hot pads for eating toast . . . I decided I needed them all.

"Excellent," Walter said, smiling beneath his black uniform cap. "This will make the organization happy, and since we're part of the organization we'll be happy. And you, Mr. Crane, as one of our regular customers back in the fold, you'll be happier too."

I didn't feel happy at all, and indignation again began to seep through my fear.

"He doesn't look happy," Martin said, but Walter ignored him.

"Mr. Crane, I'm sure you'll feel better after you sign to make the order legal and binding," Walter said, motioning with a curt nod toward the ball-point pen.

"Better than if he doesn't sign," Martin remarked.

"But he will sign," Walter said firmly.

The sureness in his voice brought up the anger in me. "I won't sign anything," I said. "This is preposterous!"

"What about this?" Walter said, and with the flash of a silver blade severed the tip of the little finger on my left hand.

I stared down with disbelief and remoteness, as if it were someone else's hand on the table.

"This is our imported Hunter's Hatcha-knife," Walter was saying, holding up the broad-bladed, gleaming instrument. "It can be used for anything from scaling fish to cutting firewood." He wiped the blade with a white handkerchief, slipped the Hatcha-knife back beneath his jacket and tossed the handkerchief over my finger. Martin picked up the fingertip itself and dropped it into a small plastic bag as if it were something precious to him. He poked it into a zippered jacket pocket.

I held the wadded handkerchief about my left hand, feeling the dull throb that surprisingly took the place of pain. There was also surprisingly little blood.

"I'm sure Mr. Crane will sign the order form now," Walter said, picking up the pen and holding it toward me.

I signed.

"Now, how much money do you propose to put down?" Walter asked, and I felt Martin remove my wallet from my hip pocket. I only sat staring at Walter, trying to believe what had happened.

"Twenty-seven dollars," Martin said, returning my empty wallet to my pocket.

Walter turned the signed order form toward him and entered the twenty-seven dollars against the $210.90 that I owed.

Martin gathered all the merchandise I'd purchased and dumped it back into the suitcase.

"So you can carry everything, we'll throw in as a bonus our Traveler's Pal crushproof suitcase," Walter said.

As I stared at him blankly I heard myself thank him—I actually thanked him!

"I'm sure Mr. Crane will be a satisfied, regular customer we can count on," Walter said. "I'm sure we can expect an order from him . . . oh, let's say at least three times a year."

"At the very least," Martin agreed, helping me to my feet.

The ride home in the van was a replay of the first ride, and it seemed like only seconds had passed when I was left standing before my house with my heavily laden Traveler's Pal suitcase. Gripping the wadded handkerchief in place tightly with the fingers of my left hand, I watched the twin taillights of the van draw together and disappear as they turned a distant dark corner.

As I walked up the sidewalk past the trimmed hedges toward my front door I tried to absorb what had happened, to turn it some way in my mind so I could understand it. Had it really happened? Had it been a dream, or somebody's idea of a bloody, macabre joke? Or had it been just what it seemed—the unprovable, ultimate hard sell?

I knew I'd never find out for sure, and that whether or not Walter and Martin had really been from Happy House, the mail-order company could expect my regular orders for the rest of my life.

The Traveler's Pal suitcase heavy in my right hand, I entered the house and trudged into the bedroom, a deep ache beginning to throb up my left arm.

There was Angela, still sleeping in blissful unawareness with her eyeshades and sleep-aid earplugs. The Happy House catalogue was lying on her chest where I'd left it, the pages riffling gently in the soft breeze from the air-conditioning vent.

Angela didn't stir as I dropped the suitcase on the floor and the latches sprang open to reveal the assortment of inane merchandise I'd bought. The loud sob that broke from my throat startled me as I stared down at the contents of the suitcase. It was all so useless —all of it!

Except for the Jumbo Magi-coated Lifetime All Purpose Garden Shears. Oh, I had a use for them!

Captain Leopold went back home for the funeral of his Uncle Joe, and found himself more than just a mourner.

EDWARD D. HOCH
Captain Leopold Goes Home

Fletcher and Connie were at the office to see him off, their faces grim. "There's no need for tears," Captain Leopold told them both. "I haven't seen my uncle in something like twenty years. He was seventy-eight years old and he had a good life. I'll fly out for the funeral and be back in the office on Monday."

Fletcher walked him down to the street. "Don't you worry about a thing, Captain. Connie and I have everything under control. Stay as long as you want. It's been a slow month anyway."

That wasn't quite true because August was never slow for the Violent Crimes Division, but Leopold thanked him anyway. He waved goodbye as the taxi pulled away from the curb, taking him to the airport, and from there on to home.

Captain Leopold had always thought of Riger Falls as home even though he'd been born in Chicago and moved from Riger Falls to New York as soon as he was old enough to be on his own. The reason was Uncle Joe Leopold, who'd raised him like a son after the Captain's parents died. He'd gone to live with Uncle Joe when he was eight, and had taken the town of Riger Falls as his own.

Its shaded streets and quiet country atmosphere were a world away from the noisy, crowded avenues of Chicago, and the young Leopold welcomed the change. Now, flying back after all these years, he looked forward to the quiet as something close to a vacation. He tried to remember Uncle Joe's face the last time he'd seen him, back in the mid-fifties when Uncle Joe's wife died. She'd been almost like a mother to Leopold and her death had saddened Joe terribly. One of the greatest surprises of Captain Leopold's young life had come when he learned a year later that Uncle Joe had remarried.

He'd never met the second wife, though she was the one who'd signed the telegram informing him of his uncle's death. Her name was Margaret, and Leopold knew only that she was a good deal younger than Joe. When the plane landed and he saw from the bus schedule that he would not reach Riger Falls before dinner he phoned her from a booth at the airport.

"We're so glad you could come," her voice assured him. "Joe was always talking about you and what a success you've become in the east."

"He was like a father to me," Leopold said. "Look, I'll be there as soon as I can, but it'll probably be after seven. I'll take the next bus."

"Henry will meet you at the station. That's my son."

"Fine." He hung up and went out to wait for the next bus to Riger Falls.

In the long evening sunshine his first view of the town was a reassuring one. The trees, the streets, the houses were all as he remembered them. Progress had not yet polluted the place where he grew up. Farther on, near the center of town, he came upon one concession to change—a sprawling shopping center with a super-market and a drive-in movie. But even here the design of the place was muted, in keeping with its quiet surroundings. Riger Falls had always been a quiet town if nothing else.

A thin well-dressed man was waiting at the bus station and he introduced himself as Henry Cole. He was a few years younger than Leopold, perhaps still under forty, but he carried himself with a round-shouldered stoop that made him seem older. "I'm Mar-garet's son by her first marriage," he explained. "I live down the old Creek Road."

Leopold remembered the area—a dirt road lined with older houses that were little more than shacks. But that was a long time ago. Perhaps things were different now. "I haven't been back in twenty years," he told the man. "Haven't seen Uncle Joe in all that time."

"He was a fine old guy," Henry Cole said. "Too bad he had to die like that."

"How did he die?" Leopold asked. The telegram had given no details.

"Hit by a car on Tuesday, right in front of his house. They didn't think he was too bad at first, but at that age it was a terrible shock to his system. Died in the hospital yesterday morning."

"Who hit him?"

"Don't know. One of them wild kids from the next county, I suppose. That's what the sheriff says, anyway."

"You mean it was a hit-and-run?"

"That's what they say. My mother was in the house when it happened. She says he just went across the street to mail a letter and then she heard this car racing down the street. And then a thump. She says the car never even slowed down."

"Was he conscious? Could he say anything?"

"I don't know. You'd have to ask my mother." He turned the car into a gravel driveway. "Here we are. Raznell's Funeral Home."

Leopold looked out the car window at the familiar white Colonial structure. "Is Jerry Raznell still around?" Jerry had been his boyhood friend all through school, until Leopold moved away to New York.

"It's his place. The father died."

Inside, in a coffin surrounded by flowers, Uncle Joe Leopold lay at rest. Leopold said a brief silent prayer and then went over to the white-haired woman who stood with the other mourners. Though they'd never met, he recognized Margaret Leopold at once from the pictures Uncle Joe had sent him.

"So glad you could come," she said, extending her hand. "Joe would be so happy to know you're back home."

"I'm only sorry it took this to bring me back."

"He often spoke of you, and how successful you are." When she spoke, the lines of her mouth gave her a certain graceful air. Twenty years ago, about the time Uncle Joe married her, she would have been a beautiful woman. Even now, Leopold thought, she bore herself with a handsome dignity.

"Had he been retired for long?" Leopold asked, remembering Uncle Joe's fondness for the little woodworking shop on the highway.

"Only about a year. And even then he could have kept going in. His health was near perfect and he still loved furniture."

"Your son told me about the accident. A terrible thing. Do the police have any idea who was driving the car?"

"None. Maybe you should talk to the sheriff about it. He might like some help from a New York detective."

Leopold cleared his throat. "I started out in New York, but I've been up in Connecticut for a good many years now. Not nearly as large as New York. But maybe I will speak to him." Some others drifted in to pay their respects, and for a time Leopold was caught up in a flow of memories, hearing the old names, seeing the half-remembered faces. It was not until after nine that he could get away. Margaret Leopold asked him to stay at the house but he declined, preferring the freedom of a motel room.

"You can use my car overnight," Henry Cole volunteered. "Here are the keys."

Leopold hesitated. "I don't know—"

"Go ahead. It'll save me taking you to the motel and picking you up for the funeral."

Leopold accepted the keys with thanks. As he turned to leave, the familiar face of Jerry Raznell appeared in the doorway. "Leopold! Good to see you! I heard you'd flown out for the funeral."

"You haven't changed, Jerry," he said, and he meant it. Always a bit on the stocky side, Raznell's added weight had helped maintain the jolly boyishness of his face. He was hardly anyone's idea of the town undertaker.

"Nor have you. A little gray at the temples, but you still look pretty fit. How's the wife?"

Had it been that long since they'd seen or talked to each other? "It was a short marriage. We got a divorce and she's dead now."

"Oh. Sorry." The grin disappeared, but only for an instant. "Say, I'm just closing up here. How about stopping for a drink? Get caught up on all these years. I'd invite you upstairs but one of the kids is sick."

"I have to check in at a motel."

"No problem. I'll show you the way. It's new since you lived here."

The motel was on the other side of town, part of a nationwide chain that had somehow discovered the rural pleasures of Riger Falls. Leopold checked in, deposited his small overnight bag on the bed, and joined Jerry Raznell in the dimly lit cocktail lounge for a drink.

"It was a shock about your uncle, huh?"

"It should have been more of a shock," Leopold confessed. "In recent years I'd almost forgotten the old man's existence. And once he was a father to me."

"We all grow up and get old. My own father died seven years ago and left me the business."

"You seem to be doing well. I noticed a new wing on the house."

"People never stop dying."

"I hear Uncle Joe got it from a hit-and-run driver."

"Yeah. Awful thing."

"Are the police investigating?"

A shrug. "You know Sheriff Potter. No, on second thought, I guess you don't. He'd have been after your time. Well, he's a good enough man, but he has his own ideas. Wild kids from the next county, he says, and a lot of people believe him."

"I gather you don't."

"I'd rather not say."

"You think it was somebody here in Riger Falls?"

Jerry Raznell looked down at his hands. "You'd better ask the sheriff about that."

"I came here to attend a funeral, Jerry, not to investigate a killing."

"I know. I shouldn't have said anything."

"You didn't," Leopold told him. "Maybe you *should* say something."

"You'd better ask the sheriff," he repeated.

Leopold downed the rest of his Scotch. "I'll do that. Thanks for the drink, Jerry."

Sheriff Potter was not in his office, but the night deputy furnished his home address. Leopold phoned first and identified himself. Shortly after ten o'clock, when he parked Henry Cole's car in front of the sheriff's neat little ranch home, the man was waiting for him.

"The wife's having her bridge club," he explained. "Come on out in the garage."

It was a double garage with one side given over to a workbench and power tools. Sheriff Potter left the overhead door open while they talked, and large moths began to circle above their heads, risking their powdery wings against the attractive glow of the ceiling light.

With his curly black hair and dimpled chin, Potter did not look like a sheriff. He was too young for one thing, and when he spoke there was something like deference in his voice. "I've heard about you, Captain. Weren't you written up in *Law and Order* recently?"

"They ran an article on our department," Leopold admitted, "about how we converted the old homicide squad into a violent crimes unit."

"I read everything I can find about police work. Not that I have much call to use it in Riger Falls."

"I was wondering about my uncle's hit-and-run death. I understand it's still unsolved."

Sheriff Potter ran his hand over the smooth wood of the work table. "Well, not exactly unsolved. For one thing, the car didn't kill him right off, you know. He died a couple days later in the hospital. Case like that, in order to get an indictment we'd have to bring doctors before the grand jury to testify that the accident was the prime cause of death."

"Wasn't it?"

"Well, the man was seventy-eight years old. Doesn't take much to kill somebody at that age, you know. A broken hip, a sudden shock—"

"Do you know who was driving the car that hit him?"

"We get a lot of kids from the next county along that road, especially on these warm summer nights. My road patrol does the best it can, but you know how it is sometimes."

Leopold sighed. "Look, Sheriff, I've been back in town only three hours and a good friend tells me to ask you about my uncle's death. Well, I'm asking you."

Sheriff Potter scratched his head. "You gotta look at these things on balance sometimes. Your uncle was a good man, but he was seventy-eight years old. He'd lived a full life. Now if some young kids out joyriding hit him and caused his death, through no real fault of their own, should their lives be ruined by it?"

"That's an odd theory of law," Leopold said. "Is that what happened?"

"I don't know what happened."

"Didn't my uncle make a statement before he died?"

"Nothing we could use. He never saw the car that hit him."

Leopold could sense he was getting nowhere with the man. If there was something strange and hidden about his uncle's death, this was not the place to learn about it. "All right," he said, starting for the door. "Nice meeting you."

The sheriff walked him out to the borrowed car. "How long you expect to be in town?"

"I'll be leaving after the funeral," Leopold said. "Sometime tomorrow."

The following morning Leopold's cousin Sara arrived in town for the funeral. She was a handsome woman in her mid-forties, a wealthy widow who had been involved in one of Leopold's cases a few years earlier. "You're looking good, Sara," he said, greeting her with a cousinly kiss.

"And so are you. It's good to see you again."

They entered the funeral parlor and he nodded to Jerry Raznell, attired in a black coat and gray striped pants, looking a bit more like a smiling best man at a marriage ceremony than a funeral director. Margaret Leopold was already seated, but she rose to greet Sara and a few other arrivals. Her son Henry Cole was not yet present.

"I'll want you to ride with me in the first car," Margaret said to Leopold. "You were very close to Joe."

He nodded and sat down next to her. Jerry Raznell came in after a few moments and said a brief prayer. Then he began reading off the list of cars and occupants. Henry Cole was behind the wheel of the first car when they reached it. He nodded to Leopold, came out, and held the door open for his mother. As Leopold climbed in he saw a blue and white sheriff's car at the end of the line. He wondered if Potter was inside it.

The service at the graveside was brief and nonsectarian. Leopold found himself standing next to cousin Sara and when it was over she said, "Will you buy me lunch? I'd feel uneasy going back to the house."

"Of course. There used to be a nice restaurant out by the falls." He drove back with Cole and Margaret to the house, then borrowed Cole's car again with the promise to return it shortly. Sara was waiting for him back at the funeral parlor.

"I'd forgotten how weird this town was," she said as she settled into the seat next to him.

"It never seemed weird to me."

"Well, that's because you lived here. I was only a summer visitor. One of the outsiders."

He drove her to the Fall View Inn, a rambling old place that had been the town's best restaurant in his youth. The prices were high, but a certain seediness had begun to set in. The antique furniture that greeted them at the entrance was covered with dust just a little too thick for mere atmosphere. The falls were still there, of course, dropping the slim trickle of water that gave the town its name.

"It was a nice service," she said. "Short and simple."

"Did you hear anything about how he died?"

"A car accident, someone said."

"Hit-and-run. He was crossing the street outside his house."

"How terrible! Even a small town like this isn't safe from it."

"I think there was something odd about his death, Sara."

"In what way?"

"I think the sheriff knows who was driving that car. But for some reason he's not doing anything about it."

She smiled at his words. "Perhaps you're just too much of a detective."

"Maybe."

"You see things where there's nothing to be seen."

He ate his lunch in glum silence after that, wondering if she could be right.

The others had gathered back at the Leopold home, in the post-funeral tradition, and Leopold and Sara joined them shortly after lunch. Sheriff Potter was there, all boyish charm, chatting with an older woman on the front porch as he sipped beer from a glass.

"Good to see you again, Leopold. Thought you might have started back before I could say goodbye."

"No, I'm still here."

The older women took Sara in tow and they disappeared into the house. Leopold and Sheriff Potter were left alone on the porch. "I think Margaret's taking it quite good," the sheriff remarked. "At least she has her son to take care of her."

"Tell me about Henry Cole. He said he lives out on Creek Road."

"That's right. Got a nice place out there. Henry's a druggist in town. Owns his own store and works hard at it every day."

"I've been driving his car around." He glanced out at the car and for the first time he noticed a dent in the front bumper where the sunlight was hitting it. He made a mental note to examine it more closely later.

"It's been sort of the family vehicle since your uncle lost his license. Margaret never did drive."

"How did he lose his license?"

"It happened last year. He went off the road at a curve and hit a fruit stand. No one was hurt and it was sort of funny, really. But he'd had some other minor accidents before that and his age was against him. The state revoked his license. So since then Henry's been driving them around."

But Leopold was only half listening to the words. He was staring across the street. Suddenly he said, "Sheriff, tell me what you see over there."

"See? What do you mean? Can't you see for yourself?"

"I want to know what you see."

"A house. A couple of vacant lots."

"What else? Tell me everything."

"Two lamp posts. A fire hydrant. A Rotary Club sign."

"What else?"

"Nothing else. What are you talking about?"

"Maybe nothing," Leopold said. He left the porch and went down the front walk to the street. Finally he came back onto the porch. "You mentioned the kids in the next county. What made you suspect them?"

Sheriff Potter shifted uneasily. "Are you back on that again?"

"If I can't get the answer from you, I'll get it from the sheriff over there."

"All right," he said with a sigh. "There was a hit-and-run death over in Sedgeville the same day Joe Leopold got it. Probably just coincidence, but I guess I figured the same wild driver did them both."

"Who was killed in Sedgeville?"

"A kid. I don't know any more about it."

Sara reappeared on the porch with Margaret Leopold. "Margaret's going to show me the garden. Want to come?"

"Sure," he agreed, glancing at the sheriff.

"You people go ahead," Potter said. "I have to get back to the office anyway. These summer weekends really bring out the drivers."

Leopold sensed that Potter was anxious to escape his questions. He followed the two women into the backyard, watching while the white-haired Margaret pulled a carrot from the earth and offered it for his inspection. "This garden was always Joe's pride," she said, a sadness in her voice. "I don't know how I'll be able to keep it up without him."

Leopold looked down the rows of flowers, past the leafy vegetables and the cornstalks that reached to his head. He remembered the garden from the days of his youth. It had always been here, always the same yet always changing. Reborn each spring.

"I must be going," Sara told the white-haired woman. "I only drove down for the funeral."

Margaret cut a few flowers and handed them to her. "I'm a widow now, like you. I hope I can be as brave as you've been."

Sara took the flowers and looked away. "I must be going," she said again.

Leopold fell into step beside her. "I'll walk you to the car."

"I was never any good at funerals," she said when they were out of Margaret's hearing. "That's why I wouldn't come back for lunch. I never know the right thing to say."

"Do any of us?" Leopold asked. "I spend my life on the other side. I'm usually concerned with who did it, but not who it happened to."

"That sounds like you think he was murdered."

"The word hasn't been mentioned."

"Are you flying back today?"

Leopold stared at the sky, debating. "First I'm going to visit another bereaved family," he decided. "Over in Sedgeville."

The Flynn house was quiet when he reached it, still driving the borrowed car. It sat subdued in the sunshine of a Saturday afternoon, an island of tranquillity unbothered by the shouting children at a ballgame just down the street.

Leopold mounted the porch and knocked gently on the screen door, seeing that the front door stood open to the warmth of the day. After a moment a gaunt middle-aged woman appeared and spoke to him through the screen. "Yes?"

"I read in the papers about the accident to your son."

"The funeral was yesterday. Who are you?"

"My name is Leopold. I was visiting over in Riger Falls. Could I come in for a moment?"

"No. My husband isn't here. I'm alone."

"Certainly," he said. "I just wanted to ask a few questions about the accident. It happened on Tuesday, I believe."

"Yes."

"Here, near the house?"

She nodded. "Right in front. He was running across the street to mail a letter for me, and of course he didn't look where he was going. He never looked." Her eyes were staring past him, seeing it again. "Who are you?"

"Did the driver stop?"

"He slammed on his brakes, but it was too late. When he saw he'd hit him, he kept on going."

"I'm sorry, Mrs. Flynn."

Her eyes refocused on his face. "It was you, wasn't it? You killed him and now you've come back!"

"No, it wasn't me. Goodbye. I'm sorry."

As he retreated from the porch she opened the screen door and started after him. "It *was* you! I remember that car!"

He opened his wallet and showed her the badge. "I'm investigating the case." That stopped her and she stood looking at him uncertainly, squinting with the afternoon sun in her eyes. "Now what about the car?" he asked.

"It was like yours. I saw it going away down the street. It was the same color."

"I see."

"Is it the same car?"

Leopold looked out at the little beige sedan by the curb. "I don't know," he answered truthfully.

On the way back to Riger Falls he pulled off the road under a stand of leafy maple trees and parked. He got out of the car and went around to the front of it, kneeling in the dirt to examine the dented bumper. He could see now that the dent extended into the chrome grillwork as well, and that it was recent. The exposed metal had not yet begun to rust.

While he was still on his knees studying it, another vehicle went by and slowed down, coming to a stop about fifty feet ahead. It was a hearse, and Jerry Raznell got out from the driver's side. "What's the matter?" he called. "Have a breakdown?"

Leopold got to his feet, brushing the dirt from his knees. "No, it's okay. I was just looking at the front of the car."

Raznell walked up to him and glanced down at the dented front end. "Did you have an accident?"

"No. It was like that."

"Henry Cole's car, isn't it?"

"Yes."

The undertaker grunted. "What are you going to do about it?" he asked.

Leopold met his eyes and something passed between them, something from the old days when they had been friends. "What do you think I should do?"

"Did you talk to the sheriff?"

"He told me nothing."

"He must have told you something. You were on your way back from Sedgeville."

"Yes," Leopold admitted. "He told me that much."

"Where you heading now?"

"I guess I'll take the car back to Henry Cole." He was staring down at the dented front end. "What do you think he ran into?"

Jerry Raznell shrugged. "A tree. A small tree."

"Or a small boy? Or an old man?"

"You really think that?"

"Don't you?"

"No."

"Mrs. Flynn recognized the car."

"Who's Mrs. Flynn?"

"I found her name in the paper. Her son was killed by a hit-and-run driver on Tuesday."

"The same day Joe Leopold was hit."

"That's right. Jerry, why are we talking in circles? We were friends once. Good friends."

"You should be heading back home soon."

"I am home, Jerry. This is my home. I came back."

"But only for the day, only for the funeral. The rest of us have to stay here after you're gone."

Leopold turned and walked around to the car door. "I'm going to see Henry Cole," he said.

As he pulled away, Jerry Raznell was still standing by the side of the road. In his rearview mirror Leopold saw him start slowly back toward his hearse.

Henry Cole, the stoop-shouldered druggist, was still at the Leopold house when he pulled up. "I brought your car back in one piece," he said, greeting the man in the front yard.

"Sure did. But I wasn't worried."

"I don't want you to think I put that dent in the front end of your car."

"No, I wouldn't think that. Did it myself last week."

"How'd it happen?"

The man glanced away, obviously nervous. "I—I bumped into another car."

"No."

"What?"

"No," Leopold said. "That's not the way it happened. Do you want to tell me the truth now?"

"I gotta be going," he said quickly. He snatched the keys from Leopold's hand and hurried to the car.

Margaret Leopold came out to the porch. "Why'd he leave in such a hurry?"

"I asked him a question he wouldn't answer," Leopold said.

The others had all departed and the house was empty now, except for the two of them. "What question was that?"

"How the front of his car got dented."

"Come up here on the porch, where we can talk. It's been a long day for me."

"A long day for all of us," Leopold conceded. He chose a wicker chair opposite her and sat down. "My cousin Sara says I'm too much of a detective, that I see things where there's nothing to be seen."

"And do you?"

Leopold shook his head. "Quite the opposite, really. I don't see things where there is something to be seen."

"What don't you see?"

"The mailbox across the street."

"What?" Her forehead creased with wrinkles. "What do you mean?"

"I stood out here this afternoon and asked Sheriff Potter everything he saw across the street and he told me. There's no mailbox. I went out to the street and looked both ways, and there was still no mailbox. And yet you told your son Henry that Uncle Joe was crossing the street to mail a letter."

"I——"

"It's a very odd lie, really, because anyone around here looking across the street would see there's no mailbox over there. I thought about that a long time, and then this afternoon Sheriff Potter mentioned another hit-and-run accident in Sedgeville the same day. I drove over there and saw the mother of the boy who was killed—Mrs. Flynn."

Her face had gone white as chalk. Her hands gripped the wicker arms of the chair. "You saw her?"

Leopold nodded. "She told me her son was running across the street to mail a letter, and then of course I was pretty sure what happened. The driver of the car slammed on the brakes, but too late. There must have been an image there in the driver's eyes of a boy darting off the curb, clutching an envelope in his hand. And he told that to you, didn't he? His image became your image, and when it came time to tell about Uncle Joe's accident, you used those same words. Letter in hand, crossing the street."

"You know it all, don't you?"

"I know it all. The recent dent in the bumper, Mrs. Flynn's description of the car. And both accidents the same day. It couldn't be coincidence. I only had to ask myself who was driving that day. Your son Henry would have been working at the drugstore, and even if he hadn't been—could we imagine him lending me his car knowing what had caused that dent? No, not Henry. And not you, of course, because you never drove. And that only left one person, didn't it?"

She stared out at the trees, and at the evening sun caught in their branches. "Yes," she answered after a while. "It was your Uncle Joe who killed the boy."

"Tell me about it, Margaret," he said quietly.

"There's not much to tell, not really. He wanted to go over to Sedgeville to look at some antiques he'd seen advertised. You know how he was about woodworking and fine old furniture. Well, Henry was busy at the drugstore and couldn't take him. But the car was here as it often was, and Joe decided to drive over there himself. He'd driven a few times since losing his license, but never as far as that. I was sick about it, but he went anyway. When he came back —" Her voice broke and Leopold put out a hand to steady her.

"Go on," he urged.

"When he came back he looked horrible. He was bleeding from the mouth and his clothes were covered with spots of blood. He said he'd hit a boy who was crossing the street to mail a letter. He'd slammed on the brakes at the last moment, and injured his own chin and mouth on the steering wheel. But then he'd panicked and kept on going, because he was driving without a license. I guess it was all that blood gave me the idea for another hit-and-run accident in front of our house. I had to protect him somehow."

"So you called for an ambulance and they took him to the hospital."

She nodded. "They said he wasn't hurt bad, but the shock of what he'd done had set in. I had to get him away. I told Henry some lie about the bumper and he never questioned it, never connected it with the accident in the next county."

"Sheriff Potter knew," Leopold said.

"Oh, yes. He's a smart young man. He knew. The Sedgeville police contacted him, of course, and he had a description of the car. He talked to the doctors at the hospital about the nature of Joe's injuries, and he guessed what had happened. He told me he would have to arrest Joe."

"And he would have, if Uncle Joe hadn't died first."

"Yes." She looked away, perhaps toward the garden in the back-yard, and her firm hands tightened on the wicker chair. "I got to the hospital ahead of the sheriff to warn Joe. But they'd given him a sedative and he was sleeping. He just—never woke up."

It was almost dark, and Leopold had to be getting back. Perhaps he could still catch the bus to the airport and a night flight home.

He stood up and said, "I must be going. There's nothing more for me here."

"No. It was good of you to come."

He paused at the steps. "Potter isn't the only one who knows. Jerry Raznell knows, too."

She nodded. "Jerry uses the hearse as an ambulance. He took Joe to the hospital after—after I said the car hit him. He was suspicious then. I think he talked to the sheriff."

She seemed suddenly old to his eyes, older than yesterday when he'd come to Riger Falls. "I suppose it's a blessing this way," Leopold said. "At his age the trial would have killed him. Or just the publicity, even if it never got to trial."

"I know," she said. "I thought of that, too."

He kissed her lightly on the cheek and went down the steps without looking back. He did not ask the meaning of her last words, because he knew. Now, remembering Jerry Raznell's suspicions, remembering his uncle's sudden death from those minor mouth injuries, remembering most of all her firm hands and the way they tightened on the chair, he knew there was one question he could never ask Margaret Leopold.

He could never ask her if, alone with Uncle Joe in that hospital room, she'd held a pillow over his sleeping face until the life drained from his old body, just minutes before Sheriff Potter arrived to arrest him.

The Yearbook of the Detective Story

Abbreviations: *EQMM*—Ellery Queen's Mystery Magazine
                          AHMM—Alfred Hitchcock's Mystery Magazine
                          MSMM—Mike Shayne Mystery Magazine
                          EXMM—The Executioner Mystery Magazine
                          87MM—87th Precinct Mystery Magazine

BIOGRAPHY
JACK RITCHIE

Jack Ritchie, whose real name is Jack Reitci, was born in Milwaukee, Wisconsin on February 26, 1922. He attended Milwaukee State Teachers College for two years, then enlisted in the Army during World War II. He returned to civilian life after more than three years' service and went to work in his father's tailor shop. It was not until age thirty-one that he started to write.

The year was 1953 and Jack engaged a Milwaukee literary agent, Larry Sternig, to help market his stories. His first sale was a humorous short story to New York's *Daily News,* which at that time used a story each day, and he was paid $50 for it. That New Year's Eve, Larry Sternig introduced Jack to another of his clients, Rita Krohne. Jack and Rita were married within a year, and they've both been writing ever since.

Rita Ritchie specializes in well-researched novels for teens, usually with historical backgrounds. She published a short-short story in *Manhunt* twenty years ago under another name, and collaborated with Jack once on a science fiction short-short, but otherwise their fields have never overlapped.

When they were first married the Ritchies lived in a log cabin on an island in Wisconsin. They later moved to a farmhouse in Fort Atkinson and now live in Whitewater, Wisconsin. The oldest of their four children was married in the summer of 1975.

When the children were small, Jack used to arise at 3 A.M. each day to do his writing. Now that they're older he keeps to a more ordinary schedule. He has written some 400 short stories of all types, though in recent years he has concentrated almost exclusively on mystery and crime stories. Four of his stories were dramatized on TV's *The Alfred Hitchcock Show* in the 1960s and others have been seen on Canadian television. Elaine May directed a feature film, *A New Leaf* (1971), produced from a Ritchie short story. But important scenes were cut from the film before release, and neither Jack nor Elaine was satisfied with the finished product.

Ritchie much prefers writing short stories to novels, but he has been working on a first novel which he hopes to finish soon. Until then there is only one book in the Jack Ritchie bibliography: *A New Leaf and Other Stories* (Dell, 1971), with an introduction by Donald E. Westlake.

In *Best Detective Stories of the Year,* fourteen Jack Ritchie stories have been published under his own name and one (in the 17th Annual Collection) under the pseudonym Steve O'Connell.

Ernest M. Hutter, who bought many of Jack's stories as editor of *Alfred Hitchcock's Mystery Magazine,* says of him, "Jack Ritchie is truly one of the masters of storytelling. He possesses a gigantic subtle wit in a succinct style which may be described best by a line from one of his own stories: 'I had the feeling (he) could have written *War and Peace* on the back of a post-card.' "

Or, as the late Anthony Boucher once wrote, "Jack Ritchie is consistently one of the most original writers (and possibly the most economic) in the crime-fiction magazines."

BIBLIOGRAPHY: 1975

I. Collections

1. Alcott, Louisa May: *Behind a Mask: The Unknown Thrillers of Louisa May Alcott.* New York: William Morrow & Co. Four novelettes originally published between 1863 and 1867, two of them under the pseudonym of "A.M. Barnard." With a long introduction by Madeleine Stern.

2. Bramah, Ernest: *Max Carrados.* Westport, Connecticut (45 Riverside Street): Hyperion Press. First American edition of this classic 1914 collection about fiction's first blind detective; one of a series of hardcover Hyperion reprints selected from books listed in *Queen's Quorum.*

3. "Carter, Nick": *Nick Carter 100: Dr. Death.* New York: Award Books. The 100th novel in Award's new Nick Carter series, together with a reprinting of the first novel in the Award series and one of the original Nick Carter short stories—this last introduced by J. Randolph Cox.

4. Charteris, Leslie: *Catch the Saint.* New York: Doubleday & Co. Two short novels about the Saint, introduced by Charteris, but actually written by a collaboration of Norman Worker and Fleming Lee.

5. Ellin, Stanley: *Kindly Dig Your Grave and Other Wicked Stories.* New York: Davis Publications. A short novel and ten stories from *EQMM,* 1963–1973.

6. Ellison, Harlan: *No Doors, No Windows.* New York: Pyramid Books. Sixteen suspense stories, 1956–1975, including the winner of the 1974 MWA Edgar award. Pyramid also reissued two collections of Ellison's crime tales, *The Deadly Streets* (1958) and *Gentleman Junkie* (1961), with new stories added.

7. Gibson, Walter: *The Shadow: The Mask of Mephisto & Murder by Magic.* New York: Doubleday & Co. Two short novels from *The Shadow Magazine* (1945), with an introduction by the author. See also #9 below.

8. Goulart, Ron: *Odd Job #101 and Other Future Crimes and Intrigues.* New York: Charles Scribner's Sons. Seven science fiction crime stories.

9. "Grant, Maxwell" [Walter B. Gibson]: *The Crime Oracle & The Teeth of the Dragon: Two Adventures of the Shadow.* New York: Dover Publications. Two novels from *The Shadow Magazine* (1936–1937), with informative introductions by the author and by his editor, John L. Nanovic. Includes the original magazine illustrations.

10. LeFanu, J.S.: *Ghost Stories and Mysteries.* New York: Dover Publications. Ten ghost stories and four mysteries, including an early locked-room tale. E.F. Blieler's introduction contains much informative material on LeFanu's mystery novels.

11. Lehmann, R.C.: *The Adventures of Picklock Holes.* Boulder, Colorado. (Box 4119): The Aspen Press. First American edition of a 1901 collection of eight Sherlockian parodies from *Punch.*

12. Stribling, T.S.: *Best Dr. Poggioli Detective Stories.* New York: Dover Publications. Fifteen stories from *EQMM* and *The Saint Detective Magazine* (1945–1957).

13. Wellman, Manly W., and Wellman, Wade: *Sherlock Holmes' War of the Worlds.* New York: Warner Books. Five connected stories, some from *Fantasy & Science Fiction,* in which Holmes and Professor Challenger foil the Martian invasion described by H.G. Wells.

II. Anthologies

1. Fish, Robert L., editor: *Every Crime in the Book.* New York: G.P. Putnam's Sons. Twenty-five stories, two published for the first time, in the annual anthology from Mystery Writers of America.

2. Hitchcock, Alfred, editor: *Alfred Hitchcock Presents: Stories to Be Read with the Door Locked.* New York: Random House. Twenty-nine stories, reprinted mainly from magazine sources.

3. _____, editor: *Grave Business.* New York: Dell Publishing Co. Fourteen stories from *AHMM,* 1959–1972.

4. _____, editor: *Murderers' Row.* New York: Dell Publishing Co. Fourteen stories from *AHMM,* 1961–1973.

5. _____, editor: *Murder Racquet.* New York: Dell Publishing Co. Fourteen stories from *AHMM,* 1959–1972.

6. _____, editor: *Speak of the Devil.* New York: Dell Publishing Co. Fourteen stories from *AHMM,* 1959–1973.

7. Hubin, Allen J., editor: *Best Detective Stories of the Year–1975.* New York: E.P. Dutton & Co. Twenty of the best crime stories published in the U.S. during 1974.

8. Kahn, Joan, editor: *Open at Your Own Risk.* Boston: Houghton Mifflin Co. Eighteen stories of mystery and horror, plus seven fact crime essays, from a wide variety of sources.

9. Liebman, Dr. Arthur, editor: *Quickie Thrillers.* New York: Pocket Books. Twenty-five brief tales of crime, horror, and fantasy.

10. Manley, Seon, and Lewis, Gogo, editors: *Ladies of the Gothics: Tales of Romance and Terror by the Gentle Sex.* New York: Lothrop, Lee & Shepard. Ten stories from the nineteenth and twentieth centuries.

11. _____, editors: *Masters of the Macabre: An Anthology of Mystery, Horror and Detection.* New York: Doubleday & Co. Seventeen stories covering a wide range, from Mary Shelley to Ellery Queen.

12. Norris, Luther, editor: *The Non-Canonical Sherlock Holmes.* Culver City, California (Box 261): Luther Norris. Three short pastiches, with an introduction by Julian Wolfe.

13. Queen, Ellery, editor: *Ellery Queen's Anthology, Spring-Summer, 1975.* New York: Davis Publications. Fourteen stories in a semiannual softcover anthology from *EQMM.* (Hardcover edition, *Ellery Queen's Aces of Mystery,* New York: Dial Press.)

14. _____, editor: *Ellery Queen's Anthology, Fall-Winter, 1975.* New York: Davis Publications. Fifteen stories in a semiannual softcover anthology from *EQMM.* (Hardcover edition, *Ellery Queen's Masters of Mystery,* New York: Dial Press.)

15. _____, editor: *Ellery Queen's Murdercade.* New York: Random House. The 29th annual hardcover anthology from *EQMM,* containing twenty-three stories from 1973 issues.

16. Slung, Michele B., editor: *Crime on Her Mind.* New York: Pantheon. Fifteen stories of female sleuths from the Victorian era to the 1940s, with introductions by Ms. Slung and a descriptive catalogue of over 100 women detectives, 1861–1974.

III. Miscellaneous Nonfiction

1. Barnes, Melvin P.: *The Best Detective Fiction: A Guide from Godwin to the Present.* Hamden, Connecticut (995 Sherman Avenue): Shoe String Press. A "narrative bibliography."

2. Coppola, Francis Ford, et al., editors: *Dashiell Hammett's San Francisco.* San Francisco, California (531 Pacific Avenue): City Publishing Co. A special issue of *City of San Francisco* magazine (November 4, 1975), published by Coppola, edited by Warren Hinckle, Coppola, et al., containing articles on Hammett by Joe Gores, William Nolan and others; an interview with Hammett's widow; and an unpublished partial first draft of *The Thin Man,* originally set in San Francisco.

3. Courtine, Robert J.: *Madame Maigret's Recipes.* New York: Harcourt Brace Jovanovich. A cookbook containing more than 100 recipes associated with the Simenon characters, with a letter-preface by Simenon.

4. Dakin, D. Martin: *Holmesian Clerihews.* Culver City, California (Box 261): The Pontine Press. A chapbook of seventy-five short poems about characters in the Sherlock Holmes stories.

5. East, Andy: *Andy East's Agatha Christie Quiz Book.* New York: Drake Publishers. Some 300 questions and answers about the Christie canon.

6. Feinman, Jeffrey: *The Mysterious World of Agatha Christie.* New York: Award Books. A brief study of Agatha Christie's life and work. Among the book's many errors is a "complete bibliography" which unaccountably omits four of Dame Agatha's sixty-five mystery novels.

7. Hahn, Robert W., editor: *Sincerely, Tony; Faithfully, Vincent: The Correspondence of Anthony Boucher and Vincent Starrett.* Lombard, Illinois (509 S. Ahrens): Robert W. Hahn. A commemorative chapbook issued by Bouchercon VI.

8. Harrison, Michael: *The World of Sherlock Holmes.* New York: E.P. Dutton & Co. Speculations on the life of the great detective.

9. Hitchman, Janet: *Such a Strange Lady.* New York: Harper & Row. A brief biography of Dorothy L. Sayers, creator of Lord Peter Wimsey.

10. Menendez, Albert J.: *The Sherlock Holmes Calendar.* New York: Drake Publishers. A calendar for 1976, showing dates of importance in the Holmes stories.

11. _____. *The Sherlock Holmes Quizbook.* New York: Drake Publishers. Thirty-four short quizzes about various aspects of the Holmes stories.

12. Pointer, Michael: *The Public Life of Sherlock Holmes.* New York: Drake Publishers. A description and a catalogue of all dramatizations of the Holmes exploits—on stage, screen, radio, television and records.

13. Queen, Ellery, editor: *Ellery Queen's 1976 Mystery Calendar.* New York: Harper & Row. A calendar featuring 135 rare photographs of mystery writers past and present, plus birth dates and other information.

14. Weinberg, Robert, editor: *The Whisperer.* Oak Lawn, Illinois (10533 S. Kenneth): Robert Weinberg. An editorial, an essay by Will Murray, and a 1938 short story by Clifford Goodrich about a minor pulp hero patterned after The Shadow. Weinberg also publishes a series of reprints of classic pulp novels from the 1930s.

15. Wright, Sean & Farrell, John: *The Sherlock Holmes Cookbook.* New York: Drake Publishers. Recipes for Holmes' favorite concoctions.

AWARDS

Mystery Writers of America
Best novel—Brian Garfield, *Hopscotch* (M. Evans)
Best American first novel—Rex Burns, *The Alvarez Journal* (Harper & Row)
Best short story—Jesse Hill Ford, *The Jail (Playboy)*

Crime Writers Association
  Gold Dagger—Nicholas Meyer, *The Seven-Per-Cent Solution* (Hodder &
  Stoughton/E.P. Dutton & Co.)
  Silver Dagger—P.D. James, *The Black Tower* (Faber & Faber)
  John Creasey Memorial Award (for the best first crime novel)—Sara
  George, *Acid Drop* (Macmillan)

NECROLOGY

1. Aarons, Edward S. (1916–1975). Prolific author of eighty mystery and
   crime novels, including some first published as by "Edward Ronns"
   and "Paul Ayres." Creator of C.I.A. agent Sam Durell who starred in
   forty paperback spy novels.
2. Barry, Jerome (1894–1975). Author of seven novels, 1941–1962, some
   about series character Chick Varney.
3. Blochman, Lawrence G. (1900–1975). Foreign correspondent and
   well-known mystery writer. Creator of Dr. Daniel Webster Coffee,
   whose short cases are collected in *Diagnosis: Homicide* (1950) and *Clues
   for Dr. Coffee* (1964). Past president of Mystery Writers of America.
4. Boswell, John (?–1975). British author of *The Blue Pheasant* and *The Lost
   Girl,* both unpublished in the U.S.
5. Busch, Francis X. (1879–1975). Trial lawyer and author of several fact
   crime books in the Notable American Trial series.
6. Carroll, Thomas D. (1926–1975). Author of *Grounds for Murder* (1966)
   and other paperback mystery novels.
7. Clifford, Francis (1918?–1975). Pen name of Arthur Hill Thompson,
   author of numerous best-selling suspense novels including *The Naked
   Runner* (1966).
8. deFord, Miriam Allen (1888–1975). Long-time mystery, science fiction
   and fact crime writer. MWA Edgar winner for her true crime book, *The
   Overbury Affair* (1960).
9. Duncan, W. Murdoch (1909–1975). Prolific British crime writer under
   his own name and the pseudonyms "John Cassells," "Neill Graham,"
   "Peter Malloch," "Lovat Marshall," and "Martin Locke."
10. Giles, Kenneth (?–1972). British author of crime novels under his own
    name and the pseudonyms "Charles Drummond" and "Edmund
    McGirr."
11. Gordon, Richard M. (?–1975). Poet and short story writer, contributor
    to *EQMM,* 1958–1972.
12. Green, Alan (1906–1975). Author of an MWA Edgar-winning first
    novel *What a Body!* (1949) and *They Died Laughing* (1952), both memo-
    rable humorous mysteries.
13. Grierson, Edward (1914–1975). British author of four mystery-sus-
    pense novels, including *The Second Man* (1956), winner of the Crime
    Writers' Association award.

14. Jenkins, Will F. (1896–1975). Famed as a science fiction writer under the name "Murray Leinster" and author of eight mystery novels, 1930–1950.

15. Margulies, Leo (1900–1975). Leading editor and publisher of mystery and science fiction magazines since the 1930s, who edited such publications as *Startling Stories, Thrilling Wonder Stories, Mystery Book Magazine* and, most recently, *Mike Shayne Mystery Magazine.*

16. Montgomery, Mary (?–1975). Author of *Somebody Knew* (1961) and other novels and stories.

17. Morrow, Susan G. (?–1975). Author of six suspense novels, beginning with *Murder May Follow* (1959).

18. O'Connor, Richard (1915–1975). Author of biographies and histories, who published suspense novels as *Frank Archer* and *Patrick Wayland.*

19. Rodell, Marie (1912–1975). Well-known literary agent, author of *Mystery Fiction: Theory and Technique* and (under the pseudonym "Marion Randolph") three mystery novels, 1940–1941.

20. Santesson, Hans Stefan (1914–1975). Leading editor and anthologist in the mystery and science fiction fields. Edited *Unicorn Mystery Book Club* (1945–1952), *The Saint Magazine* (1956–1967), *The Locked Room Reader* (1968). Published occasional short fiction as by "Stephen Bond" and "John Stephens."

21. Serling, Rod (1924–1975). Well-known television writer and host of *The Twilight Zone* and *Night Gallery.* Published some suspense-fantasy books including *The Season to Be Wary* (1967) and collections rewritten from his television scripts.

22. Short, Luke (1908?–1975). Famed western writer, also author of one borderline mystery novel, *The Barren Land Murders* (1950).

23. Stout, Rex (1886–1975). Creator of Nero Wolfe, one of fiction's classic detectives, who starred in forty-six books from *Fer-de-Lance* (1934) to *A Family Affair* (1975). Also authored non-series suspense novels starting with *How Like a God* (1929). Past president of Mystery Writers of America and the Authors Guild.

24. Thomson, H. Douglas (1905–1975). Author of *Masters of Mystery* (1931), early book-length study of the detective story in English.

25. Upson, William Hazlett (1891–1975). Creator of Alexander Botts, some of whose adventures qualify as crime tales. Last in the series was "Alexander Botts, Detective" (*Saturday Evening Post,* February, 1975).

26. Wahloo, Per (1926–1975). Swedish author of several mysteries, including (with his wife Maj Sjowall) nine popular Martin Beck novels. Winner of the MWA Edgar award for *The Laughing Policeman* (1970).

27. Wilder, Thornton (1897–1975). Pulitzer Prize-winning author whose novel *The Eighth Day* (1967) was described as a "turn-of-the-century murder mystery" by judges presenting it with the National Book Award for Fiction.

28. Wodehouse, P.G. (1881–1975). Famed humorist, creator of Jeeves and other characters, some of whom occasionally ventured into crime and mystery.

HONOR ROLL

(Starred stories are included in this volume)

Ambler, Eric: "The Blood Bargain," *EQMM*, December.
*Asimov, Isaac: "The Little Things," *EQMM*, May
Avellano, Albert: "Blue Devil," *AHMM*, March
_____: "Crime by Accident," *AHMM*, July
_____: "Like Any Other Wild Animal," *AHMM*, June
Bankier, William: "Dangerous Enterprise," *EQMM*, August
Behney, L.E.: "Dry Spell," *EQMM*, April
Berry, James R.: "Nor Any Drop to Drink," *AHMM*, November
*Boeckman, Charles: "Mr. Banjo," *AHMM*, July
Breen, Jon L.: "Hercule Poirot in the Year 2010," *EQMM*, March
Brennan, Joseph Payne: "The Murder of Mr. Matthews," *AHMM*, July
*Brittain, William: "Mr. Strang Picks Up the Pieces," *EQMM*, September
Chesbro, George C.: "The Dragon Variation," *AHMM*, August
Chisholm, Lee: "Wanted: Swinger's Housekeeper," *AHMM*, December
Cohen, Stanley: "Those Who Appreciate Money," *AHMM*, April
Colby, Robert: "Paint the Town Black," *AHMM*, November
Crispin, Edmund: "St. Bartholomew's Day," *EQMM*, February
Curtiss, Ursula: "The Right Perspective," *EQMM*, March
Darling, Jean: "Never to be Lost Again," *EQMM*, August
Davidson, Avram: "If You Can't Beat Them," *EQMM*, August
Davis, Dorothy Salisbury: "Old Friends," *EQMM*, September
deFord, Miriam Allen: "Eyewitnesses," *EQMM*, February
*de la Torre, Lillian: "The Bedlam Bam," *EQMM*, September
Deming, Richard: "The Coup," *EXMM*, August
Eckels, Robert Edward: "The Great Bread Swindle," *EQMM*, July
Ellin, Stanley: "A Corner of Paradise," *EQMM*, October
Fish, Robert L.: "The Adventure of the Odd Lotteries," *EQMM*, July
*Ford, Jesse Hill: "The Jail," *Playboy*, March
Francis, Dick: "Nightmares," *EQMM*, June
Friedman, Bruce Jay: "Our Lady of the Lockers," *New York Magazine*, August 11
Garner, Judith: "Trick or Treat," *EQMM*, July
Gilbert, Michael: "The Coulman Handicap," *EQMM*, May
_____: "Death Watch," *EQMM*, April
_____: "The Sark Lane Mission," *EQMM*, December
Gores, Joe: "Kirinyaga," *EQMM*, March
Green, Gerald: "Johnny Guts," *Playboy*, July

Peirce, J.F.: "The Appearances of Evil," *EXMM*, May

Pentecost, Hugh: "Jericho and the Unknown Lover," *EQMM*, February

_____: "The Long Cry for Help," *EQMM*, August

Perowne, Barry: "The Enigma of the Admiral's Hat," *EQMM*, March

*_____: "Raffles and the Bridge of Sighs," *EQMM*, May

_____: "Raffles on the Trail of the Hound," *EQMM*, July

Porges, Irwin: "The Mannequin Murder," *87MM*, April

Powell, James: "Bianca and the Seven Sleuths," *EQMM*, June

Powell, Talmage: "Till Death Do Not Us Part," *AHMM*, August

*Pronzini, Bill: "Private Eye Blues," *AHMM*, July

_____, and Kurland, Michael: "Quicker Than the Eye," *AHMM*, September

_____, and Wallmann, Jeffrey: "Once a Thief," *EQMM*, August

*Queen, Ellery: "The Reindeer Clue," *National Enquirer*, December 23

Rafferty, S.S.: "The Bright Silver of Maryland," *EQMM*, October

_____: "The Death Desk," *AHMM*, March

_____: "The Margrave of Virginia," *EQMM*, August

_____: "The New Jersey Flying Machine," *EQMM*, November

_____: "The Rhode Island Lights," *EQMM*, September

Rendell, Ruth: "Almost Human," *EQMM*, September

_____: "The Fall of a Coin," *EQMM*, June

_____: "Meeting in the Park," *EQMM*, December

Riddell, Marjorie: "To the Smallest Detail," *EQMM*, December

Ritchie, Jack: "Bedlam at the Budgie," *AHMM*, May

*_____: "The Many-Flavored Crime," *MD*, December

_____: "Too Solid Mildred," *AHMM*, March

Simenon, Georges: "The Inn of the Drowned," *EQMM*, January

*Sisk, Frank: "The Fly Swatter," *AHMM*, July

_____: "A Look at Mother Nature," *AHMM*, September

_____: "Pain Killer," *AHMM*, November

Slesar, Henry: "The Bottom Dollar," *MSMM*, April

_____: "The Kidnapping," *EQMM*, January

Smith, Beatrice S.: "Angel," *AHMM*, December

_____: "Obligations," *AHMM*, August

Smith, Pauline C.: "The Crazy," *AHMM*, June

*_____: "Death across the Street," *MSMM*, October

_____: "Happy as a Harp Song," *AHMM*, March

_____: "The Lyon Died in Elmcreek," *AHMM*, September

_____: "Miss Margaret's Lombrose," *AHMM*, April

Stevens, Hilary: "Reflections in a Window," *EQMM*, August

Stevens, R.L.: "The Great American Novel," *EQMM*, April

Suter, John F.: "If You Can't Stand the Heat," *Every Crime in the Book*

*Tomlinson, Gerald: "Miss Ferguson versus JM," *EQMM*, April

*Treat, Lawrence: "The Candle Flame," *EQMM*, March

_____: "V as in Vengeance," *EQMM*, August

Tyre, Nedra: "Laughter Before Dying," *EQMM*, May

About the Editor

Edward D. Hoch is a full-time writer of fiction and has published numerous short stories, as well as hardcover and softcover books in the mystery story field. "*The Oblong Room*" won him the MWA Edgar award in 1968 for best short story. His latest novel is *The Frankenstein Factory*. A short story collection, *The Thefts of Nick Velvet*, starring his series detective, will be published this year. Mr. Hoch is married and lives in Rochester, New York, with his wife.